Extraordinary Acclaim for Joe R. Lansdale's
EDGE OF DARK WATER

"A charming Gothic tale... as funny that could have been dreamed up by the Brothers Grimm—or Mark Twain."   —Marilyn Stasio, *New York Times Book Review*

"Reading Joe Lansdale is like listening to a favorite uncle who just happens to be a fabulous storyteller. This book deals with dark and strange material, but it is hugely appealing as narrated in the first person by young Sue Ellen, who shines."   —Dean Koontz

"A doozy of a read, the kind of book we call an 'all nighter.'... It's that kind of great, and it's pure-blood Lansdale, crammed to bursting with plot twists that recall the snaky bends of the Sabine River.... This sucker moves.... *Edge of Dark Water* has a dank undertow that first sucks the reader in, and then drags them down into a story that thematically encompasses everything from childhood allegiances, racial tensions, sexuality, murder, a tongueless maniac nightmare named Skunk and the four teens—three alive, one dead—who attempt to flee bad, black circumstance only to find themselves in even deeper, darker waters. It's our favorite book of the year so far, and one of Lansdale's best, ever."
    — Marc Savlov, *Austin Chronicle*

"For those new to Lansdale's work, this novel will serve as a good intro: entertaining, eerie and soaked with the East Texas period atmosphere Lansdale owns like no other writer.... Along the river chase, readers will pick up on nods to Homer, Dickey, Twain

and others, but the brooding East Texas atmosphere is all Lansdale: the specter of Skunk is like something out of a horror movie; man and nature both provide plenty of thrills and chills; the mystery of who killed May Lynn is given just enough attention; and Sue Ellen's precocious teen wisdom and bumpkin delivery provide the laughs. . . . Joe R. Lansdale could fall into the Sabine River at its filthiest point and still come out dripping nothing but storytelling mojo."
                              —David Duhr, *Dallas Morning News*

"A cast of unforgettable characters . . . truly terrifying . . . a terrific read. From its pages waft memories of *Huckleberry Finn, To Kill a Mockingbird,* and even *As I Lay Dying* with its journey to lay a soul to rest. When I reached the final page, something happened that I can't remember ever happening with a book I've read for a review. I wanted to read it again."   —Hallie Ephron, *Boston Globe*

"A coming-of-age story peopled with original and fascinating blood-and-bones characters. Inevitably, *Edge of Dark Water* will be compared to the work of Twain and Faulkner, but Joe Lansdale adds his own unique voice to this chillingly atmospheric tale of good and evil and adolescent angst. *Edge of Dark Water* has all the potential of becoming a classic, read by generations to come."
                              —Sam Millar, *New York Journal of Books*

"The strongest, truest, and most pitch-perfect narration since Huck Finn's. Marvelous and terrifying, *Edge of Dark Water* is the result of real genius at work. A masterpiece."
                              —Dan Simmons, author of *The Terror* and *Drood*

"Joe Lansdale is one of the dark kings of modern mystery fiction, a master of the genre. His name deserves to be whispered with the greats."   —John Connolly

"Lansdale crafts a perfect noir mood using time, place, and culture for a novel that pits the pretty good against pure evil. This literary thriller will add to his fan base while sating the appetite of the already converted."
　　　　　　　　　　　　　　　　　　　　　—*Library Journal*

"Edgar-winner Lansdale channels Mark Twain in this chillingly atmospheric stand-alone. Lansdale's perfect ear for regional dialogue and ability to create palpable suspense lift this above the pack."　　　　　　　　　　　—*Publishers Weekly* (starred review)

"Joe Lansdale has long been one of our finest and most difficult-to-classify writers. You can call his writing supernatural, horror, crime, or plain Southern, as long as you remember to call it great. Always a generous storyteller, in *Edge of Dark Water* he offers a beautifully spun tale of life in the sticks, friendship and mortality, and tells it with the wit, humor and pure-dee power we've come to expect of him."　　—Daniel Woodrell, author of *Winter's Bone*

"Nonstop adventures that edify, terrify and deepen the bond between Sue Ellen and Jinx. A highly entertaining tour de force."
　　　　　　　　　　　　　　　　—*Kirkus Reviews* (starred review)

"Joe Lansdale always transports me. In *Edge of Dark Water,* he takes me to the mysterious brooding landscape of Twain and Faulkner, with a compelling twist that is all Lansdale."
　　　　　　　　　—David Morrell, *New York Times* bestselling author
　　　　　　　　　　　　　　　　　of *First Blood* and *Creepers*

"Joe R. Lansdale, perhaps more than any other contemporary author, is adept at blurring and crossing the genres where his books find their homes. He is highly regarded by aficionados of mysteries, horror novels, westerns old and new, and thrillers. Any number of his novels, including his latest, have feet set firmly in all of those genres. So it is that while *Edge of Dark Water* has been compared favorably to *The Adventures of Huckleberry Finn,* it reads like a mash-up of that classic with James Dickey's *Deliverance* and, yes, the *Friday the 13th* film franchise, with the veneer of a classic murder mystery that resonates long after the last page is read. Lansdale's ear for dialogue remains pitch- and letter-perfect, and his characters are so real in their strengths and failings as to seem to leap off the pages. A dark and violent—yet funny—tale that is not to be missed."   —Joe Hartlaub, Bookreporter.com

"*Edge of Dark Water* describes a trip downriver that is one-half *Huck Finn,* one-half *Deliverance,* and entirely Joe Lansdale. If you aren't familiar with the work of this true American original and master of hillbilly noir, climb in the boat and hang on for dear life: the water is rough."   —Joe Hill, author of the *New York Times* bestsellers
Horns and *Heart-Shaped Box*

"Joe R. Lansdale's fellow Texans would call Joe a straight shooter. That's what makes his writing so good—no BS involved. Joe's work is alternately scary, funny as hell, disturbing, but always (and most importantly) memorable."
          —Bruce Campbell, author of *If Chins Could Kill*

"A dark tale of loss and despair, of growing up dirt poor, where adults are mean and children are worthless inconveniences. The story is taut and laced with humor with beautiful prose—writing that's as smooth and deep as the river that flows through town. An impressive, riveting story."
          —Julia Madeleine, *Spinetingler* magazine

EDGE OF
DARK WATER

EDGE OF
DARK
WATER

~m~

Joe R. Lansdale

Foreword by Dan Simmons

MULHOLLAND BOOKS
LITTLE, BROWN AND COMPANY
NEW YORK BOSTON LONDON

Copyright © 2012 by Joe R. Lansdale
Reading group guide copyright © 2013 by Joe R. Lansdale and Little, Brown and Company
Foreword copyright © 2013 by Dan Simmons

Mulholland Books / Little, Brown and Company
Hachette Book Group
237 Park Avenue, New York, NY 10017
mulhollandbooks.com

Originally published in hardcover by Mulholland Books / Little, Brown and Company, March 2012
First Mulholland Books paperback edition, February 2013

Mulholland Books is an imprint of Little, Brown and Company, a division of Hachette Book Group, Inc. The Mulholland Books name and logo are trademarks of Hachette Book Group, Inc.

The publisher is not responsible for websites (or their content) that are not owned by the publisher.

The Hachette Speakers Bureau provides a wide range of authors for speaking events. To find out more, go to hachettespeakersbureau.com or call (866) 376-6591.

Library of Congress Cataloging-in-Publication Data
Lansdale, Joe R.
 Edge of dark water / Joe R. Lansdale.—1st ed.
  p. cm.
 ISBN 978-0-316-18843-2 (hc) / 978-0-316-18842-5 (pb)
 1. Female friendship—Fiction. 2. Friends—Death—Fiction. 3. Loss (Psychology)—Fiction.
 4. Psychological fiction. I. Title.
 PS3562.A557E34 2012
 813'.54—dc22   2011030557

For Karen

FOREWORD

Since Mark Twain's *The Adventures of Huckleberry Finn* was first published in America, in 1885, there have been hundreds—if not thousands—of favorable comparisons to Twain's masterpiece by publishers, blurbers, and/or reviewers of "contemporary" novels. Almost all of these comparisons have been inappropriate or just plain silly since a) *Huckleberry Finn* was an unmatched novel of male adolescence, moral awakening, and an entire dark era of American history told in perfect regional and temporal vernacular; b) as Ernest Hemingway said, "All modern American literature comes from one book by Mark Twain called *Huckleberry Finn*...It's the best book we've had"; and c) Mark Twain was a genius.

Joe R. Lansdale's *Edge of Dark Water* is worthy of being compared to Twain's *The Adventures of Huckleberry Finn*. Nor are the rafts or the marvelous and terrifying river voyages in both books the primary reasons for Lansdale—and what may be his masterpiece—earning the right to this comparison to Twain's masterpiece. "Sue Ellen's" voice throughout Lansdale's novel is almost certainly the strongest, truest, and most pitch-perfect regional-temporal vernacular narration since Huck Finn's. The young protagonist's moral decisions in *Edge of Dark Water* are among the most complex (yet clearest) since Huck decided to "steal" Jim and go to hell forever for doing so. *Edge of Dark Water* evokes a time and place—the Depression era, East Texas—as powerfully as Twain's *The Adventures of Huckleberry Finn* preserved and illuminated the Mississippi River region in pre–Civil War America.

The river voyages and brilliant narratives in both books are cries from the heart of the heart of America's darkness. Both are the result of real genius at work.

Finally, if we're to quote Hemingway on how wonderful Twain's book was, we need to add his all-important caveat: "If you read it you must stop where the Nigger Jim is stolen from the boys. That is the real end. The rest is just cheating." It was (and remains) "just cheating" because Twain decided that he had to keep the ending of *Huckleberry Finn* to being "just another Boys' Book" (as was his goal for all of *The Adventures of Tom Sawyer*) in order to hold up his novel's subscription sales and library orders in Victorian America. And so, after Tom Sawyer shows up, *The Adventures of Huckleberry Finn* is just a funny and beautifully written boys' book, whether we want to admit it or not. "Jim" ceases to be the complex, human, adult Jim of the rest of the important novel and Huck becomes a mere sidekick again to Tom.

Lansdale's *Edge of Dark Water* does not suffer from Twain's forgivable failure of nerve at the finale of *Huckleberry Finn,* nor in any lack of confidence in the maturity and courage of his readership. Perhaps most important, it stands alone and confident in its own dark power and beauty and doesn't require comparisons to any other novel.

—Dan Simmons

Down the river they flowed.
All the dreams that had been dreamed
across moonless, dark water.

Anonymous

A small rock holds back a great wave.

Homer's *Odyssey*

PART ONE

OF ASH AND DREAMS

1

—⟋⟍⟍—

That summer, Daddy went from telephoning and dynamiting fish to poisoning them with green walnuts. The dynamite was messy, and a couple years before he'd somehow got two fingers blown off, and the side of his face had a burn spot that at first glance looked like a lipstick kiss and at second glance looked like some kind of rash.

Telephoning for fish worked all right, though not as good as dynamite, but Daddy didn't like cranking that telephone to hot up the wire that went into the water to 'lectrocute the fish. He said he was always afraid one of the little colored boys that lived up from us might be out there swimming and get a dose of 'lectricity that would kill him deader than a cypress stump, or at best do something to his brain and make him retarded as his cousin Ronnie, who didn't have enough sense to get in out of the rain and might hesitate in a hailstorm.

My grandma, the nasty old bag, who, fortunately, is dead now, claimed Daddy has what she called the Sight. She said he was gifted and could see the future some. I reckon if that was so, he'd have thought ahead enough not to get drunk when he was handling explosives and got his fingers blown off.

And I hadn't ever seen that much sympathy from him concerning colored folk, so I didn't buy his excuse for not cranking the phone. He didn't like my friend Jinx Smith, who was colored, and he tried to make out we was better than her and her family, even though they had a small but clean house, and we had a large dirty house with a sagging porch and the chimney propped up on one side with a two-by-four and there were a couple of hogs wallowing out holes in the yard. As for his cousin Ronnie, I don't think Daddy cared for him one way or the other, and he often made fun of him and imitated him by pretending to bang into walls and slobber about. Of course, when he was good and drunk, this wasn't an imitation, just a similarity.

Then again, maybe Daddy could see the future, but was just too stupid to do anything about it.

Anyway, Daddy had these tow sacks—about ten of them—and he and Uncle Gene had them full of green walnuts and some rocks to heavy them up, and they had them fastened on ropes and thrown out in the water, the ropes tied off to roots and trees on the shore.

Me and my friend Terry Thomas had gone down there to watch and help, because we didn't have nothing else we wanted to do. Terry didn't want to go when I told him what I wanted to do and where we were going and that I wanted him there with me, but he broke down finally and went and helped me toss bags and pull up fish. He was real nervous about the whole thing because he didn't like either my daddy or my uncle. I didn't like them, either, but I liked being outside and doing things that men do, though I think I would have been more happy with a line and a hook than bags of walnut poison. Still, I liked the river and the outdoors better than I liked being at the house with a mop in my hand.

My grandma on Daddy's side always said I didn't act like a girl at all, and I ought to stay home learning how to keep a garden and shell peas and do women's work. Grandma would lean forward in her rocker, look at me with no love in her gooey eyes, and say, "Sue Ellen, how you gonna get a husband you can't cook or clean worth a flip and don't never do your hair up?"

Course, she wasn't being fair. I'd already been doing woman's work for long as I could remember. I just wasn't no good at it. And if you've ever done any of it, you know it ain't any fun at all. I liked doing what the boys and men did. What my daddy did. Which, when you got right down to it, didn't seem like all that much, just fishing and trapping for skins to sell, shooting squirrels out of trees, and bragging about it like he'd done killed tigers. Most of that bragging took place after he got liquored up good. I'd had me a taste of liquor once, and I didn't like it. I can say the same for chewing tobacco and cigarettes and anything that's got lettuce in it.

As for putting my hair up, she was really talking about certain religious ways, and I couldn't figure that God, with all he had to worry about, would be all that concerned with hairdos.

This day I'm telling you about, Daddy and Uncle Gene was drinking a little and tossing those sacks, and the water was turning dark brown where the walnuts went in. After a while, sure enough, a bunch of brim and sun perch come floating belly up.

Me and Terry stood on the shore and watched while Daddy and Uncle Gene got in the rowboat and pushed off and went out there with nets and gathered them fish like pecans that had fell on the ground. There was so many I knew we'd be eating fried fish not only tonight, but tomorrow night, and after that we'd be eating dried fish, which is another thing I forgot to put on my list of stuff

I don't like. Jinx says dried fish tastes like stained shorts smell, and she won't get an argument from me. If they were smoked proper, that was all right, but dried fish are a lot like trying to chew on a dead dog's tit.

Walnuts didn't really poison the fish to death, but it stunned them up a mite and made them float to the surface, white bellies showing, working their gills. Daddy and Gene gathered them up with nets on a stick and put them in a wet tow sack for gutting and cleaning.

The sacks was tied to the shore with ropes, and me and Terry went down there to start pulling them in. The walnuts still had enough green in them they could be used downriver to stun more fish, so we was supposed to save them. We got hold of a rope and started pulling, but it was real heavy and we couldn't do it.

"We'll be there d'rectly to help out," Daddy called from the boat.

"I think we should cut this one loose," Terry said to me. "No use straining our guts out."

"I don't quit that easy," I said, and looked up to see what was going on with the boat. It had a hole in the bottom, so Daddy and Uncle Gene couldn't stay out long. Uncle Gene had to bail it out with a coffee can while Daddy paddled the boat back to the bank. When they had it pulled out of the water, they came over to help us.

"Damn," Daddy said, "either them walnuts has got heavy as a Ford or I've gotten weak."

"You've gotten weak," Uncle Gene said. "You ain't the man you once was. You ain't the strapping example of prime manhood I am."

Daddy grinned at him. "Hell, you're older than me."

"Yeah," said Uncle Gene, "but I've took care of myself."

Daddy let out with a hooting sound, said, "Ha!"

Uncle Gene was fat as a hog, but without the personality. Still, he was a big man in height and had broad shoulders and arms about the size of a horse's neck. Daddy didn't even look kin to him. He was a skinny peckerwood with a potbelly, and if you ever saw him without a cap it was cause it had rotted off his head. He and Uncle Gene had about eighteen teeth between them, and Daddy had most of them. Mama said it was because they didn't brush their teeth enough and they chewed tobacco. There were times when I looked at their sunken faces and was reminded of an old pumpkin rotting in the field. I know it's a sad thing to be so repulsed by your own kin, but there you have it, straight out and in the open.

We all pulled on the rope, and finally, just about the time I thought I was going to strain my guts out, up come that bag. Only it wasn't just the bag. There was something caught up in it, all swole up and white, and dangling long strands of wet grass.

"Now, wait a minute here," Daddy said, and kept pulling.

Then I seen it wasn't grass at all. It was hair. And under that hair was a face big around as the moon and white as a sheet and puffy-looking as a feather pillow. I didn't know who it was right off, till I seen the dress. It was the only dress I'd ever seen May Lynn Baxter wear. A dress spotted with blue flowers and so faded you could barely tell what color the flowers had been in the first place, and it had gone a mite short on her as she had grown tall.

Only time I'd seen her not wearing it that I could remember was when me and her and Terry and Jinx slipped out one night and went to the swimming hole for a dip. I had thought she was so pretty there in the moonlight. Not a stitch on, well formed, with moon-blond hair to her waist, and that dress hanging on a limb next to the river. She moved like she was hearing music we couldn't. I knew then she was gonna be the kind of girl that made single men turn their heads and take a deep breath and married men wish their wives would catch on fire. Fact was, she already was that kind of girl.

Terry didn't pay her no mind, and I think it's because he might be a sissy. There's a rumor he is, and part of the rumor has to do with a boy from the far end of the river that come up one summer to visit relatives. I don't know if it's true, but I don't care one way or the other. I've known Terry since we was babies, and from what I've seen of man-and-woman love, it mostly has to do with Daddy lying around and not doing much, getting drunk, and hitting Mama in the eye. One time, after he'd beat her up pretty good and went out fishing, a rainstorm come up, and I lay on my bed hoping a bolt of lightning would shoot out of the sky and hit him in the top of the head, knock them few teeth out of his skull and kill him, leaving nothing behind but his cap. I know that's mean, but that's how I was thinking.

I didn't like that Mama thought she deserved that ass-whipping. She thought a man was the one ran things and had the say. She said it was in the Bible. That put me off reading it right away.

So there lay May Lynn, partway on the shore, that dress having grown smaller on her over the years, and smaller yet on account of how she had puffed up.

"Her eyes is swole shut," Uncle Gene said. "She's been in the water a bit."

"It don't take no time at all to look like that," Daddy said. "You get drowned and don't float up overnight, that's how you get."

All of a sudden May Lynn started to flutter and leak. Gas coming out of her, and it smelled real bad, like a giant fart. Her hands was tied behind her, twisted up in rusty wire, and so were her feet, which was pulled up to meet her hands. Her skin had swelled around the wire—the wire that had gotten tangled up in our bag.

When we pulled her completely up and laid her out, we seen there was a Singer sewing machine fastened around her feet with more wire, several pieces of it twisted together to make it strong. The wire had gone deep into her wet flesh, all the way to the bone. The weight of that Singer was why all four of us was needed to pull her up.

"Ain't that May Lynn Baxter?" Daddy said.

He had just figured who it was, his ability to see into the future dragging its feet until the future had arrived. He turned to me for an answer.

I could hardly get the words out of my mouth. "I reckon that's her."

"She was only a girl," Terry said. "She was our age."

"Age ain't got nothing to do with living or dying," Uncle Gene said. "But no doubt about it, she's twisted her hips for the last time."

"I reckon we ought to do something," Daddy said.

"I think we ought to cut our rope free and push her back in," Uncle Gene said. "She ain't gonna get no deader if she ain't found, and her daddy won't have to know she's dead. He can think she run off to Hollywood or something. Wasn't that what she was always saying she was gonna do? I mean, it's like a dog dies and you don't tell the kid, and they think the dog is living with someone else, or something like that."

"She doesn't have any real family," Terry said, not looking at her, but looking out at the river. "We were her only friends, me and Sue Ellen and Jinx. She isn't a dog."

Daddy and Uncle Gene didn't look at him. It was like he hadn't said a thing.

"We could do that," Daddy said. "We could push her back. She wasn't known to be of much account anyhow. And they're right. She ain't got no real family, with her mama and brother dead, and her daddy in love with the bottle. It wouldn't do no harm to just let her sink. Hell, he didn't miss her much when she was alive, and with her dead, he still won't miss her."

"You ain't pushing her back," I said.

Daddy took note of that. He turned and looked at me. "Who you talking to, little girl? You ain't talking to your elders like that, are you?"

I knew it might mean I was going to get a thrashing, but I stood by my guns.

"You ain't pushing her back in."

"She was our friend," Terry said, and I saw tears in his eyes.

Daddy reached out and slapped me on top of the head with the palm of his hand. It hurt. It made me a little dizzy.

"I'll make the decisions around here," Daddy said, and leaned his face close to me. I could smell the tobacco and onions on his breath.

"You didn't have any reason to strike her," Terry said.

Daddy glared at Terry. "Don't be talking above your raising."

"You aren't my daddy," Terry said, stepping out of range, "and if you push May Lynn back in the water, I'll tell about it."

Daddy studied Terry for a moment. Probably judging distance, wondering how fast he could reach him. It would have required too much work, I reckon, because the tension drained out of him. Daddy Don Wilson wasn't one for expending energy if he didn't have to, and sometimes even if he had to.

Daddy twisted his withered mouth a little, said, "We was just funning. We ain't going put her back, are we, Gene?"

Uncle Gene looked Terry over, then me.

"I suppose not," he said, but the words sounded to me as if they had been burned real good and were mostly charred.

Daddy sent Terry into town to get the constable, but didn't let him take the truck. He made him walk. It would have been easy enough to have loaded the body in the back of the truck and driven us all into town, but that would have been too damn convenient, and that wasn't Daddy's way. And he didn't like Terry on account of he figured he wasn't the way he thought a man ought to be. Uncle Gene had a truck, too, but he didn't offer it, either. I think he just didn't want a dead gal in the back of it.

I sat on the shore and looked at May Lynn's body. It was gathering flies and starting to smell and all I could think of was how she was always clean and pretty, and this wasn't a thing that should have happened to her. It wasn't like in the books I had read, and the times I had been to the picture show and people died. They always looked pretty much like they were when they were alive, except sleepy. I saw now that's not how things were. It wasn't any different for a dead person than a shot-dead squirrel or a hog with a cut throat hanging over the scalding pot.

Shadows came tumbling through the trees and over the water and you could see a bit of the moon shining on the river; it looked like a huge face floating up from the bottom. The crickets had started to saw at their legs pretty seriously, and there was a louder gathering of frogs that came with the dark. If I hadn't been staring mostly at a dead body, it would have been kind of pleasant. As it was, I felt numb, the way your arm will get if you sleep on it, but I felt like that all over.

Daddy built a fire a ways from the body to sit by while we waited on Terry and the law, and Uncle Gene gathered up the fish and carried them up to his truck. He took them to be split up with us, and to take the rest over to his house and his wife. Since he and Daddy had gone to pulling at a jug before he left, he was lit up good, and I figured if he didn't wrap the pickup around a tree in the dark, when he got home he'd make his wife, Evy, clean the fish, and then he'd give her a beating. Uncle Gene said he liked to give her one a day when he could, and one a week when he was busy, just to let her know her place. He had even offered to give me one a couple of times, and Daddy thought it might be a good idea. But either Mama was there to stop it, and ended up getting beat on by Daddy instead of him beating on me, or he eventually played out on the idea because it got in the way of his drinking.

Anyway, Uncle Gene decided it was best to go home, and left Daddy to his business.

Daddy tried to get me to come over and sit by him near the fire, but I stayed where I was. In dark places he liked to touch, and it made me feel strange and uncomfortable. He said it was a thing fathers did with daughters. Jinx told me that wasn't true, but I didn't need her to explain it to me, because I could tell inside of me it wasn't good. I sat away from the fire, and though it was a warm enough night, the fire did look inviting. But all I could think about was how Daddy was. How his breath smelled of whiskey and tobacco most of the time. How when he was really drunk, the whites of his eyes would roll up from the bottom like a frightened horse. How if he tried to touch me he'd start breathing faster, so I just kept my place in the shadows, even when the mosquitoes started to show up.

"You and that sissy boy going to stir things up don't need stirring," Daddy said. "We'd pushed her back in the water, we'd be home by now. Most things you decide to deal with you could skip."

I didn't say anything to that.

"We should have kept a fish or two to fry on the fire," he said, like maybe it was my fault Uncle Gene had packed them all up and toted them off. There were still a few that had washed up to the bank, but he wasn't willing to leave the fire and go get one to clean and cook. And I wasn't about to do it. All I could do was think about May Lynn and feel sick, and I had to keep my eye on Daddy cause the drunker he got the bolder he got, and the harder he talked. You never knew when he might do something stupid or scary. That's how he was. He could be laughing and having a good time, and the next thing you knew he'd pull a pocketknife and threaten to cut you. He didn't look like much, but he was a known hothead and knife fighter, and was supposed to be good with his fists, and not just when he was hitting women and children. He was also known to tire out quick and start looking for a place to nest.

"You think you got it hard, don't you, baby girl?"

"Hard enough," I said.

"I tell you what hard is, that's when your own father sets you out the door and locks it and won't let you come back for a night or two. And when he does, it's just because cows needed milking and eggs needed gathering, and he wanted someone to hit."

"Well, now," I said. "The apple didn't fall far from the tree, did it?"

"You ain't never milked a cow in your life," he said.

"We ain't never had one."

"I'm going to get one, and when I do, you'll milk it. You'll do same as I did."

"It's a thing to look forward to," I said, and then I shut up. The way he twisted his head and turned the jug of hooch in his hand told me it was time to be quiet. Next thing I knew that jug would be flying through the air, and he'd be on me, his fists swinging. I just sat there and kept watch and let him suck his liquor.

The moon was high and the night was settled in heavy as stone by the time we seen a light coming over the hill on the trail that split down between the thick woods that led to the river. Along with the light came the rumble of a truck, the crackling of tires over a pocked road, and the swish of close-hanging limbs dragging alongside of it.

When the truck was down the hill and still a good ways from the water, it stopped, and I could hear Constable Sy Higgins pulling on the parking brake. He left the motor running and the lights on. He got out of the truck like a man climbing down from a tall tree with a fear he might fall. Terry got out of the other door and came down quickly. When he was close to me, he said so no one else could hear, "He's drunk. I had to get him out of bed, and he didn't want to come. He said it wouldn't have hurt to just push her back in the water."

"That's the law for you," I said. "Now if we could get the clergy here and the mayor, we'd have the perfect pile to smell."

Constable Sy sauntered down the hill with a flashlight shining in front of him, even though the headlights on the truck were bright enough to see how to thread a needle. He made toward the fire, his belly bouncing before him like a dog leaping up to greet him. Daddy got to his feet, staggering a little. They were drunks together.

"Where is she?" Higgins said, pushing his fedora up on his head. When he did, I could see his hard face and the patch over his eye. Way the shadows fell, it made that eye look like a black tunnel. Rumor was he'd had it scratched out by a black woman he raped. The holster that held his gun was said to be made out of an Indian's hide, and had been passed on to him by Indian-fighter relatives. It was probably just a story.

Constable Sy hadn't even bothered to look around and find May Lynn. It wasn't like she was hidden in the woods under a tarpaulin. All you needed was one good eye to find her. A blind man would have noticed her right off.

Daddy led him over to the body while me and Terry watched. Constable Sy shined the light around on her and the sewing machine lying nearby. He said, "She's squatted to pee for the last time, but I think maybe the sewing machine can be salvaged."

Daddy and Constable Sy snickered together.

"Wasn't nothing wrong with her," I said. "She's the one murdered. She's the one that's had something done to her. There ain't a thing funny about it."

The constable shined his flashlight on my face. "Girl, you ought to know children ain't supposed to speak unless spoken to."

"That's what I tell her," Daddy said.

"I ain't a child," I said, dipping my head and squinting my eyes against the light. "I'm sixteen."

"Yeah, well," the constable said, moving the light from my head to my toes. "I can see you ain't as much a kid as I remember."

I don't know how to explain it, but that light running up and down me wasn't any different than a hot yellow tongue; it made me feel kind of sick.

"Why don't you and your girlfriend there go sit down out of the way?" Daddy said.

That made Constable Sy snicker, and Daddy liked that. I could tell the way he stood a little straighter and his chest went out. There wasn't nothing made him feel better than belittling somebody, unless it was hitting somebody upside the head that didn't expect it.

Terry sighed, and me and him went over and sat down on the ground by the fire. Constable Sy went to his truck and got an old blanket out of the bed, and then he and Daddy, using the toes of their boots, sort of kicked poor May Lynn onto it, wrapped her up, carried her, and put her in the constable's truck bed. When they dropped her back there, it sounded like someone tossing a big dead fish on a smooth flat rock.

"You could have done this yourself," Constable Sy said. "You could have brung her in and we could have looked at her in the morning."

"I'd rather your truck stank than mine," Daddy said.

2

May Lynn didn't have a mama anymore, cause her mama had drowned herself in the Sabine River. She had gone down with some laundry to soak, and instead wrapped a shirt around her head and walked in until the water went over her. When she came up, she wasn't alive anymore, but she still had that shirt around her noggin.

May Lynn's daddy was someone who only came home when he got tired of being any other place. We didn't even know if he knew his daughter was missing. May Lynn used to say after her mama drowned herself her daddy was never the same. Said she figured it was because the laundry around her mother's head had been his favorite snap-pocket shirt. That's true love for you. Worse, her brother, Jake, who she was close to, was dead as of a short time back, and there wasn't even a family dog to miss her.

The day after we found her, May Lynn was boxed up in a cheap coffin and buried on a warm morning in the pauper section of the Marvel Creek Cemetery next to a dried patch of weeds with seed ticks clinging to them, and I suspect some chiggers too small to see. Her mother and brother were buried in the same graveyard, but they hadn't ended up next to one another. Up the hill was where the people with money lay. Down here was the free dirt, and even if you was kin to someone, you got scattered—you went in anyplace where there was room to dig a hole. I'd heard there was many a grave on top of another, for need of space.

There were oaks and elms to shade the rest of the graveyard, but May Lynn's section was a hot stretch of dirt with a bunch of washed-down mounds, a few with markers. Some of the markers were little sticks. Names had once been written on them, but they had been washed white by the sun and rain.

The constable ruled on matters by saying she had been killed by a person or persons unknown, which was something I could have figured out for him. He said it was most likely a drifter or drifters who had come upon her by the river. I guess they had been carrying a sewing machine under their arm.

He didn't make any effort to search out her murderer or find out why she was down there. For that matter, there wasn't even a doctor or nobody that looked at her to be sure exactly how she was killed or if she had been fooled with. Nobody cared but me and Terry and Jinx.

The service was conducted by a local preacher. He said a few words that might have sounded just as insincere if they had been spoken over the body of a distant cousin's pet mouse that had died of old age.

When he was through talking, a couple of colored men put the plain box down in the ground using ropes, then started shoveling dirt in the hole. Outside of the colored men, and the preacher and the seed ticks, we had been the only ones at the funeral, if you could call it that.

"You'd think they was just taking out the trash, way that preacher hurried up," Jinx said, after they left.

"Way they saw it," I said, "that was exactly what they was doing. Taking out the trash."

Jinx was my age. She had her hair tied in pigtails that stood out from her head like plaited ropes of wire. She had a sweet face, but her eyes seemed older, like she was someone's ancient grandma stuffed inside a kid. She wore a dyed blue flour-sack dress that had some of the old print faintly poking through, and she was barefoot. Terry had on some new shoes, and he had gotten from somewhere a man's black tie. It was tied in a big knot and pulled up tight to his neck, making him look like a bag that had been knotted near the top. He had enough oil in his black hair to grease a truck axle, and it still wasn't quite enough to hold his wild mane down. His face was dark from the sun, and his blue eyes were shiny as chunks of the sky. None of us was happy with what had happened, but he was taking it especially hard; his eyes were red from crying.

"No one will make a concerted effort to discover what happened to her," Terry said. "I think a search for the truth is out of the question."

I loved to hear Terry talk, because he didn't sound like no one else I knew. He hadn't dropped out of school like me, as I was having problems with it being so far and no way to get there and I didn't like it much anyhow. My mother, who was pretty good educated, didn't like that I had quit, but she didn't get out of bed to make much of a complaint against it; that might have required her putting on her shoes.

Terry liked school. Even the math part. His mother had been a schoolteacher and gave him extra learning. His father had died when he was young, and as of recent his mother had taken up with and married an oilman named Harold Webber. Terry didn't get along with him even a little bit. Webber made Terry's mother quit teaching school to be home with the kids, and then she started a seamstress business, but he made her kill that, too, and toss out all her goods, because he believed a husband took care of his wife and she shouldn't work, even if she liked the work she did. In the end it was all about the same anyhow, as jobs, especially for women, had become as rare as baptized rattlesnakes.

Since that marriage, Terry had a look in his eyes like a rabbit that was about to run fast and far.

Jinx could read and write and cipher some, same as me, but she hadn't learned it in school. Coloreds didn't have a school in our parts, and she had been taught by her daddy, who had gone up north to work for a while and learned to read there. He said it was better in the north for coloreds in some ways because people acted like they liked you, even if they didn't. But he come back because he missed his family and being in the South, since he knew right off who the sons of bitches was; there wasn't as much guesswork involved in figuring who was who.

But when times got bad, that didn't keep him from heading north again. He hated to do it, he told Jinx, and meant it, but he had to go up there and make some money and mail it back to her and her mother.

None of us was happy in East Texas. We all wanted out, but seemed stuck to our spots like rooted trees. When I thought about getting out I couldn't imagine much beyond the wetlands and the woods. Except for Hollywood. I could imagine that on account of May Lynn talking about it all the time. She made it sound pretty good, even though she had never been there. Still, that's where I wished to be. But as I had learned from Jinx, shit in one hand and wish in the other and see which one fills up first. She said the same thing about prayer, but I had never taken it on myself to test the notion.

We decided to go to May Lynn's house and see if her daddy was there so we could let him know the bad news, tell him he missed the funeral. Our guess was if he was home, he would know by now, but it was something to do, and to tell it true, if he wasn't home, we wanted to take a look around. I can't explain it, but I guess we didn't want to let go of May Lynn just yet, and going where she lived seemed a way to keep her memory warm.

With her dead, a lot of hopes I had were gone. I always figured May Lynn just might go off to Hollywood and be a movie star, and then she'd come home and take us back with her. I never could figure why she would do that, or what we might do out there, but it beat thinking I was just gonna grow up and marry some fellow with tobacco in his cheek and whiskey on his breath who would beat me at least once a week and maybe make me keep my hair up.

None of this kind of thinking mattered, though, because May Lynn didn't become a star. Truth was, as of late, we hadn't known her very well ourselves. By the time she showed up in the water wired to that Singer sewing machine, I reckon I hadn't seen her for a month. I figured it was similar for Terry and Jinx.

Jinx said she thought May Lynn had come of the age to think hanging with colored kids might not lead to stardom. Jinx said she didn't hold it against her, but I had doubts about that. Jinx could hold a grudge.

As to what happened to May Lynn, I had ideas about that. Nobody loved a picture show the way she did, and she'd hitch a ride with anyone if they'd get her into town on Saturdays to catch a show. Men were always quick to pick her up. Me, I'd have had to lay down in the middle of the road and play dead to have them stop, and even then they might have run over me, same as they would a dead possum. Could be May Lynn got a ride with the wrong person; an angry Singer sewing machine salesman. It was a stretch, but I figured it was better detective work than Constable Higgins had done.

To get to May Lynn's house from our side, you either had to walk ten miles up to the bridge and cross over and walk about ten more on the other side along the edge of the river, or you could cross by boat to the far bank and walk right up to her house. It would save you hours.

We used Daddy's boat, the one with the little hole in the bottom, and while me and Terry rowed, Jinx used a coffee can to bail the water out. After a while, I took a turn and she rowed.

Trees leaned way out over the river and there were long vines and dangles of moss hanging near the surface of the water. There was the usual turtles and water snakes swimming about, long-legged birds diving down to take fish out of the water, and those little bugs that flittered along the water's surface like dancers.

We had been going along for a ways when Jinx said, "You hear that?"

"Hear what?" Terry said. He was still wearing his knotted tie, but he had slid the knot down so that it was no longer tight against his neck.

"That knocking sound," Jinx said.

We stopped rowing and listened. I faintly heard it.

"That's trees striking and rubbing together in the wind," Terry said. "They've grown up too close to one another, and that's the sound they make. See how brisk the wind is?"

I looked at the trees, and they were blowing right smart. The water was wind-rippled, too.

"It might be the wind doing it," Jinx said, "but that ain't trees knocking together. Them's bones."

"Bones?" I said.

Jinx pointed toward the riverbank, where briars and brambles twisted tight around the trees. "Somewhere back in the thicket there is where Skunk lives. He hangs out bones on strings, and when the wind blows, they bang together. Human bones. That's that sound you hear, them bones."

"There isn't any Skunk," Terry said. "That's an old wives' tale. Like the goat man that's supposed to live in the woods. It's just a tale to scare children."

Jinx shook her head. "Skunk is real. He's a big old colored man that's more red than black, with twisty red hair; he wears it wild, like it's a bush. They say he keeps a dried-up bluebird hanging in it. He's got dark eyes as dead and flat as coat buttons. They say he can walk softer than a breeze and can go for days without sleeping. That he can live for weeks sipping water from mud holes and eating roots and such, and that since the only baths he ever had was when he fell in the river, or when he got caught out in the rain, he stinks like a skunk and you can smell him coming a long ways off."

Terry let out a laugh. "Don't be ridiculous."

"He's part Indian—Seminole or Cherokee or something—and that's why he's red-touched. He's a tracker used to live in the Everglades over in Florida. He's a stone killer. Ain't nobody bothers Skunk unless they want someone caught, or dead is more likely. He chops off hands and takes them back to prove he's done the business he was hired to do."

"Even if there is a fella with a bird in his hair, and his name is Skunk," I said, "I don't think that's bones from his place rattling. Terry's right; that's treetops knocking together. I've heard that sound before, and not just in this place."

"Well," Jinx said, "he moves his place around. And if that is trees, not bones, it don't mean Skunk ain't out there. I know people that have seen him. I know one man told me he hired Skunk because his wife run off and he wanted Skunk to find her. He said Skunk must have misunderstood or didn't care. All he brought back was her hands, chopped off right at the wrist with a hatchet. Old man told me the story said he didn't ask where the rest of her was, and he paid up, too. What Skunk wanted from him wasn't money. He wanted all the man's blankets and the food he canned for the winter, and his biggest, fattest hunting dog. Old man gave it to him, too. Skunk carried that stuff off in a wheelbarrow, the dog tied to a rope, walking alongside him. Old man said Skunk didn't use no hunting dogs because he was better than any of them. He figured the dog was for dinner."

"And he's got a big blue ox named Babe," Terry said. "And he can rope a tornado and ride it like a horse."

Jinx was so mad she almost stood up in the boat.

"He ain't like no Paul Bunyan or Pecos Bill," she said. "You're making me mad. He ain't no story. He's real. And you better watch out for him."

"It wasn't my intention to make you angry, Jinx," Terry said.

"Well, you done made me angry," Jinx said. "Big angry."

"Sorry," Terry said.

"Go on, Jinx," I said, soothing her ruffled feathers. "Finish telling about him."

"He don't talk much, unless it's to who he's gonna kill. They say then he can't talk, just makes funny sounds. I know cause Daddy told me he knew a fella had got away from Skunk, just by accident. That Skunk had been hired to get him, found him, tied him to a tree, and was gonna cut his throat and chop off his hands. The tree this fella was tied to was up against the bank next to the river. It was an old tree, and though this fella wasn't thinking about it on purpose, he was pushing with his feet to get away from Skunk. The tree was more rotten than it looked, because there was ants at the base, and they had gnawed it up. This fella told Daddy he could feel them ants on him, biting, but he didn't hate them none, because they had made that old tree rotten, and with him pushing with his feet, pressing his back into the trunk, it broke off. He went backward into the water. When he hit, the log floated, spinning him around and around, him snapping breaths every time he was on top of the river. Finally the log come apart altogether, and that loosened the ropes and he swam out to a sandbar and rested, and then he swam across to the other side. Course, none of it done him any good. Daddy said that later, after he told him about it, he wasn't seen no more. Daddy said it was because he didn't have sense enough to go up north or out west, but had stuck around. He figured Skunk finally got him. Skunk ain't no quitter, though he can wander off from a trail for a while if he gets bored. He gets interested again, he comes back. He always comes back, and there ain't no end to it until he's got whoever he's after."

"Why was Skunk supposed to be after this man?" Terry asked.

"I don't know," Jinx said. "Someone hired Skunk to get him, and Skunk got him. Reckon he chopped off his hands and gave them to whoever hired him, or maybe he kept them himself. I don't know. As for what was left of the fella, I bet he rotted away in the woods somewhere, never to be seen again."

The boat was drifting lazily toward the bank. We started paddling again.

"He's in them woods," Jinx said, not through with her Skunk business. "In the dark shadows. He don't do nothing but wait till someone wants to hire him. He's out there somewhere, in his tent made of skins, all them bones hanging around it, rattling in the breeze. He wraps all those bones in that tent and straps it to his back and moves about, sets up camp again. He's waiting till someone wants him. They got to talk to one of his cousins to go up in there and find him, because he won't let no one else come close, and they say even his cousins are afraid of him."

"How did he get the way he is?" I asked her.

"They say his mama couldn't stand him no more cause he was

crazy, and so when he was ten, for his birthday, she took him out in the river and threw him out of the boat and hit him in the head with a paddle. He didn't die. He just got knocked out good and floated up on shore. He took to living 'long the riverbank, and in the woods. Later, his mama was found with her hands chopped off and her head had been stove in with a boat paddle."

"How perfect," Terry said, and he laughed.

"You laugh, you want," Jinx said. "But you better believe it. Skunk's out there. And you run up on him, it's the last running you gonna do."

3

Finally we come up on the spot by the river where May Lynn had lived, paddled the boat up there, and leaped out on the bank. Terry had hold of the rope that was tied to the front of the boat, and he looped it around a stump by the water. Then for insurance we all dragged the front end of the boat out of the water so the hole in the bottom was on dirt.

Just before we started up to the house, Jinx looked out over the river and pointed. Jinx was a big pointer. She was always pointing out this and pointing out that. Every time we were there Jinx would point out that spot. It's where May Lynn's mother went into the river with a shirt wrapped around her head.

"It was right there," she said, as if we didn't know.

We walked up a hill, which was slick with pine needles. The house was on top of the hill and it was raised on a bunch of leaning creosote posts; it was up high like that so that when the river rose it wouldn't float away. With the way it leaned, I reckoned it wouldn't be long before the whole shebang was shoved off and went tumbling downhill and into the river, about where May Lynn's mama had gone down.

When we got to the top of the hill, just so we wouldn't surprise May Lynn's daddy and get our teeth filled with shotgun pellets, I called out, "Hallo the house."

No one answered, but we waited a minute anyhow. Just in case he might be napping off a drunk. There was an outhouse farther up the hill, and there was a ditch that ran off from it out into the water, which was the plumbing. What went in the hole in the outhouse went down the hill through that open ditch, and into the water. Terry studied the toilet for a while, then said, "That isn't very sanitary. You should keep your body leavings away from water. It's standard knowledge. You dig a pit, not a runoff. That's lazy."

"Her old man is lazy," I said. "What else can you say?"

We had been standing below and near the house, waiting to see if anyone came out. When they didn't, we called out again, all three of us calling at the same time. Still no one answered.

There were some steps going up the ten-foot rise to the weathered, sagging porch, and we walked up them. They shook as we climbed. The sides of the steps were fixed onto the platform by wooden rails, and where there should have been a step at the top there wasn't one. You had to stretch your leg out and climb carefully onto the landing, which wobbled when we climbed up on it.

We called out one more time, but still no one answered. Except for Cletus Baxter, there wasn't anyone left to answer. There had been May Lynn's brother, Jake, but he came to an end about a year back. Word was he robbed banks, but according to most he knocked off filling stations. He hid out down in the Sabine bottoms between station jobs and nobody would tell the cops on him. It wasn't that he was all that well liked, but he was one of the river people, and he had a gun and bad temper and at any moment either one of them could go off.

Course, Constable Sy Higgins knew he was there, but he didn't care because Jake kept him paid up. Constable Sy, according to folks I heard talk, was always glad to hear Jake was about a new job of stealing, cause it meant the constable was going to have a fresh supply of whiskey, or a new eye patch.

As for Jake, before the real law could close in on him, if they were ever going to, he come down with a cold and got pneumonia and died right in the house.

When no one came to our knock at the door, Terry said, "What in the world are we doing here? May Lynn is back at the graveyard."

I was the only one that had ever actually met Cletus Baxter. All of us had been in the house a few times to see May Lynn, but when Terry and Jinx were with me, Cletus was never there. When I had seen him, he hadn't so much as acknowledged me with a fart or a nod. Her mama we had all known; a quiet, thin woman with hair the color of damp wheat, a face like all the sadness in the world.

Even Jake we had all seen, a dark-eyed man with a handsome face marred by a scar across his right cheek where an old shotgun had blown apart on him when he was about our age. He was friendly enough, but always eyed us like we might be young feds out to gun him down for stealing twenty-five bucks from a filling station.

"It is funny," I said. "Here we are, and I don't know what for."

"We is just plain nosey, that's what for," Jinx said.

I knocked on the door again, and this time it moved. We all stood there looking at the crack that was made when it did, then I reached out and pushed at it, and went inside just like I had been invited.

Terry and Jinx followed.

"This isn't right," Terry said.

"It sure ain't," Jinx said.

Neither of them turned around, though. They kept coming after me.

The house was just one big slanting room that was sectioned off by blankets hung up on ropes so the blankets could slide back and forth. The biggest section was for May Lynn's daddy, and there were several blankets stretched across the house for his part. One of his blankets was pulled back and I could see a cot in there and a little table with a Bible on it that was stuffed full of papers. When I looked more closely, I saw they were cigarette papers for rolling. There was a tin of Prince Albert on the stand, too, and all over the place—the table, the bed, the floor, and even on the one wooden chair—there was specks of tobacco, like dirty dandruff flakes. I remembered I had watched him roll a cigarette once, and his hands shook so bad from being on the end of a weeklong drunk, he scattered tobacco everywhere.

Part of the room had been divided for a cooking place, which was a woodstove with a pipe that ran out a hole cut into the wall by a window. Over the window was curtains made of the same blue flowers that had been on May Lynn's dress.

May Lynn's part was sectioned off by blankets, and it wasn't much. If Jake had ever had a section, it had been taken over by his old man. It was hard to believe four people had ever lived there.

We moved May Lynn's blankets aside and took a peek. She had a little feather mattress on the floor, and it was stained by water and sweat. There were two near-flat pillows on the mattress. One of them had a pillowcase made of the same material as her dress and the kitchen curtains. The other didn't have a case. There was a dresser with a cracked mirror up against the wall. It had belonged to May Lynn's mother, and it was the only piece of real furniture in the house.

On top of the dresser was a huge stack of movie magazines. There was a chair by the dresser and one at the end of the bed. May Lynn used to sit in one chair and I would sit in the other, and she would show me the magazines and the people in them. They seemed like people from a dream, like angels descended from heaven. They didn't look like anyone I knew except May Lynn, even if she didn't have the clothes for it.

Jinx touched the magazines, lifted them, said, "These here all put together is heavy enough to sink a boat."

"She certainly loved them," Terry said.

"I figured she'd go off someday and become a movie star," I said. "I figured anyone could do it, it was her."

Terry sat down in the chair at the end of the bed and picked up one of her pillows. He said, "It smells like her. That drugstore perfume she wore." He put the pillow down and looked at us. "You know, May Lynn really ought to go to Hollywood."

"She's a whole lot dead," Jinx said, sitting down on the mattress.

"She should still make the journey," Terry said, and crossed his legs. "It's all she ever wanted, and now she's ended up buried in a hole like a dead pet. I don't think that's how it ought to end for her."

"And I don't think I ought to stink when I'm straining in the outhouse," Jinx said, "but so far it don't work no other way."

"We could take her to Hollywood," Terry said.

"Say what?" I said.

"We could take her."

"You mean dig her up?" Jinx said.

"Yes," Terry said. "She won't dig herself up."

"That's certainly true," I said.

"I mean it," Terry said.

Me and Jinx looked at one another.

Jinx said, "So we dig her up and carry her and the coffin all the way to Hollywood on our backs, and when we get there, we go over to see the movie people and tell them we got their next star, a dead body that don't look nothing like May Lynn used to look and has a smell about her that could knock a bird out of a tree and kill it stone dead?"

"Of course not," Terry said. "I'm merely stating the obvious fact that we haven't got so many friends that we should not care about a dead one. I think we have to dig her up, give her a funeral like they used to give heroes in ancient Greece. You know, burn her on a funeral pyre and gather up her ashes; the ashes can go to Hollywood."

"She ain't a Greek," Jinx said.

"But she was a kind of goddess, don't you think?" Terry said.

"What she was was a river-bottoms kid that was very pretty that came up dead with a sewing machine tied to her feet," I said. "You're crazy, Terry. We can't dig her up and set her on fire, take her ashes to Hollywood."

"It's the principle of the thing," Terry said.

"How's that?" Jinx said.

"It won't mean anything to her, you're right," Terry said. "Being dead takes the fun out of things. I know. I once had a dog that died and I prayed that he'd come back to life, but he didn't. And I finally decided God had brought him back, but hadn't let him out of the hole. I went out and dug him up to help him out, only he was still dead and not looking very good."

"I could have told you how that was going to turn out," Jinx said.

"It isn't like any of us want to remain here," Terry said.

"That's true," Jinx said. "I do, I'm gonna end up wiping white baby asses and doing laundry and cooking meals for pecker-woods the rest of my life. And if that's what I got coming, I might do like Mrs. Baxter and wrap a shirt around my head and go in the river."

"Don't even say that," I said.

"I just did."

"Well, don't say it again."

"There isn't anything for us here," Terry said. "You can't really grow here. Not the way we should. We stay here, there will always be some kind of weight on our heads, holding us down. I like the idea of taking May Lynn's ashes to Hollywood and sprinkling them around where she'll always be a part of it. May Lynn had an adventurous spirit about her, and I think she was no more than a few months shy of departing from this place."

"She should have hurried up," Jinx said.

"We have a chance to leave," Terry said. "All we have to do is reach out and embrace it. Together we can make it work. We can help each other achieve that goal."

"What you need is a good meal and some sleep," I said, looking at Terry.

Terry shook his head. "No. What I need is a shovel and some friends to help me dig her up. Then we burn her and the magazines together. It's symbolic that way."

"Symbolic?" Jinx said.

"Then we put the combined ashes in a jar—"

"A jar?" Jinx said.

"Or some kind of container," Terry said. "Then we float down the river to a good-sized town, catch a bus, and head for Hollywood."

"A bus?" Jinx said.

"Stop being a mockingbird," Terry said, frowning at Jinx.

"That sounds crazy," I said.

"I like crazy better than I like being around here," Terry said.

"That's two of us," Jinx said.

They both stared at me, waiting for agreement, I suppose.

"Let me think about it," I said.

"I know you," Terry said. "You aren't really going to consider it. You're just saying that so I'll shut up."

"While you think about it," Jinx said, "me and Terry are gonna be setting May Lynn on fire with them magazines, and by the time you've decided one way or the other, we'll be in a boat, maybe one without a hole in the bottom, on our way to Hollywood with that gal in a jar."

"I know this much," I said. "The Sabine River don't go to Hollywood."

"Yeah, but we'll arrive there somehow," Terry said.

I could almost see the wheels in his head turning.

He lifted his head and his lips curled at the edges. "There's the barge. We could take the barge. It's big enough to live on."

"It's too big for some of the narrow spots," Jinx said. "We might go better by patching up the boat, or getting some other one."

"I bet we can get it through those spots if we put our backs into it," Terry said.

"The barge, as you call it, ain't nothing more than a raft," I said.

"You could actually dock it against the bank at night and sleep on it," Terry said.

"I want to think about it," I said, feeling the pressure, hoping the whole thing would go out of his and Jinx's head by the time we got back across the river.

"What's to think on?" Jinx said. "You told us you can't even sleep good for watching for your daddy coming into your room."

I nodded, thinking about how I usually slept with a piece of stove wood in the bed next to me, my door locked, one eye open and an ear cocked. "That's true."

"Well, then," Terry said.

"I got some things to do at home first," I said, still thinking it was all going to be forgotten in a short time, but actually beginning to warm to the idea.

"All right, then," Terry said. "We can all go home and prepare, and if either of you have any money, now would be a good time to bring it."

"I have a quarter," I said. "That's it."

"I got the teeth in my head," Jinx said.

"I have a few dollars," Terry said. "But what we really need is a plan."

4

—⁓—

We gathered up the magazines, and decided it was okay because May Lynn told us her daddy always thought her wanting to be in the movies was silly, told her wanting to be on a screen dressed up like a hussy in tight clothes and wearing makeup like war paint wasn't any plan for a grown woman. That meant those magazines would soon be burned up for fire starter or tossed out to rot when he came back and found out she was dead. I figured that portion of the house would become his, too, littered with cigarette papers and tobacco crumbs.

Anyway, we took them, and as we was stuffing them into a couple of pillowcases, a writing tablet with a red cardboard cover fell out and hit the floor. Jinx picked it up and said, "Look here."

Scrawled on the front of it in May Lynn's handwriting was the word DIARY. The writing was in pencil, and it was so rubbed over, and the cover so dark to begin with, you could hardly see the word.

"You think we should peek inside?" Jinx said.

"We shouldn't," I said, "but I know we will."

"If we're going to steal her body and set her on fire and take her ashes to Hollywood," Jinx said, "I think we must go in for the whole hog, including the squeal."

"Not here, though," I said, switching my viewpoint instantly. "We can go somewhere, sit, and read it. I don't want her daddy showing up, and us having been housebreakers and thieves right out here in the open. Criminals, I think, should act in privacy or the dark."

"Perhaps we ought to burn it with the magazines," Terry said, taking the diary from Jinx's hands so deftly I figured it was a full minute before she realized she wasn't holding it no more. "She isn't here to say we can look at it."

"That's the proper thing to do," I said. "Burn it. But is that what we're gonna do?"

Jinx said, "We all know we're gonna look at it, so we should get on with it."

"I thought it might be good manners to at least act like we wasn't," I said.

Going home right then went out of my mind like a bird that had been let loose from a cage. We decided to go someplace private and read the diary. But when we went out of the house, Terry, still clutching the diary, left me holding the pillowcase full of magazines and went to the outhouse.

"Don't you read none of it in there," Jinx said.

"I won't," Terry said.

"Leave it," I said.

"Nope, cause I trust me not to read it," he said. "But you two, I don't."

"That wasn't very nice," Jinx said, as Terry went into the outhouse and closed the door.

* * *

Not too far downriver there's the barge, the one Terry said we ought to steal. It's staked out like a Judas goat to an old cypress stump in the middle of the water. It's really just a big raft, but everyone calls it a barge. There's a tree branch that has sprouted off the stump and it grows tall and green and puts out shade at one end of the barge. Midday and dead summer, the shade looks green because of the way the sun shines through the leaves and lays on the rough planks nailed over the logs. The barge is tied to the stump with thick twists of weathered rope, replaced from time to time by someone with fresh rope and the desire to do it. Where the barge sits, the water is wide. The barge can hold a fair number of people on it, and it was put there by someone long ago that's been forgotten. Whoever built it made it solid, and the wood has held and hasn't rotted. The bottoms of the logs and boards used to make it are coated in creosote. Everyone uses it, and no one has moved it for at least ten years. Storms and high water have been unable to tear it up, even if on occasion the water has risen higher than the rope that binds it. Sometimes when the water is way up, the roped end of the barge stays down, and the loose end floats to the top and you can see that end sticking out of the water. When the water settles, it's like nothing ever happened. Sometimes when I walk along the river and look out at it, I can see frogs on it, or long yellow-bellied water snakes and sometimes water moccasins, looking thick and stumpy and evil and ready to bite.

Whoever gets there first uses it as a place to picnic, fish, and swim. At night, kids skip the shorts and skinny-dip there. It's said there's been a few babies made there on blankets when the night is deep and the water is smooth and the moon is shining a silvery love light. And I don't doubt it.

There have been a lot of drownings around the barge, and

there's been talk about setting fire to it so folks won't go out on it. But the thing is, people will always go in the water, and they'll always drown, and they don't need a barge to do it. Some even do it on purpose, something May Lynn's mother proved without a barge. As for wearing a shirt over your head, you can do it or not—it's not expected.

We paddled and bailed our boat on down the river until we came to the barge. There was no one there, only the shade.

We climbed out of the boat onto the barge and pulled the boat up behind us. It was tough work, but we did it. Under the shade of the leafy limb we sat down, and Terry opened the diary. There were a number of pages torn out of it, and doodles in the margins. Terry started reading it aloud. It wasn't written the way she talked, but instead she had tried to make it proper. It made me sad. It had some truth to it, but it also had a lot of things that might not have happened—things that May Lynn felt certain would occur someday. Like going to Hollywood and being discovered in some soda shop or such, and then becoming a big star. She told how this had happened, when I knew it hadn't. She hadn't never got out of East Texas, let alone to Hollywood.

She talked about us in passing, like you might point out you seen a redbird the other day. I won't kid you, that bothered me a little. I figured we was worth more than a spotty mention. Here we was going to her funeral and planning on burning her up and taking her out to Hollywood, and we didn't get no more consideration than that. I felt the story of her life, even with lies, might have given us a bigger role.

The shadow was spreading wider by the time Terry came to the part in the diary that made our plans, everything we had talked about, real. It was a part that caused me to cry inside and made me scared a little, though I can't tell you exactly why. It was the part that sealed the deal about us going to Hollywood.

It was the part that would change our lives and make it so nothing would ever be the same again.

It was a page or two about her brother, and there was a photograph of her stuffed inside the diary. It was a good one, but she had ways about her a photograph couldn't hold; even in that old faded flower dress she looked like a million bucks. And there was another thing inside of the diary, a little map put down on thin paper. This map, along with things we read in the diary, let us know that her brother, who we knew to be a thief, was a bigger thief than we thought; though I guess she could have made the whole thing up, like some of the other stuff she had written down.

May Lynn wrote about her brother: "This isn't something I should put down, because it is a scandal to the family." But she was doing it anyway, because it was her diary, she said, and she could write what she wanted. There was no one to see it but her and the lamplight.

Her take on Jake's theft wasn't what I expected. She said Jake gave her some of the money he stole. Her daddy got some of it, too, and that she was always glad to see Jake coming, not only because she loved her brother, but she liked that he had money. She thought soon he'd give her more than just enough for perfume and a picture show; maybe enough for some new clothes and a bus ticket to Hollywood.

The diary said Jake had mostly centered his attentions on service stations and little stores until he took in a partner named Warren Cain, and because of that he got his courage up. They came to a little town that had a bank, and he and Cain went in there and robbed it at pistol point, jumped in the car and drove off, and came here to the river bottoms to hide away. There wasn't any more mention of Warren Cain, but a few pages later, May Lynn wrote how before Jake got the chest sickness and died, he buried all the money he stole cause her daddy kept sniffing around, trying to lay his hands on it, and Jake knew he'd drink it up, quicker than a cat can jump.

"Jake gave me a map," she wrote,

so I could find the money. He may just be out of his head and none of what he says is true, and the money may be all gone. And what he says about how I need to be careful may not be anything to worry about. I asked what it was I should be careful of, and he said getting killed. When I asked by what, or who, he began to roll his eyes up in his head, as if something might be standing on the ceiling. I guess it was. I guess it was the Angel of Death that he saw, because it wasn't more than a minute after he done that, that his eyes glazed over and I realized he had quit breathing and was gone on.

If the money really is there, I'm going to try and find it and go off to Hollywood to get my start. I think God must want me to have this money, or he would not have let my brother rob banks and bury it and then die. I thank God left this money for me.

When Terry quit reading, he said, "That is an interesting conclusion."

"Sounds to me like stealing," I said. "And if God left her the money, then he's a thief, too."

"It sounds to me like a way to get out of this hellhole," Jinx said. "And though I ain't no thief under normal situations, I knew where that money was, I'd be on it like stink on a dead possum."

"We can follow the map," Terry said.

"What if it's just one of her tales?" I said. "The diary is full of them. And it's even missing pages, for some reason."

"I presume that was her way of editing it," Terry said. "Writing things about yourself and putting them in a diary can even be difficult. There's always some part of you, I suppose, that fears someone will see it."

"Like three friends who stole it from her house," Jinx said.

"Like that," Terry said. "I think a lot of this is more like a novel, or a long short story. Maybe she started out to write a diary and there just wasn't enough to talk about that was interesting."

It certainly had in it all manner of nonsense about how she had been writing big movie stars and they had been writing her back, and how she had sent a picture of herself in and a producer liked the way she looked and wanted her to come on out. All of that was just foolishness, and nothing else, but some of it I knew to be true. Some of it was about things I knew had happened.

"Well, now," Terry said, "we know Jake was a robber, isn't that correct? And she has written down a detailed map that she said she got from her brother on his deathbed, so—"

"All we got to do," said Jinx, "is take that map and follow it, see if it leads somewhere, and then split up the money and run like bastards."

"Not exactly what I had in mind," Terry said. "But it has occurred to me that with Sue Ellen's quarter, and your 'nothing but teeth,' Jinx, and me having a few dollars, we might not get far, or however far we manage to go there might be very little comfort to it. But once we get downriver, to a town, money can make things a lot better. So we go and see if the stolen money is there, and if it is, we take it. Then we do what I said about the body. Burn it up and carry her ashes out to Hollywood. It's what she wanted."

"It's stolen money," I said.

"We don't even know what bank it came from if we wanted to give it back," Terry said.

"See there?" Jinx said, nodding quickly several times. "We ain't really got no other choice."

"We could give it to the authorities," I said.

"Constable Sy?" Terry asked.

"There's bound to be someone else," I said.

"There might be," Jinx said, "but I don't want to find them suckers. Constable Sy would just take it for his own self. I want to do what Terry wants to do, and I say we do it on the cheap, and if there's money left over we split it. And if you're all that bothered about it, Sue Ellen, I'll take your cut."

"Say there was bank money," I said. "Why didn't May Lynn take it and go off on her own?"

"Maybe she wasn't ready," Jinx said. "Maybe she couldn't figure out the map. That don't mean the money ain't there and that she didn't plan to take it. Now that I think on it, we ought to take a bus. I don't like water all that much. I can swim, but not so good, and there's snakes and such. On a bus, I have to ride in the back in the colored part, like dirty laundry, but at least I'm a whole lot less likely to drowned or get snakebit."

"And where do we catch that bus?" Terry said.

"Gladewater," Jinx said. "That's how Daddy goes. He walks across the Sabine River bridge, catches a ride to Gladewater, then gets the bus there, takes it up north to Yankee land. We'd take our bus out west."

"Your daddy has a car," I said.

"Now he does," Jinx said. "But that's how he went the first time. By bus."

"Best way for us to arrive in Gladewater is to take the river," Terry said. "It's quicker than walking, and more certain than a ride, and we don't have to wonder who it is we're riding with. Catching a ride might be why May Lynn's dead. She may have caught it with the wrong kind of person. I say we take the money and steal her body and burn it up, and jar it up, and then float down near Gladewater, walk in and buy tickets at the bus station, and proceed to Hollywood."

"There's some sense in that," Jinx said. "And when we get to Gladewater and take the bus, we can use some of the money to buy lunches to tote with us. I've always wanted to buy a lunch. Though you'll have to buy it for me. There's that whole colored thing about going into cafés and such."

"Don't worry," Terry said. "It'll be taken care of." He looked at me. "You aren't saying much."

"I'm sitting here considering on my life of crime and how it could help me buy a lunch for a bus trip."

"It's money that has already been stolen," Terry said. "It's not like you stole it."

"If I take it, it would be like stealing, because that's exactly what I'd be doing. Stealing from a thief wouldn't make me any less a thief."

"The thief is dead, and so are his heirs," Terry said.

"There's the father," I said.

"He doesn't count," Terry said.

"Why's that?" I said.

"Because I don't like him, and if you get right down to it, you can't be an heir to stolen money. Not legally, anyway."

"I'm glad that puts us on such solid legal ground," I said.

5

W e pushed our boat off the barge—or what I call a raft—
back into the river, and paddled it to land. After we got on ground,
we pulled the boat up under a tree and found some dried brush to
lean on it. It wasn't much of a hideaway, but it's what we had.

Before we left out of there, we sat down under a tree and got
out the map and turned it ever which way trying to figure out
what it meant. It might as well have been written in Greek. We
could make out what must have been May Lynn's house and the
river drawn on it in a squiggly line, and above it a rise in the land
that was familiar. Finally there was a couple of thick lines with little lines drawn between them. We figured that had to be railroad
tracks. Beyond the tracks, there were some humps, and there was
a line written out that said MALCOLM CUZINS. Neither the humps
or the name meant anything to us.

We walked away from the river and the bottomland, made our
way back to where May Lynn's house stood. We went wide of it
toward the woods.

The woods were thick and it took us a while to thread through them and climb up a big hill. We finally got on the trail that went out of the bottoms, ending us up on a field where cane grew. It was highland cane and it wasn't as good as bottom cane, but it was still good enough. It was a big patch that covered a lot of acres, and the stalks were thick and tall. The cane had turned slightly purple, and I knew once it was stripped the sugar inside of it would be sweet.

I had a pocketknife, and I cut down a stalk next to where the field started, then cut it into three pieces. It took some work, but we all got our pieces frayed and that gave us the pulp to chew on. It was sugary, and it was something to keep us happy and busy while we walked. I figure when you got right down to it, we weren't fresh thieves after all, but had had plenty of practice in the cane fields and watermelon patches. Heck, I had started my life of crime sometime back, but had just then realized it. The natural move forward would be to take stolen bank money and spend it on a trip to Hollywood with a dead girl burnt up in a jar.

We followed the map and came to a low cut of pines, and on the other side of the pines was the train tracks. On the far side of the tracks was more trees. Most of them was pecan and hickory nut and might have once been part of an orchard, but were now wild and unpruned. There was a nice breeze blowing, and we could smell the scent of the trees on the wind, and there were birds in the trees, mostly red-winged blackbirds; they were as thick there as leaves.

There was a rumble and the train rails began to vibrate. We stepped back in the pines, in the shadow, and waited. A train came chugging by, screeching on top of the rails. I thought maybe that ought to be the way we should get out of there, by hopping a train. But it was traveling fast as it went by, and none of the boxcar doors was open; it was an idea that passed from my mind quickly. I figured if I grabbed at the train my arms would get jerked off.

Still, it was mighty pleasant watching the train go by, all those boxcars clacking along, and while it rolled I thought of May Lynn. I guess it was the train moving away from us, heading anywhere but where we was, that made me think of her. That and our plans, of course.

I remember once sitting in her house on her mattress on the floor, and she had been talking about the movies and her plans to star in them, and then she said something to me that dove out of the air like a rock and felt like it hit me in the back of the head.

"Sue Ellen," she said, "what is it you want to do with your life?"

Until she asked that, I didn't even know I had the chance to think about anything different than what I was doing at the moment, but with her telling me all her plans, and then asking me that question, certain feelings I had started rising up to the surface like a dead carp. I knew then I wanted out of what I was in, and I wanted something else other than what I had, but the miserable thing was, I didn't know where I wanted to go or what I wanted to do.

We laughed and talked about this and that, about some boys we knew, none of them particularly interesting, and May Lynn said she sure thought Terry was cute, but there was that whole sissy problem. We combed each other's hair, and her mama, a few months short of her dip in the river and moving like she was some kind of animal dying slowly, cooked us some grits, and we had them with no butter and no milk. I remember thinking then that May Lynn was the most wonderful person in the world, and certainly the most beautiful. But what made me feel really good while eating grits with no butter and no milk was that she had spoken to me like I could have plans and ought to have plans, and that my life could be better. Right then and there I believed it myself a little. Not so much you could write a song about it, but some. I didn't know what I was going to do, but I knew it would be something. I can't say that stealing money and going by raft down the dirty Sabine with May Lynn's ashes in a jar had been any part of those plans, but I knew then that I wasn't going to be settled with life as I knew it; wasn't going to end up like Mama, drinking cure-all and taking a whacking from her husband and thinking it was as natural as the course of the river.

I looked up from thinking about all this, and saw the train moving on down the line and out of sight. We stood there looking where it had gone, and then we looked at the map again and determined that we at least knew where the tracks were. Beyond that it was all mighty confusing. The little humps — and there was bunches of them in several rows on the paper — and the name Malcolm Cuzins didn't make no sense whatsoever.

As we crossed the tracks and went under the trees, the red-winged blackbirds took flight. They looked bloodied as they rose in a whoosh, and they filled the sky like a cloud, then they was gone.

"Well," Terry said, looking at the map. "I fail to make sense of it. I can't determine what these humps mean. And the name written on the map is a mystery to me."

Jinx and I were equally baffled, and we kept looking at the map like it would all come to us eventually, but it didn't. Fact was, I was getting a bit of a headache.

"There's nothing out here but a few trees," I said. "I think there's an old graveyard over there, and beyond that there's a road."

"I remember that ole graveyard," Jinx said. She nodded at me. "We was up here once, when we was little kids. We seen some of them graves then."

"I barely remember," I said.

"I told you there was haints there and that they'd grab you up and pull you down in the ground," Jinx said. "I thought you was gonna pee your pants."

"That wasn't very nice," I said.

"That's what made it funny," she said.

We looked around for a while, then gave up and went back down to the cane field and cut us another piece of cane.

As we ate the pulp from the cane and walked, I said, "I think our Hollywood plans would be on the too-early side without that money. So I think we don't burn May Lynn up and put her in a jar and head out just yet. My guess is we might make Gladewater, but beyond that we'd be hard-pressed to go on."

No one said anything for a long while, but I'm pretty sure, like me, they could hear our plans crackling away like dry paper on fire.

By the time we worked our way back to the boat, the sun was starting to drop out of sight behind the trees, and the shadows were long and dark across the ground and on the water. Frogs was getting louder and so were the crickets. We paddled our way across the water current, and by the time we got to the other side, the water was high in the leaky boat, in spite of me and Jinx taking turns bailing.

As we got out of the boat, pulled it on shore, and pushed it under some trees, Jinx said, "One thing we gonna have to say for sure. This boat ain't no damn good. We go downriver, we'll have to take the barge, otherwise we'll be tuckered out in a couple hours. The boat will fill up and sink to the bottom of the river. Catfish will be living in our skulls before a week passes."

This statement went uncontested. Everything we talked about seemed like so much wind now. Talk is cheap and exciting, but when you get right down to doing something, money is usually needed. Planning is often better than going through with the actual plan. Expectations, I once heard an old man say, were a little like fat birds: you might as well kill them before they fly away.

We split up and headed our own ways. As I walked, the shadows stretched. I realized it would be dead dark long before I got home. Even though I had grown up in the bottoms, there was lots of tales about things down in them that gave me a case of the nerves. Mostly they was stories about things that came out at night and was angry and hungry and carried you off and sucked the centers out of your bones. Ever hoot of an owl or crack of a limb or the scratching of brush moved by the wind made me jump a little. To top things off nicely, it began to lightning in the east, stitching up the pit-black sky like a drunk seamstress with bright yellow thread. The wind rose and made the trees sigh and whip even more, and before long, drops of rain were falling on me. By the time I got near enough to our house to see a light in the window, the rain was coming down hard as tossed gravel, and the wind was whipping the willows along the riverbank like a teacher smacking a rowdy student's butt with a switch.

In the yard, I was startled by one of the free-ranging hogs that came around the side of the house and grunted at me, perhaps hoping I had an apple or something. It was the big black-and-white one. I started to reach out and pet it, but since it was gonna be eaten in the fall, I hesitated. It never set well with me to get friendly with something I planned to have on a plate with a side of new potatoes and collard greens. I felt it was proper to have a solid understanding between person and hog that no friendship was involved, though if the hog had known the true nature of its arrangement, I'm sure it would have found reason to depart for parts unknown, maybe taking the other hog and chickens with him. Besides, petting a wet hog, be it friend or supper, is stinky business.

Daddy was home. I could see his banged-up pickup parked in

the yard. I walked up on the porch and it creaked, and that made me nervous. It wasn't that Daddy cared when I came in, and much of the time he might not know I was gone. But to wake him could set him in a bad temper, and then the razor strop would come out. I wasn't up for dodging his blows, or, for that matter, dodging his grabbing hands.

On the porch there was a stack of firewood piled close to the house. I picked me up a good stout piece that fit my clenched fist, opened the door, and stepped inside. Our house wasn't no kind of showplace, but it was big. It had been built long before the river changed course. Daddy had it handed down to him when his father died—who, according to word I had heard, was no better a person than he was. But Daddy's grandfather was a solid gentleman with money he had brought down from the North back in the eighteen hundreds. Word was he had earned it in shipping somehow, and then decided he'd had enough and had gone down south. He had built a sturdy house and barn and sheds that his son, and now grandson, had let go to ruin by neglect.

Some years back the river changed and it had taken away a lot of the outbuildings. I had heard about the flood of 1900, and how it had killed families, and how back then our house sat high on a hill. Then the river rampaged through like a pack of wild Indians. It stole the soil and carried it off, and the water had climbed up to where there was once high ground. Where solid earth had stood, there was a bend in the river now, rising high on the bank, maybe a hundred feet from our two-story house. I liked to imagine that the water that had carried those outbuildings away had put them back together at the bottom of the river with the help of the catfish, and that the barn I had never seen had mermaids living in it; and that the outhouse was being used by water monsters with lots of long, sticky legs and whiplike tongues that was forked at the tips.

It was a shame, really, what Daddy and his daddy had let happen

to the place. Now the big house squeaked when you went upstairs, and you had to watch your step where it had rotten spots.
In the main room, which was large, it was too cold to be there
in winter. The fireplace leaned away from the wall, and outside it
was held up by a big stick that looked ready to break at any moment. Around the cracks in the bricks the wind came through like
a burglar, and in the summer, so did the snakes and frogs and all
manner of vermin.

There was only three of us in the house, and Daddy and Mama
mostly avoided one another. They had little to say except simple
stuff about chickens and hogs, and as of late, there was less of that.
Daddy spent a lot of his time somewhere else, and Mama didn't
care. She took to bed often, lay propped against cotton-stuffed
pillows drinking cheap cure-all she bought from a man that traveled the country in a dusty black car. He always wore a big black
hat and had black clothes and boots, and his shirt was the color of
flour paste. He had been around for years and looked the same.
Some said for twenty years, but others said a son had taken over
the father's position. There were even those who said he was the
devil. I had seen him, a tall, whip-lean man in a black hat and
a smooth black suit. His face looked like it had been cut out of
wood, and his chin was long and pointed.

"Devil don't need no car that runs on gas," Jinx had said. "So he
ain't no devil. And there ain't no devils or angels anyhow."

Jinx was certain on the matter. Me, it depended on if it was
Tuesday or not. I had a tendency to believe all manner of things
on a Tuesday. I know this: what the salesman sold to Mama was
certainly devilish. It was a mixture of alcohol and most likely laudanum. It went for a quarter, and may have cost him a dime. It
was money we couldn't afford, but she bought the stuff by the box
and sucked it like a baby will suck a bottle.

Daddy had his whiskey. Mama had her cure-all. It made her

deep dream, she said, and the dreams were fine and bright and there was no river near the door. In those deep-down dreams, she said, me and her lived in a good way in a clean white house on high, dry land. Daddy was shaved and dirt-free and upright, wasn't missing so many teeth, and lived the way he should. When she woke, she said, it was like she was in a nightmare, and everything that mattered was stepped on and messed with or mistreated, but a few long swigs of the cure-all took her back to where she liked to live. It hurt to think I was losing Mama to twenty-five cents a bottle and a lying dream.

The light in the house was a lantern burning on a nightstand near the window. Mama had lit it and left it for me. I was glad for the light, but thought it was damn dangerous to let it burn like that, being near the curtains. Then again, Mama's judgment was missing a step these days. I blew out the lantern and looked out the window. The rain had gone away as swift as it had come, and the clouds had parted, and the apple-slice moon was giving out shiny light that looked greasy through the glass; it made the yard shimmer like a wet nickel.

I started upstairs with my stove wood, feeling my way along the rail by experience. Daddy didn't leap out on me. I watched the bad boards, and made it to the top of the stairs without one of the steps breaking and dropping me through like a gallows. Upstairs, it was musty where the old carpet had rotted. Rain came through a hole at the end of the hall, and sometimes so did pigeons. Daddy was always planning to fix it, but when it came time to buy boards, he bought whiskey instead.

The thing I did like was having a room of my own with a lock on the door. Most river people didn't have such a thing, and even Terry, who had come from better circumstances, slept on a pallet in their living room, along with four other kids, who had come as a package with his mama's new husband.

I started to go in my room, but stopped and went down the hall, where Mama stayed. The door was cracked. When I looked in, I could see her shape on the bed, and I was surprised to see another. Even in the dark, I could tell it was Daddy. The moonlight, though thin, lay on his face and made it look as if he was wearing a mask. He was halfway under the covers and had his head turned toward me.

Mama had had far too much laudanum, and that was a fact. Otherwise she would never have let him in to sleep with her, even if it was only to lie at the foot of the bed as a foot warmer.

As I stood there looking, Daddy opened his eyes and saw me. He didn't move. He just kept looking at me. After a while, he smiled, and the few teeth he had held the moonlight.

I frowned, smacked the stove wood against my open hand until his smile went away, and then I closed the door and walked off.

I dug in my overalls for my key, unlocked my door, pushed it shut, and locked it. I took off my clothes, pulled on my night-gown, shoved back the covers, and crawled in bed with the stove wood beside me. I lay there with the moonlight poking through the thin curtains over my window. I patted the stove wood like it was a bark-covered cat. I thought about Mama and Daddy together, something that ought to have been right, but wasn't. They had been as distant from one another in recent months as the moon is from the earth, and now this.

I came to the conclusion that on this night, in Mama's laudanum dreams, he may have been a white knight on a white charger, and she had, so to speak, opened the castle doors and let him in. Bless her heart, the laudanum lied. Yet who was I to judge? Even a root hog has its needs, and I suspect even a root hog has its dreams.

The bed was soft and I was tired. I lay there half awake, half in dream. I dreamed of me and Jinx and Terry, sailing down the Sabine River until we came to Hollywood, sailing right out of darkness and into light, gliding down a wide, wet street of water. On either side of us, standing on golden bricks, were handsome men and beautiful women, all movie stars, people we had seen in films. They waved at us as we drifted by and we waved back, sailing along on our stolen raft with a big white bag of stolen money with a black dollar sign on it. Next to the bag was May Lynn's ashes in a golden urn.

Along the street, on either side, all the people—knowing who May Lynn was and what she might have been, knowing all the movies she didn't make, the life she didn't live—stopped waving and started to cry. We sailed quietly down the street, out of their sight, into shadows black as crows.

6

Next morning I awoke to the sound of a mockingbird outside my window, perched on a cottonwood limb. It was imitating a songbird, and it sounded as happy as if the song belonged to it; the mockingbird is a kind of thief, same as I planned to be. The big difference was he seemed happy about it and I didn't, and I hadn't stolen anything yet, outside of cane and watermelons.

I lay there for a while and listened to it sing, then got up and dressed, unlocked my door, and went out carrying my stove wood. I wanted to see Mama, but I feared Daddy might still be there. I went downstairs and looked out the window and saw his truck was gone. I rummaged around in the warmer over the stove and found a biscuit hard as a banker's heart, and ate that, careful not to break any teeth.

Back upstairs, I knocked on Mama's door and she called to me to come in. It was dark in the room—since last night someone had pulled the curtain—and I went to the window and pushed it open slightly. Sunlight draped across the bed, and I could see Mama with the covers pulled to her chin, her head propped up on the pillows. Her blond hair was undone and flowed out from her like spilled honey. Her face was white as milk and her bones poked against her skin more than usual, but even so, she was quite beautiful. She looked like a doll made of china.

Dust was spinning in the sunlight, and the bottom of the comforter was fuzzed with it. Cobwebs lay in the corners of the room, thick as ready-to-pick cotton. A bit of the outside breeze came in through the cracks in the wall and moved the floating dust around. It wasn't anything some elbow grease and about twenty-five pounds' worth of lumber and a hammer couldn't fix, but none of us were having at it. We lived there like rats hanging on to a ship we knew was going down.

Mama smiled at me as I sat down in a stuffed chair by the bed. The chair smelled damp and old, like a wet grandma.

"I'd like to get up and fix you something to eat, baby," she said, "but I don't feel up to it."

"It's all right," I said. "I had what I think was a biscuit."

"It's the medicine," she said. "It makes me woozy. I just don't feel up to anything, with it or without it."

"I know."

She looked at me for the longest time, as if she was trying to see something beneath my skin, and then she came out with a confession. "Your daddy was in here last night."

I wasn't sure why she told me, but I said, "Oh," like I didn't know what she was talking about. It was knowledge I would have preferred to have tucked away someplace where I couldn't touch it, like down at the bottom of an alligator pit.

"I'm so ashamed," she said, and turned her head away from me. "I shouldn't even be telling you, you're just a young girl."

"I know some things you might not think I know."

Actually, I had an idea she had seen me, or Daddy had told her, and she felt obliged to explain herself.

Slowly she shifted her head on the pillow and looked back at me. "I don't really remember all that well, but this morning I knew. He had been here. In the night."

"That's all right, Mama."

"No," she said. "No, it isn't. He isn't any good."

We sat that way for a while, her looking at me and me looking at the floor.

After a time, I said, "What if I wanted to go away?"

"Why wouldn't you want to go away?" she said. "There isn't anything for you here."

This wasn't exactly what I expected, and I had to let that roll around in my head for a moment before I was certain I had heard what I thought I had.

"No, ma'am, there ain't nothing here for me."

"Isn't," she said. "Don't use 'ain't.'"

"Sorry," I said. "I forget."

"Actually, you haven't had enough schooling to know better, and I haven't exactly furthered your education by lying in bed, but I'm not up to much, you know. There was a time when I thought I might be a teacher, or a nurse."

"Really?"

"Sure," she said.

"Mama, if you had a friend got drowned, and you found her body, and she always wanted to go to Hollywood to be a movie star, would it be wrong to dig her up after she was buried, burn her to ashes, take them downriver to Gladewater in a jar, catch a bus, and take her out to Hollywood?"

"What?"

I repeated myself.

"What are you talking about? Who is this girl you would dig up?"

"May Lynn."

"The beautiful May Lynn?" she asked, like there were dozens of them.

"That's the one."

"My God, is she dead?"

"Daddy didn't tell you?"

She shook her head.

"You been kind of out of touch," I said. "She was found with a sewing machine tied to her feet yesterday and was buried today. I would have told you last night, but you was out of it."

"Don knew about this?"

"Yes, ma'am. He and Uncle Gene and me and Terry found her in the river."

"Oh my God," Mama said. "She was so young. And it hasn't been that long ago she lost her brother, and before that her mother."

"She was my age," I said. "She never did go nowhere. She wanted to, but she never did."

"Your daddy was there when she was found?" Mama asked, as if I hadn't already explained it.

"He was."

"He never said anything to me."

"No surprise. He wanted to push her and the Singer back in the water."

"He doesn't like problems," she said, as if that explained all his actions.

"I guess not," I said.

"And now you want to go away?"

"I don't know what I want. Me and Terry and Jinx—"

"You still seeing that colored girl?"

"I am."

"Oh, it's all right," Mama said. "I'm not speaking against her. I'm just surprised you aren't like everyone else."

"Everyone else?"

"Way it usually goes is children, colored and white, play together until they get grown, and then they don't associate. It's how it is."

"Thanks for thinking highly of me," I said.

"I didn't mean it that way, Sue Ellen. I just meant it's not the standard way things work out in these parts, or most parts, for that matter, and there's the whole problem of how she's affecting your speech. You talk like a field hand."

She paused, seeming suddenly to have taken hold of what I had said about May Lynn.

"You said you want to dig up your friend and burn her up and take her ashes to Hollywood?"

"I said that, yeah, but am I going to do it? I don't know."

"That's pretty crazy," she said.

"You should know," I said, and hated it as soon as I said it.

Mama turned her face away from me.

"I didn't mean nothing by it," I said. "I'm sorry, Mama."

Slowly she looked back in my direction. "No. It's all right. I wasn't very thoughtful before I spoke. And I suppose I'm not one to judge anyone in any manner, am I?"

"You're all right."

"No. No, I'm not. Listen. I don't know that you should dig up and burn anybody. I'm pretty sure that's a crime. I think there's a list of weird crimes and that's on the list, along with eating out of the toilet and the like. It's just not done. So forget that. But I think it would be good for you to leave. I haven't got the gumption for much of anything anymore, not even being a mother, but you ought not to stay here. Something happens to me, there's just you and your daddy . . . and you wouldn't want that."

"I don't want to leave you here with Daddy," I said, "let alone myself. He's still got a pretty good left hook."

"Don't stay on my account," Mama said. "I let him in last night, though I don't remember it all in a solid kind of way. It was the cure-all. It keeps me confused. And I get so lonely."

"That stuff doesn't cure a thing," I said. "It just makes you drunk and dreamy, and gives you excuses. You ought not drink it anymore."

"You don't know how things are," she said. "It makes me feel good when I feel bad, and without it, I feel bad pretty much all the time. You should go. Forget digging up anybody, that's a bad idea, but you should go."

"I told you, I don't want to leave you with Daddy."

"I can deal with him."

"I don't want you to have to," I said.

Mama considered on something for a long time. I could almost see whatever it was behind her eyes, moving around back there like a person in the shadows. Time she took before she spoke to me, had I been so inclined—which I wasn't—I could have smoked a cigar, and maybe grown the tobacco to roll another.

"Let me tell you something, honey," she said. "Something I should have told you maybe some years ago, but I was ashamed. I didn't want you to know what kind of woman I was."

"You're all right."

"No," Mama said. "No, I'm not all right. I said that before, and I mean it. I'm not all right. I'm not a good Christian."

It wasn't Tuesday, so I wasn't all that high on religion.

"All I know is, if something works out, God gets praised," I said. "If it don't, it's his will. Seems to me he's always perched to swoop in and take credit for all manner of things he didn't do anything about, one way or the other."

"Don't talk like that. You've been baptized."

"I been wet," I said. "All I remember was the preacher held my head under the river water, and when he lifted me up he said something while I blew a stream out of my nose."

"You shouldn't have such talk," she said. "Hell is a hot and bad place."

"I figure I could go there from here and feel relieved," I said.

"Let's not discuss it any further," she said. "I won't have the Lord spoken ill of."

She smoldered for a time. I decided to let her. I sat there and checked out the tips of my fingers, looked at my feet, and watched dust floating in the air. Then she said something that was as surprising as if she had opened her mouth and a covey of quail flew out.

"The man you call Daddy," she said, "well, he isn't your daddy."

I couldn't say anything. I just sat there, numb as an amputated leg.

"Your real daddy is Brian Collins. He was a lawyer and may still be. Over in Gladewater. He and I, well, we had our moment, and then . . . I got pregnant with you."

"Then Don ain't my daddy?"

"Don't say 'ain't.'"

"Forget the ain't shit. He ain't my daddy?"

"No. And don't cuss . . . what a foul word. Never use that word . . . I been meaning to tell you he isn't your daddy. I was waiting for the right time."

"Anytime after birth would have been good."

"I know it's a shock," Mama said. "I didn't tell you because Brian isn't the one who raised you."

"It's not like Don did all that much raising, either," I said. "My real daddy . . . what was he like?"

"He treated me very well. He is older than me by five years or so. We loved one another, and I got pregnant."

"And he didn't want anything to do with you?"

"He wanted to marry me. We loved one another."

"You loved him so much, you come over here and married Don

and let me think he was my daddy? You left my daddy, a lawyer and a good man, and you married a jackass? What was you thinking?"

"See? I told you I was a bad mother."

"Okay. You win. You're a bad mother."

"Listen here, Sue Ellen. I was ashamed. A Christian woman having a child out of wedlock. It wasn't right. It made Brian look bad."

"He said he'd marry you, didn't he?"

"I was starting to show," she said. "I didn't want to get married to him like that, even if it was just in front of a justice of the peace. He had a good job and was respected, and I didn't want that to be lost to him because I couldn't keep my legs crossed."

"He had something to do with the blessed event."

She smiled a little. "Yes, he did."

"So to stay respectful, you left him and came here and ended up marrying Don while you were showing, and now here we are, me toting a stick of stove wood and you a cure-all drunk."

"I was seventeen," she said. "I wasn't thinking clearly."

"I'm seventeen."

"You're sixteen."

"Close enough."

"You aren't the way I was when I was your age. You're strong. Like your real daddy. You have a determination like he has. You're hardheaded in the same way. He wanted to marry me no matter what. I ran off in the dead of night and caught a ride and ended up with a job in a café. I met Don there. He wasn't so ragged and mean then. He wasn't an intellectual or financial catch, and no one thought so highly of him that if he married a pregnant woman it would matter. I decided I could deal with that with him, but not with Brian. He deserved better."

"You didn't think you was good enough?"

"Were good enough," she said. "It's 'were.' That's the proper word."

"You been sleeping up here and wandering around in a vapor of cure-all, but now you have time to fix my English?"

"Brian was a good man and it would have changed things for him."

"What about me?" I said.

"I was young. I wasn't thinking clearly."

"That's your hole in the bag? You were young?"

"I wanted you to have a home. Don said he didn't care whose child it was. He just wanted me. I thought he meant it, and things would be okay, and Brian could go on with his life. Next day after our wedding, Don got drunk and blacked my eye and I knew who he was. But I was stuck. He got what he wanted, and then the hell began. It's gone on now for over sixteen years. He has times when he's like the man I met, but then he has more times where he's the man I know now."

"And here you are, wearing hell's overcoat and happy to have it."

"I think Don has done the best he could," she said. "I think, in his own way, he loves me."

"I know this, Mama—Jinx don't have to go to bed at night with a stick of stove wood."

"I stayed for you."

"No, you didn't," I said, leaning forward in the chair. "It was for me, we'd been long gone a long ways back. You stayed because you're too weak in the head to do anything else. Weak before you took that damn cure-all. Weak and happy to be weak. You're just glad he don't hit you as much as he used to, and when he does, not as hard. He's got you in a bottle now, and he can pour you out and use you when he wants to. That ain't right, Mama. You left me to deal with him while you was floating on some cloud somewhere. I don't blame the cure-all for it, Mama. I blame you."

I could see my words had stung like a bee, and that made me happy.

"You're right," she said. "I am a quitter. I quit the man I loved. I quit life, and I married a quitter, and I've pretty much quit you, but I didn't mean to."

"Now that makes it all better."

"I didn't mean to hurt you," she said.

"Somebody meant it," I said. "You wasn't swigging cure-all back when you got pregnant and run off. Tell you what. I'll leave you a good stick of stove wood by the bed. When you ain't drunk on your medicine, which is about fifteen minutes a day, you can use it on him. I think a good shot to the side of the head is best. Rest of the time, you can float in the clouds and he can do what he wants, and you can pretend you don't know or understand. But you ain't fooling me, and let me say 'ain't' again. Ain't."

I got up, picked up my stove wood, hesitated, and laid it on the chair by the bed.

"Here's the wood," I said. "I can put it beside you if you like."

"Honey, don't be mad."

I had moved to the foot of the bed and was starting for the door. "I was any madder the house would catch on fire."

I went out and slammed the door and went to my room and slammed that door and locked up and cried for a while. Then I got tired of crying, as I could see it wasn't helping a thing. I decided I was so mad I wanted to wear shoes. I got some socks that only had one hole in each foot, put them and my shoes on, and went downstairs and outside, started walking briskly along the river's edge.

7

By now the sun was pretty high and the air was hot and windless and sticky as molasses. I didn't know where I was going right then, but I seemed to be getting there fast, and was pretty sweated up over doing it.

I walked for hours, and eventually came to the spot where we had found May Lynn. I don't know if I went there on purpose, or if I just ended up there, but I came to it.

I walked close to the bank and looked down at the Singer sewing machine that had been left there. I bent down and had a closer gander at it. Where the wire had been tied was bits of gray flesh with flies on it. The killer had bent the two ends in such a way as to tie a knot and then a little stiff bow. It was like what he had used was ribbon, not wires.

I wondered if the murderer thought that was funny. I kept thinking how the man I thought was my daddy, and Constable Sy Higgins, had jerked her feet loose from the wire and hadn't bothered trying to untwist it off of her. I could still hear the bones in May Lynn's feet snapping. I remembered how the wet skin stripped off her feet like sticky bread dough and stayed on the wire.

I shooed the flies away, and as I did something moved inside of me that made me feel funny; something that felt like a wild animal trying to find a place to settle down. I started walking again.

I walked until the trees and brush thinned and there was a wet clay path that went up a grass-covered hill like a knife cut in a bright orange sweet potato. When I got to the top of the hill, there was another clay road that wound off of it, and it led to the top of another hill, and on top of that hill was a small white house that looked as fresh as a newborn calf. There was a small green garden out to the side of it with a fence around it to keep out the deer and such, and way out back was a little red outhouse. It looked so bright and perky I had the urge to go up there and use it, even if I didn't have to go.

The red clay, being wet from the night before, stuck to my shoes and made my feet heavy. I got off the path and took off my shoes and wiped their bottoms across the grass until they were clean. I put them back on and stayed on the grass as I climbed the hill. On the top of the hill it was flat and there wasn't any grass. The ground had been raked, and there were bits of gravel in the dirt that Jinx's daddy had hauled in. In front of the house there was a horseshoe drive and no car in it. The car would be up north with Jinx's daddy.

The house was very small, maybe two rooms, but unlike our huge house, it was in fine shape and the roof looked to have been shingled not too long ago. The shingles were made of good wood, split perfect, laid out and nailed, tarred over to keep out the rot. I knew Jinx's daddy had done it before he went back north. It was always his way to keep things fresh and tight.

There were a few chickens in the yard, but there wasn't any

livestock. Jinx's daddy mailed money home to them, and unlike most anyone else around the bottomland, they bought all the meat they ate, except for chicken now and again, and some fish. They mostly had the chickens for eggs, and since they didn't have any kind of set place for them to nest, they had to be alert as to where the eggs had been laid, or otherwise, you wanted an egg for your breakfast, you might have a bit of a treasure hunt before you could crack one in the pan. I knew that for a fact, as I had to do exactly the same thing at home.

I was almost to the door when I saw Jinx come out of the house carrying a basket with laundry piled high in it. She had her hair out of her usual braids and knotted up behind her head in a thistle-like pile and tied off with a piece of white cord. She was wearing a man's blue work shirt, overalls, and shoes that looked as if they had room for another pair of feet in them.

She called out to me and I followed her to the backyard and the wash line, which was strung between two tall posts. There were clothespins in the basket, and I helped her hang the wash. We hung it carefully and neatly, and while we moved down the line, we talked.

"I'm wanting to go on that trip we talked about," I said.

"I wanted to," Jinx said. "Then I get to thinking about Mama here with just my little brother. Now that I'm home and not out there on the river, this seems all right to me."

"Not me. What I got is a big house that's about to fall down around my ears, a drunk mother, and a jackass I have to fight off with a piece of stove wood that I thought was my daddy, but he ain't. So I reckon I'm coming from a place now that I wasn't coming from yesterday."

"What's that you say?" Jinx said, pausing with a clothespin she was about to clamp to a pair of underpants. "That part about he ain't your daddy."

"That's it. He ain't my daddy. There's a fellow named Brian Collins in Gladewater, and he's my daddy. He's a lawyer."

"Shut your mouth."

"It's true."

"Ain't that something," Jinx said.

"It's the best thing that's happened to me in a long time, finding out that old son of a bitch ain't my kin."

"He did raise and feed you, though," Jinx said.

"No, Mama did what there was of that, then she took to bed and hasn't done much since I been big enough to tote my own water. I guess what I'm saying, Jinx, is I'm going away, even if I have to go by myself."

Jinx let that comment hang in the air like the wash on the line. We moved along, hanging clothes, and when we got to the end of the hanging, she said, "When you leaving?"

"Soon as possible. What I want is to look at that map another time, see I can figure out where that money is, nab it, burn May Lynn to a cinder, stick her ashes in a jar, and head out. I get through here, I'm going to find Terry and talk to him, get the map, and see what I can do from there. For me, it's die dog or eat the hatchet. I'm heading out quick. I want away from here and soon as I can go. Mama has pretty much given up. She told me as much. Gave me her blessing to light out. Besides, right now I'm feeling a little less than friendly toward her, her waiting till now to let me know Don ain't kin. It's like she told me, 'Oh, by the way, those legs, they don't belong to you. I stole those from someone when you were born, and now they're asking for them back.'"

"Maybe she thought you'd handle it some better when you was older," Jinx said.

"All I know is it's a good thing to know he's not my kin, and Mama says my real daddy is a good man."

Jinx nodded, picked up the empty wash basket, started back

toward the house with me following. "You ought to keep in mind you ain't never seen your real daddy, and your mama ain't seen him in sixteen years. He might be same as Don. Might be worse. Might even be dead."

"Don't say that," I said.

"I'm not trying to mess up where your heart is right now, but as your friend, I'm just giving you a warning. Sometimes when things are bad, they don't get better. They get worse, and when you think they can't get no worse, they do."

"That's not a very forward way of looking at things," I said.

"No. But it's a way that often comes to pass."

"I hope that isn't true."

"By the way," Jinx said, grinning at me, "you giving them back?"

"What?"

"The legs your mama borrowed."

Terry lived in town, which wasn't much more than a handful of buildings that looked to have been stolen away by a tornado and set down on a crooked street so that they didn't line up good. His house was off the main street and down a blacktop road. It was a pretty nice house, good as Jinx's, and larger. There was a house on either side of it, and unlike the downtown, they were lined up even and similar in the way they looked. All the houses along there had a little front yard and a backyard and some flowers out front, and on this day, in Terry's front yard, there was a kid. He was a short, fat kid with carrot-colored hair and green snot on his face that had dried in a long trail that reached to the corner of his mouth, like the runoff from an outhouse.

There was a white fence around the yard and a swinging gate. I pushed through the gate and waved at the kid. It was one of Terry's stepbrothers. Terry hated all his step-kin. I think what he mostly hated was that he was no longer the center of attention since his mama got remarried. After that, he always had a feeling of being left out in the rain without a hat. I didn't think he had it so bad myself, but I guess it's what you compare it to.

The kid in the yard was called Booger by Terry and most everyone else, including his daddy and his stepmother. I figure it was a thing that would follow him even when he was grown up, like a cousin of mine who was called Poot. I suppose it beat being called Turd, especially if the tag had some kind of truthful connection.

"Is Terry here?" I asked Booger.

Booger eyed me as if he was sizing me up for a meal. "He's out back with a nigger."

The apple didn't fall far from the tree. Terry said his new daddy was the sort of man that was still upset he had to pay colored people a nickel for a couple hours' work and thought he should be able to find them for jobs at the same place he bought mules.

"Thanks," I said.

"Did you know boys and girls got different thangs?" the boy said.

"Yep," I said.

I went out back. There was a big pile of wood near the fence, and next to the wood was Terry. Closer to it yet, with ax in hand, was a big colored man. He was splitting a piece of stove wood in half over a log, and he was doing it with the ease of a fish swimming in water. I stood and watched while he did it, it was such good work. He had his shirt off and he was well muscled, and his skin was the color of sweaty licorice. I had been noticing a lot of things about men lately, white and colored, and some of what I noticed made me nervous and anxious.

Terry wasn't wearing a shirt, either, and I noticed that right off as well. He wasn't as muscled as the colored man, but he looked pretty good, and I remember thinking in that moment that it wasn't such a good thing he was a sissy.

Terry was grabbing the pieces as they were halved and piling them on a wheelbarrow. He was doing this quickly and with great skill to avoid the rising and swinging of the ax. He looked around and saw me and nodded. I knew he had chores to finish, so I went and sat on the back porch. I heard the door open behind me, and Terry's mama came out. She was a fine-looking person with dark, short hair that had a perm in it. She sat down on the steps beside me, said, "Sue Ellen, how are you?"

"I'm fine, ma'am."

I didn't look at her direct, as I figured if I did I would look guilty, considering the plans I had might include her son.

"It's been so long since I've seen you," she said.

"Yes, ma'am."

I had to look at her now. It was manners. I put on my best lying face and turned it to her. When I did I saw she looked a little less full of juice than when I had seen her last; still pretty, but something she needed had been sucked out of her, and I had the impression that if I touched her hard she might fall apart, like a vase that had been badly glued back together. Still, compared to my mama, she was as solid as a mountain.

According to Terry, what was sucking out the juice was his stepdaddy, who he said was well-heeled but had all the personality of a nasty dishrag. He told me once, "Stepdad didn't become rich by charm. He became rich by discovering oil on some land he bought and by building a brick-firing company that hires most of the people in town that are being hired. After that, he didn't need to be charming. He just had to have his wallet with him."

"How do you think Terry is?" she asked me.

"Ma'am?"

"Do you think he's okay?"

"Yes, ma'am. I guess so."

"I think the new arrangements bother him."

That was like saying I think the selling of one of our children to buy a pig might have been a bad idea. But since I was thinking about even newer arrangements for him, I didn't know what to reply, other than, "I suppose that's so."

After a bit, the colored man stopped chopping and picked his shirt off the woodpile and wiped his face and chest with it and then put it on. Terry pushed the wheelbarrow over to the porch and started unloading it, piling wood under the porch's overhang.

The colored man came over, smiling and shuffling. Jinx said that was how colored did if they didn't want to have a visit from the Ku Klux Klan. She said you never knew when it would be decided you were being uppity in the presence of a white, and being uppity could cause you to come to grief. To add to that, it was probably pretty well known that Terry's stepdad had a white robe and hood hanging in his closet.

The colored man didn't say anything, just stood there smiling, like a jackass waiting for a carrot. It made me feel funny, seeing a grown man act like that.

Terry's mama stood up and smiled and handed him something she had in her hand. He took it without looking to see what it was, and went away. When he was gone, she looked down at me and said, "I think that was worth more than a nickel, don't you? He chopped a lot of wood and it's hot."

"Yes, ma'am," I said.

"I gave him a quarter."

"Well worth it," I said.

Terry finished up with the wood and came over and sat by me on the porch steps. I could feel the heat off his body and I could smell his sweat.

"Well," his mama said, still standing on the steps. "I'll leave you two to visit. But don't forget your other chores, Terry. You know how your daddy gets when they're not done."

"He's not my real father," Terry said.

"You don't mean that," she said.

"I do mean it."

"Well, it'll take a little time to adjust."

"By the time I adjust, the world will be made anew," Terry said.

"We won't discuss it right now . . . Sue Ellen, it's good to see you."

"Thank you, ma'am."

She went in the house.

I said, "You hurt her feelings."

"I know," he said. "I didn't mean to. It's not her I don't like. It's that man she married and all his kids. The smartest one of them barely knows to get in out of the rain, and only does so with considerable encouragement."

"I'm wanting to look at that map again," I said. "I'm wanting to find that money."

"You sure?"

"I am. Jinx might come, and she might not. But I want to go."

"When?"

"Tonight."

"I think I got in too big a hurry the other day," Terry said.

"You don't want to go now?"

"No. I want to go. But I think we should find the money, and then we have to dig up May Lynn and burn her, and I need to do some work on that barge so it can run cleaner down the river."

"You know how to do that?"

"I know how to do a lot of things. My real daddy taught me things, and he taught me how to teach myself about things I don't know. He taught me how to study, and my mama taught me the same."

"How much studying you need?"

"For what we have in mind, little to none. But I need time.

Burning a body takes more time and work than you might think. You need a real serious fire, and we have to have it someplace where we won't be seen. I have an idea for that, but I'd rather not discuss it until I've had time to consider on it awhile. Thing we should do first is determine if the map is real, and if it is, we have to find out if there's any money buried out there."

"Then we steal it."

"You're reconciled with that idea now?" he said.

"If 'reconciled' means I'm fine with that idea, I am."

"That's about the size of it," Terry said.

8

Terry got the map from a hiding place in the house, put on a shirt, and then we took a walk down the street. There was a graveyard nearby, and we went there. It was a private place to talk. We sat where we often sat, on a metal bench under a spreading oak tree in view of the Confederate dead; rows and rows of sun-shiny stones that held down old rebels who had been shot or died later of wounds, or old age, or disappointment.

We unfolded the map and stretched it out between us and looked it over.

"What I can't figure," Terry said, "is what these humps are. Everything else on the map seems accurate, but I can't make them out, and then there's the name written here, Malcolm Cuzins."

I nodded, said, "I figure we can go back there and look things over more carefully and see what we can come up with. Maybe if we look again, something will jump out that fits this. I thought it might mean hills, but after we got to where we was going, there wasn't any hills. There's nothing out there but a few trees and—"

And then it hit me.

I looked at Terry. "We are the dumbest people that ever walked on a spinning earth."

"How do you mean?" he said.

"Look out there," I said, waving my hand toward the graves.

He looked.

"Okay. A bunch of dead people with rocks on their heads."

"That's it, the stones," I said. "We been overthinking things."

"You mean that old graveyard up in the pines?"

"Well, I don't mean this one. Sure. Those humps on the map could be gravestones."

"But the tombstones there have mostly been removed by vandals," he said. "Or broken up."

"Yeah, but that don't mean these humps don't mean a graveyard. That would be a way the map drawer could remember things. A graveyard is supposed to have gravestones, even if it don't. There might even be a stone or two left up there we ain't seen, and one of them might have the name Malcolm written on it. The money might be there."

"You know, Sue Ellen, you may be correct. We should check it out. We might get lucky."

"I figure luck is either a plan or an accident," I said. "What we have is a plan."

We went over to see Jinx and helped her finish up her chores. She got us some boiled eggs and wrapped them in a black-and-white checkered cloth and put them in a syrup bucket. We borrowed one of her daddy's shovels and she told her mama we was going digging for fishing worms, and the three of us lit out. We used the leaky boat again and paddled across the river, not too far down from May Lynn's house.

Following the map the way we had gone before, we got to

where the graveyard was, stopped, and took a breather. Underneath the trees there were shadows, and the shadows lay where the graveyard was said to be. It was supposed to be haunted by the ghosts of those buried there. Some said it was a graveyard full of slaves, others said it was the graveyard of a family long forgotten. Some claimed Christian Cherokees had been buried there.

It was cooler in the shadows and the trees dripping cool water from the rain of last night made it even cooler. There were no gravestones visible, but there were slumps in the ground where aged graves might have been. There were no fresh diggings, however, and after poking around with the shovel, we finally wore out looking, stopped, and sat down on the ground under the pines. Jinx pulled the eggs in the cloth from the bucket, and we took one apiece and started peeling. We ate and thought and listened to birds.

The boiled egg was good but dry, and I was wishing for some water, when Terry said, "Look here."

He pushed the rest of the egg into his mouth and stood up, talking around his chewing. "I'm sitting on an old gravestone."

Me and Jinx got up and took a look. It was a rock that had a name carved on it, and some dates. It had fallen over, or maybe had been placed flat to begin with. The name on it wasn't Malcolm Cuzins, but still, my heart beat faster.

We went back to looking around with a new fire in our bellies, and before long, Jinx said, "You gonna like this."

Me and Terry went for a look-see, followed Jinx's pointing finger. Near a crop of poison ivy there was a slight slope, and through a split in the pines above there was so much sunshine coming in it looked as if it was being poured from a bucket. What it was pouring on was a stone. It had fallen over but was supported by a mound of dirt. It was easy to miss and had near-blended into the pine needles on the forest bed. There was a name on the stone, and the sunlight made the name stand out.

It read: MALCOLM CUZINS.

"Ain't that something?" Jinx said. "Here we was just looking and looking, and we sat down to have a boiled egg and we found it."

"It's God's will," Terry said.

"Or we found it because we had a map and was looking around," Jinx said.

I grabbed up the shovel, knocked the poison ivy back, and started digging. I could tell pretty quick that the dirt had been moved and not too long ago. My first thought was May Lynn might have got to the money already, but then the shovel clicked on something; I dropped it, got down on my hands and knees. So did Jinx and Terry. We all started scraping the dirt back with our hands.

As we dug, the day slipped away, and I heard a whip-poor-will call from somewhere over the hill. We kept digging.

My fingers wrapped around something solid, and I called out. Terry and Jinx started helping me dig there, and in no time at all we came upon a large piece of crockery. It had a tight cover on it, and when we felt around the lid, we realized it had been sealed with wax.

We dug more, knocked away the dirt around it, and lifted it out. It was a small crockery pot, but heavy enough. Terry pulled out his pocketknife and trimmed around the waxed-on lid until the wax was loose enough we could get the lid off. There was a bag inside with a blue-and-white flower pattern on it. I pulled it out. I recognized it as a match to the pillowcases and curtains and May Lynn's dress. It was pretty heavy. It was tied shut with a string. Before I could loose the string, Terry went at it with his pocketknife. We opened the bag and looked inside.

It was full of greenbacks, and even a bit of change. There was a daddy longlegs in there, too. He was dead and dried up, like a salesman's heart.

"Oh, hellfires," Jinx said.

"That's a lot of money," I said.

"I don't mean that," Jinx said. "Looky there."

She was pointing at something in the grave. It was right under where the crockery had been. We had been so excited we hadn't noticed. It was a row of teeth, and they was partly coated in clay.

"Well," Terry said. "It is a graveyard. You are going to find bones."

"Yeah, but look there," Jinx said, and pointed again.

Down a ways was a hand. The hand still had some flesh on it, and there were worms digging into it.

"Them worms would have done chewed up anyone buried long ago," Jinx said. "This fella may not be fresh as this morning's milk, but he's fairly new to the ground."

"She's right," Terry said. He stood up, got the shovel, and started gently digging around the body. It took a long while, but in time it was uncovered. It was a man in a brown-and-white pin-stripe suit, lying slightly on his side with his knees pushed up toward his middle. The teeth we had seen was in a skull. A lot of him was missing, but he didn't need any of it back.

The white stripes on his suit had turned the color of the red clay, and there wasn't any shoes on the feet, just brown silk socks with blue clocks on them. There were still strips of flesh where the face had been, and on the skull was a brown narrow-brimmed hat. It was crushed up, but it was easy to see that, like the suit, it had been something that cost money and most likely went with a new cigar and gold watch chain.

Terry got down on his hands and knees and looked the body over. He said, "It still has an odor about it. You're right, Jinx. He hasn't been in the ground all that long."

Terry opened the man's clay-caked coat. When he did, way it stuck to the rotting body, it made a sound like something ripping. He reached inside the man's coat pockets, but there wasn't anything in them. He fumbled through the outside pockets and found some threads and a button. He pulled off the hat, and when he did the man's skull crumbled somewhat. You could see that the back of his head had been crushed. Terry took the hat, which was dark in the back, and shook it into some kind of shape. He looked inside of it and let out his breath.

"It has his name stenciled on the inside band," he said. "Warren Cain."

He showed it to us. I let out my breath.

"Wasn't that name in May Lynn's book?" I said.

"That was the man her brother was running with," Terry said. "The one who helped him rob the bank. Now we know what happened to their partnership."

"And if that ain't enough, they took his dadburn shoes," Jinx said.

"Jake would be my guess," Terry said. "It would make sense they came here to bury the money, and an argument ensued——"

"Ensued?" Jinx said.

"Started," Terry said. "And when it did, it turned ugly, and Jake killed him, buried him, and put the money on top of him. My assumption is they had already dug the hole for the money, and Jake didn't want to dig another. Probably caught him from behind with the shovel."

"Maybe there wasn't an argument, and he planned to kill him all along," I said.

"Either way makes sense," Terry said. "He killed him, hid the money on top of him, and took his shoes because he liked them. He'd have probably taken the hat and the suit, too, if he hadn't covered them in blood by hitting Warren with that shovel."

"That's all tough on the dead man and all," Jinx said, "but maybe we ought to count the money. Ain't like he's gonna get any deader."

We counted it twice. There was close to a thousand dollars. When we put the money back in the bag, it was on the edge of night.

"It's like we done dug up a pirate's chest," Jinx said.

"It is at that," I said.

Jinx cleared her throat, said, "You know, that's a lot of money even if we don't burn May Lynn up."

"We have to stick to the plan," Terry said.

"Do we?" I said.

"We do," Terry said. "She's why we found the money."

"We sure gonna use a lot of it going out to that California," Jinx said. "We could use a lot of it someplace closer."

"That sounds greedy," Terry said. "If not for her we wouldn't have known about the money, and when it comes right down to it, it's not our money."

"When it comes right down to it," Jinx said, "it's not her money, neither. Nor her brother's. It come from a bank."

"Do you think her daddy knows where it's buried?" I asked.

Terry shook his head. "He did, he would have already dug it up and drank it up. He's not exactly a salt-away-for-a-rainy-day sort of individual. Jake told May Lynn where it was when he was sick because he didn't want anyone else to know. She obviously didn't have time to dig it up and leave before things went wrong."

"Think she knew about the murdered man?" I said, nodding at the hole.

"I don't know," Terry said. "I think when Jake realized he was dying he had her draw up the map and didn't tell her his bank-robbing buddy was here under it. Listen, we want to get out of here, don't we?"

Me and Jinx nodded.

"Here's our chance," Terry said. "And we ought to take May Lynn with us."

"She's pretty snug in the graveyard," Jinx said.

Terry gave Jinx a hard look. "She's our friend."

"Was," Jinx said.

"Should we forget her because she's dead?" he said.

"I ain't forgetting her," Jinx said. "I remember her real good. But what I'm saying is she's dead and there's a lot of money in that bag and I don't think she had plans to share it with us."

"Does that matter?" Terry said.

"You got the bus tickets to get, the food for going out there, someplace to stay, and so on," Jinx said. "It can run into some expense, and I'm not sure that's how we want to spend the dough."

"May Lynn didn't want to end up buried in some hot plot of dirt in the pauper's section of the local graveyard," Terry said, "and I don't think we should let her."

I have to admit, thinking about digging her up and setting her on fire and going all the way out to Hollywood to dump her ashes seemed less appealing now that we had a huge bag of money. I was a little ashamed of myself for thinking that way, but there you have it.

"Well?" Terry said. "That's not what we want. Is it?"

"No, I reckon not."

Jinx's face twisted up, then slowly straightened out. "Okay," she said, and the word struggled out of her mouth like a rat out of a tight hole. "Sure. Let's burn her up and haul her out."

"Good," Terry said. "It's decided."

9

We started back with Terry carrying the bag full of money from the crockery pot. When we got to the cane field we stopped and I cut us another snack. I figured since we had gone over deep into theft, we might as well go whole hog and hit the cane again.

The night was growing thick, and we left the cane field and went through a run of trees and out into a meadow of wild grass. It was a slightly different path than we had gone before, and the moonlight made the grass look like shiny water; the wind rustled it like someone shaking hard candy in a paper bag.

By going that way, we came down right behind where May Lynn lived. As we neared her place, you could hear the river run, and you could see the house near it creaking in the wind. Cletus was home, because we could see his old truck parked in the trail that ended up against the house. Course, if the truck wasn't there, it didn't mean he wasn't home. Sometimes he lost his truck when he got drunk and got brought back by someone and dropped off, least that's what May Lynn had said, and I didn't have any reason to doubt her. It's why I had been careful to want to call out to the house earlier, to make sure he knew we was there if he was home. He struck me as a man might shoot first and ask questions later.

Jinx spied the outhouse not far from us.

"I'm gonna have to stop and use the toilet," she said.

"Can't you wait?" Terry said.

"I can wait, but you won't like it about the time we get to the boat."

"Well, hurry up," Terry said. "We'll wait over by that tree." He pointed at a big elm on the hill above the river.

Jinx darted across the way and inside the outhouse and closed the door.

Terry and I walked over to the elm, sat down under it, side by side, our backs against the trunk. Terry put the bag of money between his legs and looked off toward May Lynn's house and the truck parked by it. He said, "Think he knows about May Lynn by now?"

"I don't know, but I'm not in the mood to tell him anymore. Especially since we dug up the money his son stole and we're thinking about digging his daughter up. I don't know I could look him in the eye."

"I don't care," Terry said. "With that money, we can get out of here."

"Split three ways it won't last long," I said. "It's a good start, but that's all it is."

"That's all I want," Terry said. "A good start. I'm like a bird with someone's foot on its tail. I can't fly. Stepdaddy has heard rumors about me, about me and a boy who came to visit before he married my mom. Those rumors are not true. But because he thinks it, he treats me bad and talks to me bad, and he hurts my mother's feelings. He's sucking the spirit out of her, like she's nothing more than a sugar tit. And how come he's made up his mind about me? How come so many people have? Do I seem like a sissy to you?"

I mulled that over.

"I do!" he said. "I can tell the way you're thinking it over."

"Well, you are very good-looking and you have good manners. I don't see you with a lot of girls."

"You're a girl," he said.

"But we're friends," I said.

Terry shook his head. "Looks are not my choice, and there are lots of people with good manners."

"Not crossing my path," I said.

"That's the only reason you think I'm a sissy?"

I shook my head. "No. May Lynn. You didn't look at her the way other men did. You didn't even take notice when we went skinny-dipping; you hardly even looked."

"You noticed her, or you wouldn't be asking me why I didn't notice her," Terry said. "So do you like girls?"

"Sometimes, between me and you, I think I could have liked her. She looked like some kind of ice cream dessert. But no, I'm kidding. I reckon I'm inclined to men and a life of misery."

"Not all men are miserable," Terry said. "A man and a woman can be friends and be married."

"Mama and Don aren't friends," I said.

"Yeah, and that's precisely the reason they don't get along," Terry said.

"You got me there," I said.

"That time we went skinny-dipping, when May Lynn was naked as a nymph, I noticed. I noticed plenty. I was on the sly about it, but I noticed. Thing is, May Lynn liked to use that body of hers for power, and I didn't want to give it to her. I didn't want her to know I liked what I saw. I don't want anyone having power over me. Anyone. In any kind of way."

Before I could fully get in line with this new information, I saw a man coming up from May Lynn's house, trudging in the moonlight. He was heading for the outhouse. He had on a ragged hat and overalls and clodhopper boots with the laces untied. He had about him the look of a scarecrow that had climbed down from its pole.

"It's Cletus," I said, knowing it was the first time Terry had actually ever seen him.

We stood up but stayed in the shadows under the tree. Still, bright as the night was, he would have seen us easy had he looked that way, but he had his head down and was walking fast. He was a man on a mission.

He came to the outhouse, tugged on the door, and it didn't open. Jinx had thrown the swivel lock inside. It wasn't the sort of lock that would hold if someone was serious against it; it was more of a friendly reminder that someone was inside.

May Lynn's old man stepped back and looked at the outhouse like it was strange to him. He said, "Who's in there?"

"Just passing by," Jinx said. "I'll be out right soon."

"Is that a nigger in there?" he said. "You sound like a nigger."

"No," Jinx said. "I'm white."

"Better not be no black ass on my outhouse hole," he said.

There was a long pause, and then the side of the outhouse bumped, and bumped again. A board came loose with a screech and popped out. Then another. Jinx shot out of there like a cannonball, causing the boards to fly completely off. She came charging toward the tree where we stood, pulling an overall strap over her shoulder as she ran.

Behind her came Cletus, running at a good pace, his loose bootlaces flapping.

I suppose the polite thing to do would have been to wait on Jinx, but we didn't. Terry grabbed the bag, and we broke and ran like a couple of rabbits, leaving her to catch up. When I looked back over my shoulder, she was almost up with us, but Cletus was closing in fast.

"Hey, hey," Cletus yelled. "That there is my bag."

He had recognized it even in the dark.

We ran over the ridge and down to the river, and then we ran along its edge. When I looked back again, Cletus wasn't slowing, and he had picked up a big stick. About that time, Jinx tripped and fell against the riverbank.

"I got you now," Cletus yelled, and in fact he did.

I stopped and turned, saw him bring the stick down on the back of Jinx's head as she tried to get up. It was a good solid blow, and it wasn't meant to aggravate or wound. It was meant to kill. Jinx went down with her nose in the dirt, her heels flipping up like two startled birds.

Cletus dropped his club and grabbed her up and pulled her to the edge of the water and stuck her head under. Jinx started flailing her arms and legs and sputtering.

Cletus looked at us. "You two better come back, or I'm gonna drown this little nigger. If she's anything to you, you better come back."

I found a rock by the river, about the size of half a cantaloupe, dug it free with my fingers, hefted it in my hand, and started running at him. I seen then that Terry was running up alongside me, and he had the bag of money in one hand and a short, stubby stick in the other.

Cletus was pushing Jinx's head under the water again as we came running up. He was yelling at Jinx, even though she didn't have the pillowcase. "Why you got my pillowcase? You better tell me. Better give it back."

I came up on him and brought the rock down with both hands. I hit him on the forehead with it, just as he turned to look at me.

It knocked him onto his side and his hat come off. It wasn't an entirely successful attack. The rock slipped out of my hands and fell down and hit Jinx in the small of the back. Cletus tried to get up, one hand holding his bloody head.

Then Terry was on Cletus with the stick, swinging it like a madman. Cletus grabbed Terry around the waist, driving him over Jinx, who still lay on the ground, trying to get her hands underneath her. So far, she had only managed to get her face out of the water.

When Terry was knocked back, the bag came out of his hand and came open and a bunch of that money puffed out of it like goose feathers from an old mattress.

Cletus came down on top of Terry with his fist raised, and then he saw the money scattered about, said, "That's my money."

Jinx, who had found her feet and her energy, got hold of Terry's dropped stick and swung it. It was one heck of a swing. I could hear the wind coming off of it; it made a sound like an owl swooping down on a mouse. The blow caught Cletus in the back of the head. His noggin jumped up like it might come off his neck, and then he bent his head forward, shook once, and down came that stick again. Man, that was some hit. You could probably have heard it all the way to Gladewater. It caused Cletus to let out with a kind of bark like a startled dog, and then he fell off Terry.

Jinx jumped on Cletus again, and was hitting his knocked-out self every which way with that stick, hitting him faster than a woodpecker can peck. I ran over and grabbed her and hugged her and the stick to me. She started sputtering and struggling like a greased pig.

"You'll kill him," I said.

"That's what I'm trying to do," she said.

I jerked her back and fell on the ground. She struggled on top of me.

Terry went over and looked at Cletus.

"He's good and out," he said.

"I hope he's dead," Jinx said, still struggling. "Called me nigger, and messed up my toilet, and hit me in the head, and stuck my face in the water. Damned old cracker. I don't want to never be called nigger no more by nobody. I'm sick of it. I'm sick of it. I can't stand this goddamn place. I can't stand no goddamn place."

"Jinx," I said. "Now quit it. You ain't gonna hit him anymore."

"What if he wakes up?"

"You can hit him then," I said.

"All right then, let me go."

I let her go, and she jumped right up and ran over there to whack him again with the stick. Terry caught her arm, said, "That's enough, Jinx. He's nothing more than an old fool."

"That's as much our money as it is his," Jinx said, trying to jerk her hand free of Terry. "It don't matter who stole it first. Besides, he didn't even know where it was. We was the ones figured it out and dug it up."

Finally, I came up behind her and helped him hold her, and after a while, Jinx got herself together, and started breathing shallow again. Terry let her go, but not before he took the stick from her.

"Let's gather up the money before he wakes up and Jinx becomes a murderer," Terry said.

We got the money stuffed back in the bag, and right before we left out, Jinx kicked Cletus in the head as hard as she could. We had to pull her off of him and drag her along the riverbank, her cussing a blue streak, flailing her arms and legs like a centipede on a hot rock.

10

The Sabine River is long, but it ain't that wide in the places I know. It's not like I hear the Mississippi is, which can be more than a mile or so across. The Sabine is a brown run of water that twists its way along dirty banks, underneath lean-over trees and all their shadows. It's deep in spots, not real deep in most, but there's a right smart amount of water to carry boats and to sink them. There's plenty of water to drown in. It's a dark old river and it's the Kingdom of the Snake; home to the water moccasin in particular, a thick, nub-tailed serpent with a bad attitude. I thought about that as we came ashore on the other side and dragged the leaky boat out of the water and under a weeping willow.

Our plans had changed. There wouldn't be a lot of time to do much more than take off. I wasn't firm on what had become of the idea to burn up May Lynn's body, but I was sure Terry had that still tucked away in the back of his mind. We had all cared about May Lynn, but Terry, who had always seemed less close to her than me, had really taken all this to heart; he seemed the most bothered by her death, the unfairness of it all. It wasn't that I had moved on, but I couldn't figure how there was any way to rectify what happened. Wasn't any way for me to know who done it or how to get them nabbed if I did. Jinx, she had cared for May Lynn, too, but she was someone who looked at things pretty straight on, or so it seemed to me. I figured her view was, dead is dead, and that's sad, and she felt bad about it, but she wasn't going to worry about if May Lynn got burned up and hauled anywhere if she could avoid it. That business was Terry's plan.

We decided to let Terry hang on to the bag full of loot, go home and put together a few possibles, meet back quick at this spot, and head out. As I watched my friends go their own ways in the dark, I was having second thoughts, some of them due to thinking about days and nights on the river. Bad as my life was, it was the life I knew. And though Mama had lied to me and disappointed me all my life, and my daddy wasn't my daddy at all, I still thought maybe I ought to reconsider. Maybe we could give Cletus the money and let bygones be bygones. Going off to Gladewater to find my real daddy, then out to Hollywood, was a good thing to think about, but I wasn't so sure it was a good thing to do, even if there was stolen money in the deal—though secretly I was thinking I might get a share of it for a nice dress and shoes and my hair done up like I'd never had it, and maybe I'd buy one of those hats women wore that looked like it ought to have come with a quiver of arrows and a couple of Robin Hood's Merry Men.

Anyway, there I stood on the riverbank, thinking these thoughts, considering what Terry had told me about himself not being a sissy, feeling confused. Just about everything I thought I knew about my world had changed. And then it hit me. All of a sudden I couldn't walk or stand no more. I started to cry.

There was a log nearby, and I went over and sat on it and kept crying. It wasn't a long cry, but it was a good one. Pretty soon I was cried out, and not exactly sure what it was I was crying about. I sniffed like a little kid, sat there till I was sure I was done with it, got up, and started walking quickly toward home, feeling stupid for wasting valuable time sitting on a log.

As I neared our house, I saw there wasn't no lights on, but out by the side of the house was three pickups. Don's truck, Uncle Gene's, and, damn it, Cletus's. I was considering my next move when someone stepped out of the dark between the trees and touched my shoulder and stuck a hand over my mouth.

"It's me, Sue Ellen," a voice said, and of course, I recognized right off it was Mama. "Be quiet now."

She took her hand from over my mouth and grabbed my shoulders.

"What are you doing out here?" I said.

"I knew this was your way to come, so I waited on you."

"But why?"

"Cletus has come for you, and Constable Sy is coming, too. I heard Cletus telling Don and Gene about how you stole some money. That isn't true, is it?"

"There's more story to it than that," I said. I thought, So much for Don's "sight." He got all his information secondhand.

"Come on," Mama said. "Let's walk back a ways and find a place to talk."

Fact that my mama was out of the house was amazing enough, but before we walked off to that place to talk, she stepped back in the shadows and picked up a tow sack and half-dragged it after her. I took it away from her and carried it myself, cause she was as weak as a newborn pup and it was a heavy sack. Surprised as I was, I didn't ask her about why she had it or what was in it.

We walked back to the log I had sat down on to cry. When we got there, Mama was so tuckered out and breathing so hard that I felt bad for her, but it seemed like a good idea to put some space between us and the house. When we were sitting on the log, I put the tow sack between my legs, said, "What are they saying about me?"

"I heard Gene drive up. I looked out the window. Then I saw Cletus follow up in his truck. Cletus must have gone to Gene first, cause they are closer friends, and then they came to the house. Since the window was open, I could hear them talking. Cletus said you and a boy and a colored girl stole some money from him. He said the colored girl hit him in the head to get it. That would be Jinx, I suppose. The boy would be Terry."

"He doesn't know them," I said. "They were never at May Lynn's when Cletus was."

"Yes, but that won't be hard for them to figure out. Don knows who you run with, and he hates Terry."

"True enough," I said. "But that's not entirely right about what happened."

"Did you steal money?"

"We stole stolen money."

"Stealing is stealing," Mama said.

"I know that, and to tell you the truth, I can live with it."

She didn't argue with me. She sat there waiting for me to say more, so I told her all about it, including how there was a body under the money, and who it was. I told her how Jinx had been chased and hit, and how she fought back, and how we helped her. I told her we planned to dig May Lynn up, unless something changed in the next few hours.

Mama sat silent for a long time after I finished telling my story. "A body?"

"Yes, ma'am."

"I'm so weak," she said, and for a moment I thought she was going to slide off the log.

"I'm sorry, Mama," I said. "I said some things to you I shouldn't have, and now I'm a thief and pretty soon a grave robber."

She shook her head. "No, I'm not weak from what you've done. I'm weak from living the way I have. Lying in bed so much hasn't done me any good, either. I should never have left Brian, and I should never have settled."

"You were protecting him," I said.

She shook her head again. "I didn't think I was good enough for him. I wasn't never good for anything, to hear my mama tell it, and when I met Brian, for a moment I thought I might be worth something. Then when I got pregnant, I felt bad, and dirty. I didn't want to make Brian dirty. But mostly I believed I got pregnant because the Lord was telling me who I was, and that I was being punished, and that my lot in life was always to be an unhappy one."

"Thanks," I said.

"Not how I meant it, dear. I come to the conclusion just this morning that if he's a loving God, he wouldn't do that kind of thing, and he isn't punishing me at all. I'm punishing myself. I listened to those men talking, and I heard Don say he didn't care what happened to you. He said that after Cletus said if they got the money back, he'd give Don and Gene some of it. Offered them fifty dollars apiece, but Don argued him up to seventy-five apiece. He said they couldn't help him find you, he'd hire that colored man that lives in the woods."

"Skunk?"

"Yeah. Skunk."

"There ain't no Skunk."

"I have heard different," Mama said.

Mama also believed in signs and angels and ghosts, so I didn't take her thoughts on Skunk seriously.

"Seventy-five apiece, huh?" I said.

"That's what Cletus finally offered," she said.

"Considering it's a thousand dollars missing, that's not that good a deal," I said. "But at least I know how much I'm worth, along with Jinx and Terry. Did Cletus mention it was stolen and there was a dead body under it in a once-nice suit?"

"He didn't."

"Well, I guess selling me out for a hundred and fifty dollars between the two of them is better than Don and Gene doing it for nothing," I said. "That's the stepdaughter rates, I figure. I wonder what they'll trade their own kin out for."

"That's a lot of money in these times," she said.

I stared at her.

"I didn't mean he should do it. Just saying."

"You ought to get back before they miss you," I said. "I got to warn Terry and Jinx."

"I'm not going back. I'm going with you," Mama said.

"You are?"

"Why I brought the bag," she said. "It's got some things for both of us in it. I even put your good dress and shoes in there."

"Thank goodness for that," I said. "I hope you brought the dresser from my room. The one with the mirror."

"You might need that dress along the way," she said. "You never know who you might meet."

"Traveling with us, that makes you a thief, too."

"Then we will all be thieves together," she said. "You see, Sue Ellen, today, as the cure-all wore off, I had a dream of a big black horse, and it was following me along this riverbank. It was a big horse, and just kept getting closer. And then I saw this white horse up ahead, in the brush, and somehow I knew if I could get to that white horse, and swing on its back, that it would ride me away from the black one."

"Maybe it's a nice black horse," I said.

"I don't think so, hon. I don't think so."

"Did you get to it?"

"I woke up. So no. What now?"

* * *

It sounds pretty bad, but I left Mama sitting on that log and went to warn Terry first cause he was the closest. Mama just didn't have the strength for a lot of scouting around. I left her there thinking about horses.

It took me a while to get out of the river bottoms and into the crooked-built town. I went along, watching carefully, and as I was walking to Terry's place, trying to figure how I could get to him without being discovered by his stepfamily or his mama, down the road he come, walking in the moonlight, moving in such a way it looked as if he had one foot in a ditch and the other on something slick. He had two shovels slung over his shoulder. He saw me and raised his hand.

When we met up, I spilled out all that Mama had told me. I didn't mention she planned to go with us. I thought I'd save that tidbit.

"Damn," Terry said. "I assumed I'd already have May Lynn dug up by the time you and Jinx showed. I knew pretty soon Cletus would put two and two together as far as Jinx and myself went, so I started making trips. That's how I hurt my ankle. Stepped in a hole."

We started walking together in the direction of the graveyard where May Lynn was buried.

"Trips?" I said.

"I've already been to the graveyard, and I carried a tarp out there to put the body on. I've made three trips, taking supplies we'll need. I have a wheelbarrow there as well. I've been busy. But I haven't dug up the body yet. Why I brought the shovels."

"Jinx is probably there by now," I said.

"Works out right," Terry said. "By the time they come to tell my mama and the stepdummies what's what, we'll have May Lynn dug up, and they'll have no idea where we are. I got a surprise in store, too."

It took us about a half hour to get to the place where May Lynn was buried. When we got there, Jinx was sitting on the ground by the grave with her little bag of goods. When she saw us coming she sprang to her feet.

"It done took you long enough," she said.

"I was here before you," Terry said.

"I figured that, all this stuff being here," Jinx said. "But still, I been waiting and thinking Cletus would be after me like a pig on a mushroom since he knows Sue Ellen and she knows us."

"Good figuring," I said. "That is, in fact, in motion."

I filled Jinx in quick-like. She said, "Mama, she knows I'm going. I couldn't just leave her. I told her."

"How'd she take it?" I asked.

"She took it good," Jinx said. "She took it so good I almost stayed. She told me I might ought to go even if I hadn't stole nothing; that there's not a thing here for me, and that maybe there's something out there. She said a colored girl might have a chance out in California or up north, but here there wasn't nothing but raw fingers and tired bones. I'll write her when everything blows over—Daddy, too, where he's working up north. I almost figure I'm doing it for them, giving myself a chance. Besides, me having hit that white man with a stick upside the head isn't going to set well around here."

"I reckon that's right," I said.

"Take a shovel," Terry said, handing me one of them.

I took it, and me and Terry started digging.

After a while I traded out the shovel with Jinx, and as I was sitting on the ground beside the grave, it really hit me. We was digging up May Lynn's dead body.

I was startled out of my thoughts when Jinx's shovel hit the lid of the coffin. Jinx and Terry stopped for a moment. Jinx said, "We're standing right on top of her."

"We have to rake the dirt clear, prize up the lid, and take her out," Terry said. "I brought gloves for it. They're in the wheelbarrow."

I got the gloves, and by the time I done that and looked in the hole, the wooden coffin lid was visible. Terry was pushing the last of the dirt off it with his hands. The coffin was made of wood so cheap it looked as if you could spit through it.

Jinx climbed out of the hole. Terry took the tip of the shovel and pushed it under the edge of the box, and started prying it up. It didn't resist much. The nails squeaked like a rat, the lid lifted and cracked in the middle, and a stink came out from under it big enough and strong enough to deserve some kind of government promotion.

I turned and threw up. When I looked back in the grave, I could see the lid was off and I could see the body in the box. They had tossed her in on her side. She was thinner now and darker, and she still had on that old dress, which had sort of melted into her. She wasn't blowed up no more. She had popped and gone flat against the bone. You could see where water had leaked in from below, making the bottom of that coffin come apart in places. If the wood had been a penny cheaper, she'd have fallen through the underside of it before she was in the ground.

"Those sons a bitches," Terry said. "This thing wasn't good for a day in damp ground."

He reached in his back pocket and took out a handkerchief and tied it over his nose. Me and Jinx didn't have a handkerchief, so we had to depend on scrunching up our faces and trying to think about something else. But me and her got down in the hole and yanked May Lynn out. When we did one of her arms come off, and I had to climb out and throw up again. By the time I got back down there, Jinx was throwing up in the grave.

Terry didn't so much as cough, but when we finally got her out of the hole, he wandered off a ways and puked. I glanced at May Lynn, and her face was dark as old pine sap. There were no eyes cause bugs and worms and groundwater had done been at them, and she had been full of river when we pulled her out, so she looked way worse than that dead man under the money bag; and she hadn't been near as long gone as he had. It didn't seem right.

After a bit, Terry come back and helped us load the body into the wheelbarrow. We put the tarp down first and put her on top of it. We had to bend her some to make her fit, and she came apart a little more, and something fell out of her that I couldn't recognize. Terry used the shovel to put it in the wheelbarrow. Jinx brought over her arm and laid it on top of the body. Terry folded the tarp over her on both sides and at the ends.

"Now what?" I said.

"The brick kiln," he said.

11

Now, there's no use going into all of it, but what I will say is it's a wonder we didn't end up being caught. I guess we didn't because it was late and we didn't see anybody but a couple of dogs. They came out to smell the dead meat and Jinx threw rocks at them and ran them off.

We took turns pushing the wheelbarrow, and it wasn't no real chore, because what was left of May Lynn seemed as light as a new loaf of bread, without the freshness. The night was clear and the wheelbarrow squeaked a little. Her stench made us push the barrow along quite smartly.

Terry guided us to the back of his stepdad's brick company. We stopped under a window, and me and Jinx made a cradle with our hands, and Terry stepped up on it and pushed at the window till it come up. He wriggled inside, and in a moment the back door opened to let us in. I pushed the wheelbarrow through the door.

I guided the barrow between rows of stacked bricks, and finally we came to a spot along the wall with a dozen brick beehive kilns. They all had metal doors on them, and there were some handles

on the doors—wooden ones in metal slots—and on the wall between each door was a dial.

Terry fumbled a match out of his pocket and lit it to a twist of
paper that had been lying on the floor. He turned one of the dials,
opened a metal door. There was a hiss like a surprised possum. It
was gas shooting up from a grate on the bottom of the kiln. Terry
stuck the flaming paper through the grate, touched a spot inside,
and the hissing turned to a whoosh; the heat from it nearly singed
my eyebrows. The fire rose up and licked out with blue and yellow tongues, and in an instant, I was sweating.

"We got to wait a little bit," Terry said, and closed the door.

There were some stacks of bricks, and we used them to sit on.

"It'll have to heat to a very high temperature," Terry said.
"When it does, she'll burn hot and rapidly. Her body will turn to
ash, bones and all."

I don't know how long we waited there, but I know I was nervous the whole time. I kept expecting the constable and those
mean old former kin of mine to burst in on us, but they didn't.

Finally, Terry stood up and pulled on his gloves, which he had
stuck in his belt, and opened the door; the flame inside was twisting and rolling. Using gloves and the shovels, we lifted the tarp
with May Lynn's body folded inside it, along with the broken-off
arm and the dark part we didn't know, out of the wheelbarrow. Together we carried the tarp to the open beehive, stuck the
corpse in at the feet, and shoved. The flames went to work immediately. They licked at the tarp like they was hungry. Terry
slammed the door. He looked at us. His face was popped up with
sweat balls from the fire, and he looked like he was barely there
with us.

"Someone ought to say something," he said.

"I'm sorry it's so hot in there," Jinx said.

"Something else."

"Goodbye, May Lynn," I said. "You've been a good friend up until we didn't see you much anymore, and maybe you had your reasons for that. And we thank you for the map and the stolen money, which has shown us a way to go. I hope you wasn't hurt too long before you died. I hope it was quick."

"I hope so, too," Terry said, and made a choking sound. "You're going to Hollywood, May Lynn."

We pushed the wheelbarrow back to the graveyard and covered up May Lynn's grave with the shovels. We loaded our supplies on the wheelbarrow, along with the shovels, and left. The graveyard was on the way to the river bottoms, so it had been best to leave the stuff there, and Terry, on one of his early trips, had put the bag of money in a lard bucket and buried it near May Lynn's grave. He dug it up and we loaded it and the rest of the stuff on the wheelbarrow, right next to a small sealed cardboard box we had taken from the brick company and put May Lynn's ashes in.

We headed out, and when we got into the woods, close to where our boat was, which was also close to where Mama was, I laid it on them.

"Mama not only told me about Cletus coming to the house, she's going with us."

"Say what?" Jinx said.

By that time, we were coming down a little rise, and they could see Mama sitting there in the moonlight on the log. She turned and looked at us and our squeaking wheelbarrow.

"Wasn't you the one talking about a yellow dog and a goat?" Jinx said.

"She ain't neither," I said.

"No," she said. "But there sure is a right smart lot of us now."

* * *

After we loaded the boat and pushed the wheelbarrow off into the Sabine, Terry cut three long poles with a hatchet he had in his bag. We stretched the poles across the boat so that they stuck out long on either end, then we got in and Jinx held them in place while me and Terry paddled downriver to the raft. Mama used the can to bail out water.

"It took you a while," she said. "I thought you had gone on without me."

"We had to burn May Lynn up," I said.

"You actually did that?" she said.

"In a brick dryer," Terry said.

"Yeah," Jinx said. "We got her somewhere in a box."

"Oh my," Mama said.

When we come to the raft, or barge, if you prefer, we loaded onto it. It was a good thing, too, cause we had been tight in the boat, and the water was coming through the bottom worse than ever, even with Mama bailing fast as a spinning windmill in a high wind. We took the paddles and pushed the boat away from the raft; it was already taking on heavy water by the time it drifted away from us.

After we was good and fixed, Terry got his hatchet and went to cutting the rope that held our ride to the tree. When it come loose, the raft turned sideways a little, then straightened itself and started to move forward in the slow but steady current of the river.

I looked back at the boat we had left behind us. It was tilting up slightly at one end, but mostly it was just low in the water. It got lower as I watched, and I'm sure within a few moments I would have seen it go down. But I never got the chance. The raft shifted a little as the river bent around a sandbar, and we had to go to work with our poles to guide it through the shallows. Then the river carried us beyond the bar and around a bend, and out of sight of the sinking boat.

PART TWO

THE KINGDOM OF THE SNAKE

12

It was such a bright night we could see the river good as day. We could make out sandbars and easily pole around them. We could see the spaces between trees clearly, and the moonlight lay on the tops of them like some kind of fuzzy halo. Slats of soft shadow fell over the water as if they was window blinds. Even the sticklike heads of turtles poking out of the water was easy to see.

After we had gone a ways, the river became straight and wide, and we saw a deer swimming across it wearing a rack of antlers on its head big enough to hang a rich man's winter coats and a couple of hats.

Mama sat in the middle of the raft with her knees drawn up and her arms wrapped around them while the rest of us poled. The box holding May Lynn was near her, and she had her head turned, looking at it, knowing what it was, I guess, though we hadn't actually pointed it out as May Lynn's resting place.

She wasn't doing nothing to help, and we didn't expect her to. Hell, we hadn't planned on her going, so it was hard to have expectations. And what we all knew from just looking at her was she was weak and sick and could have been wrestled to the ground by a playful kitten. I was even afraid harsh language might knock her out.

I don't know exactly how long we poled along like that, but we seemed to be making good time, and Terry said he figured we was five to seven days away from Gladewater, depending on circumstances and how hard we worked at it.

After a long while I began to feel hungry and in need of sleep because it had been one busy day, but I didn't want to be the first to call out, and didn't have to. We come to a place where the river went pretty thin, and Terry said, "Look over there."

What there was to see was a little pool off the straight of the river. You had to be in just the right spot to see it. Too soon and all you saw was a big overhanging cypress and some droopy willows, and if you looked too late, you was past it. It was a shiny pool and didn't look stagnant or mossy. It was a pretty good size, about twice the size of the raft. The water flowed into that place, turned around, and flowed out, keeping the spot clean and fresh, and from the dark of the water I figured it was deep, too.

"Go there," Terry said.

Me and Jinx poled in that direction. It was a hard turn in that fast water, but we poled hard enough we got some speed up, and the raft glided into that little pool and bumped up against the shore.

I held my pole to the bank to keep us from floating back, and Terry took a hammer and nails from his bag. He drove a couple of long nails, darn near spikes, into the front of the raft, then got a rope out of the bag, uncoiled it, wrapped it around the nails, and bent them over a bit of the rope with the hammer. He tied off the rope to the roots of the cypress—those roots being considerable and sticking out from the bank for some ten feet, coiling down and around like fat snakes twisting into the water.

"We didn't go too far before we holed up," I said.

"I believe we have a good start," Terry said. "And they don't know how we're making our run for it. Except maybe they'll think by boat, since we stole your daddy's. It's missing, they might figure we're going that way, but my first guess is they're going to think the bus, and they'll go to the bus station in Gladewater. That we caught a ride with someone. But we won't be there, and they won't know when to expect us."

"He ain't my daddy," I said.

"What?" Terry said.

"Ain't my daddy's boat, cause he ain't my daddy," I said.

"No," Mama said. "No, he isn't. And Don, he's pretty much a quitter. Something doesn't work out immediately for him, he'll leave out. That's been my experience in more ways than one."

I tried not to mentally count the ways, but I said, "Why he fishes with poison, 'lectricity, and dynamite is because it takes the waiting and trouble out of things."

"It doesn't matter, we have to rest, and it's better that we don't wear ourselves thin right at first," Terry said. "We're most likely better off traveling by day than night, even if we can be seen. The moon will be less bright tomorrow night, and even less so as we go. We're more probable to end up getting wedged up on something or turning the whole thing over when we can't see. During the day, we can journey more rapidly, even if we can be observed more easily."

None of us argued. We were tuckered out.

Terry had stuffed a couple of blankets in his bag, and Mama had thought to do the same, and so had Jinx. They were all thin blankets, but there wasn't much need for them on a nice night like it was. The boards that had been nailed over the logs were nice and smooth from years of people walking on them, so it was easy to stretch out and cover ourselves and get comfortable. Mama chose the middle of the raft, and I ended up close to her. She was warm, and she put her arm around me. The crickets sawed and the frogs bleated and the wind blew and the mosquitoes took a night off; the water beneath the raft rocked lightly.

"He didn't want to be the kind of man he is," Mama said in my ear.

"What?"

She was talking soft, and though Jinx and Terry might could have heard her, I'm sure they couldn't have understood her.

"Don. I think he got broken early on, like me, only he was broken more. He came from a family that inherited much and his father turned it into less. The beatings he got took a toll, and, like me, he never thought he was worth anything. My family sure didn't know what to do with me. It wasn't that we didn't get along, it's that they seemed to be somewhere else even when I was there. I never told you much about them, my mother and father."

"You said they died of smallpox," I said.

"Yes. They did. But before they died, they might as well have been dead. Me and Don was the same to you. We didn't do you any good, that's for sure, but you haven't become like us, and I'm not sure why."

"I reckon you did your best," I said. "But you still get to choose how you want to act and go, don't you?"

"You do. But not everyone chooses well."

"That's on them," I said.

"I know. I wear my mistakes like a coat, only it's heavier," Mama said.

"You did what you could, I guess."

"I did what I could do, but it wasn't much. I want to do better now. Don isn't just a man without hope anymore. He's a man without heart. I can stand one, but I can't stand the other. Between what went on between us, him hitting me, there were moments that were very nice. Then it would start over. I got so I lived for the in-betweens."

"What you said about Daddy—I mean Don—being a quitter," I said. "You believe that?"

"I do," she said. "But I been wrong before. Maybe he has more juice in him than I suspect. I know this, though: Gene isn't a quitter, and neither is his pal Cletus, and certainly not Constable Sy. Neither will quit when he thinks he can get something for free, or when he thinks he can manage some kind of bargain in his favor. Those two will work themselves to death to get a free thing, and do nothing for something they can have for honest work. They'll chase this money till they get it, or there's no way for them to have it. I'm certain of that. I have known them as long as I've known your daddy, and I know that much about them. Somewhere inside Don I used to think there was a good man pressed flat. I thought he might blow up to size again at some point, but he didn't. He wasn't always bad to me, honey. There were times when he was good."

"You said that," I said. "It doesn't comfort much."

"It's just those times got farther and farther apart, and I think he's been flat so long he's going to stay that way. What makes me proud of you is that you didn't let either of us mash you down. You spring right back, and you got hopes. I used to have hopes, and I'm trying to remember what that's like, and I'm trying to make sure you keep yours."

"I'm trying," I said. "But he was always bad to me, and wanted to be as bad as he could."

"I guess I knew that."

"Why didn't you do something?"

"Because I didn't have the spirit."

This wasn't a very satisfying answer, but I knew it was the best I was going to get. I decided I had to start with her this very night, and call it a new beginning. She touched my hand, and then was quiet. I snuggled in close. I felt like a sad old dog that had finally been petted.

During the night, we all awoke to Mama on the edge of the raft. She was lying on her belly with her head hanging over, puking. When she got what was in her out in the river, I got her back to the center of the raft and covered her and hugged her close, but she trembled like she was cold, which didn't make no sense, as it was a warm night.

"I'm needing the cure-all," Mama said. "That's what's happening. I didn't bring any of it with me. I should have cut it back, not quit cold turkey. I'm so sick. I thought I heard God calling to me, but it was a whip-poor-will. I dreamed about that black horse again, and I saw the white one, but it was running in front of me, too fast to catch."

"You'll catch it in time," I said.

She trembled for a while, but finally got still, and me and her both slept.

We was all up with the sun. Mama felt considerably better, and with the light I felt happier about our possibilities.

Mama, like Terry, had come well prepared. She had some hot-water cornbread patties in a bucket in her bag, and she gave us all a couple of them, and we drank water from a canteen Terry brought. It seemed the best cornbread I had ever eaten and the sweetest water I had ever drunk. Mama, I noticed, drank a little water but ate nothing.

After untying, we poled back onto the river and started out again. It was good water and the river was straight. We went along right smart-like and didn't have to do anything much until the raft started to drift to one side or the other, then we'd have to push off hard to get back to where the water was swift and straight again. But with the current like it was, and the raft well built, we stayed mostly in the middle and kept making good time. It was hard sometimes to even feel like we was moving. Might not have known that was the case if I hadn't looked toward shore and seen trees and such go by.

About the time the cornbread began to wear off and the sun was starting to get high and turn hot, we heard singing. It was sweet and it was loud, and there was a choir full of it.

"It's as if angels have come down from heaven," Terry said.

"Yeah," Jinx said. "Or a bunch of people singing."

It was pretty, though, like the songs was dancing over the water. As we drifted on, the singing grew louder. We finally came in sight of where it was coming from. A bunch of white people gathered on the edge of the river. Many were near the bank, but the rest went up a little slope of grass that at the peak was yellow with sunlight. A lot of the people were dressed up — at least, they was as well dressed as they got in East Texas — and down by the water was a barefoot man wearing black pants and a white shirt with the sleeves rolled up. He was waving around a big black book. A man dressed about the same way was standing beside him with his head down, the way a dog will do when you're scolding it.

But it wasn't a scolding. I realized what it was when I figured it was Sunday. I had sort of lost count of the days, but now I knew what day it was because of what I was seeing. It was a bunch of Baptists and they was attending a baptism. I knew because I had seen it before. It had been done to me, but I was so young I didn't really remember much about it.

Someone was about to get dunked in the river. Way the Baptists saw it, that dunk in the river made sure you was going to heaven, even if before or later you knew a cow in the biblical sense or set fire to a crib with the baby in it. Once you was dunked and a preacher said words over you, heaven was assured and Saint Peter was already brushing off your seat and stringing your harp. Since most everyone in these parts was a Baptist, the fields and the prisons being full of them, it seemed like a pretty good deal.

As we cruised by, we saw the singers lift their heads to look at us. The children waved. Some of them got smacked by their folks on account of it. The preacher, his light hair shiny as gold in the sun, dragged the man standing next to him out into the water. The tails of their shirts floated up.

Passing them, we looked back and seen the man holding his nose, falling back into the preacher's arms, being lowered down.

Mama, who had turned around to watch it all, said, "He has been baptized."

"Like us, he can pretty much commit any crime he likes and he'll be redeemed," I said.

"Hush," she said. "It isn't exactly like that."

We sailed on past the church folk.

The water was brisk because of all the recent rain, and the river bent a lot, and sometimes when it bent and became narrow, the raft would turn so that the rear end became the front end, and there was no fighting it with our poles because it was so deep. We switched to paddles, but it was like trying to use ice cream sticks to get the job done.

Eventually, we come around a twist in the river and the raft started going around and around and finally it twirled down a little offshoot. All we could do was just keep our places and hope we didn't tip. It turned shallow, though, and it got so we could use our poles again. In time we was able to push ourselves up against the shore. I jumped off and tied the raft to an oak.

Finished, I sat down on the ground. After I'd been on the water for that long, the earth felt funny underneath my butt, like I had been on a merry-go-round and had gone too fast and had been thrown off.

Everyone got off the boat and sat down. Mama dug around in her bag and came up with more cold cornbread and water. The cornbread was still good and the water still tasted sweet. Even Mama ate this time.

When we finished eating, none of us was eager to get back on the raft, though there wasn't a discussion about it. We just sat there thinking to ourselves, and not saying anything. Terry took a clean white cloth sack from his goods and opened the box with May Lynn in it, poured the ashes into the bag, and tied it off.

Mama said, "Is that . . . her?"

"Yep," I said.

Terry stored the bag and we all went back to sitting and not talking. Then as we sat, we was startled by a voice.

"What are you doing here?"

I leaped to my feet, along with everyone else but Mama, who once she got seated was slow to move.

It was a man standing on the rise above us. He had the sun at his back, so all we could make out was a dark human shape. It was like the light behind him was coming out of him, shooting into the sky.

"Did you build your raft?" the shape asked.

"What was that?" I asked.

"I said did you build your raft?"

"We kind of borrowed it," I said.

"It looks like that raft upriver," the shape said. "The one tied out to a stump."

"It does look a lot like it," Terry said.

"They practically twins," Jinx said.

"I'm pretty sure that's the same raft," the voice said, and the man moved down the slope toward us. As he did, with the hill at his back, and the sun hanging more above than behind him now, we got a chance to check him over good.

He was tall and thin with that kind of yellow hair that when it grays just looks more blond; the sunlight showed us that his hair had started to do just that, around the temples and at the front. There didn't seem to be any oil in it, and it had most likely been slicked back wet with water and had sun dried. The wind moved it around on his head like old corn shucks.

He was wearing a white shirt and black pants muddy at the bottom, and some worn shoes that folded over on the sides. He was maybe in his forties and nice-looking. He smiled and showed us he had all his teeth. In my world, finding someone with all their teeth, both ears, and their nose on straight by the time they reached forty was as rare as finding a watermelon in a hen's nest. Mama was an exception, and of course all three of us kids, but we still had a pretty good hike to go before we made forty, if we did, and Mama was still a few years off of it herself, though she treated her teeth well and was good about keeping herself washed and her few clothes clean.

As he came down the hill he kept smiling. He wasn't a big fellow, and I figured after what I had seen Jinx do when she was mad, if he got to be a bother, we could just sic her on him with a boat paddle.

When he was down close, he turned his head and looked at Mama. It was like a fire lit up behind his eyes. I looked at her, too. She looked very pretty that morning. Like a goddess on a trip, recovering from an illness. Her long, dark hair was glossy in the sun, her face white as oats. Her head was turned up to look, and except for her sad eyes, she seemed much younger than her thirty-something years. I always knew she was pretty, but in that moment I realized she was beautiful, and I knew then why Don had wanted her, why my father had loved her. I wished I was as pretty as she was.

"We took the raft cause we had to," Mama said.

"I'm not in the judging business," the man said. "I think too many people are judged. Though I have to say, 'Thou shall not steal.' "

"Ain't nothing says 'Thou shall not borrow,' " Jinx said.

The man smiled, and all of a sudden I knew what I should have known right off when I seen what he was wearing and his muddy pants bottoms. He was the preacher that had done the baptism.

He came down closer, and when he did, I eased over close to a pretty good-sized rock that was by the water, measured in my head if I could throw it fast enough and hard enough to bean him a good one on the noggin, if things called for it. But he didn't show any need for that. He came down smiling and stood by the water and put a hand to his chin and gave our raft a real good once-over.

"It's hard to steer, isn't it?" he said.

"A little," Terry said.

"More than a little," Jinx said. "It's as ornery as a Shetland pony."

"Oh, those Shetlands bite," the preacher said. "I can tell you that."

"It's a raft," Terry said. "Not a pony."

"Yes," the preacher said, "but the young girl and myself were speaking metaphorically."

"Got that, Terry?" Jinx said. "That's how we was speaking."

"I understand that," Terry said. "But I'm not speaking metaphorically."

The man turned his smile on Mama. "Are all these but the little colored girl your family?"

"Only Sue Ellen," she said, and nodded in my direction. "The others are friends of my daughter."

"And friends of yours?" he asked.

"I suppose they are," Mama said. "Yes. They're friends of mine."

"Well, now, I suppose if they are friends of a lady lovely as yourself, then they should be friends of mine. I'm Reverend Jack Joy. The last name is real. I didn't make that up for religious reasons, though I certainly see myself as a man of joy, eager to raise a joyful noise in the name of the Lord."

"I'm Helen Wilson," Mama said, "and that's my daughter, Sue Ellen, and the colored girl is Jinx and the young man is Terry."

"No last names for you two?" he said, smiling at them, which is a thing he did plenty of.

"First names are fine," Terry said.

I realized then that Mama might have been a little too eager to share, us being fugitives and all.

"It's turning off a hot day," Reverend Joy said. "Would you like to come up to my house and have some tea? One of my flock, not a half hour ago, brought me a block of ice that she carried in her car all the way from Marvel Creek, about half of it melting into the floorboard before she got to me. And she brought a platter of fried chicken. Ice and chicken are all laid out in the icebox. If there's enough ice, I might could churn some ice cream, though I can't make promises there."

"What you doing down by the river, then, if you got all that up there?" Jinx said.

"I wasn't hungry yet, and I came to see if the water was up. I was thinking about a little fishing later, and I wanted to see how the water was."

"How is it?" I asked.

"High. Come on up and have something. It's a good reason to get away from the river and the sun for a while. I didn't really want to fish all that bad anyhow."

"We just ate," I said.

"Just the tea, then," he said.

"We got to be on our way," I said.

"I understand you being cautious," Reverend Joy said, "you people not knowing me. But I've been a reverend in these parts here for two years, and so far, I haven't shot or eaten anybody."

"It is turning off hot," Mama said, smoothing her hair. "I could have a glass of tea, and hold something to eat in abeyance. Maybe that ice cream."

I looked at Mama, surprised. She was flirting. I had never seen her do it, but I had seen May Lynn go at it, and she was a master, so I recognized it for what it was. Still, Mama doing it was as strange to me as if I had looked into the mirror and discovered for the first time that I was actually a hippopotamus wearing a derby hat.

"Good, then," Reverend Joy said. "I'll just lead the way."

"We can't leave the raft," I said.

"Sure you can," Reverend Joy said. "It's tied off good. And after we have some refreshment, I've got a bit of lumber and such, and I think we can make you a rudder. You're going to go down the river, a rudder would make it a whole lot easier to control your craft. Way I figure, the current, which is strong there, pulled you right off the main river. After you have something cold, maybe a bite to eat, you can set right off again."

Except for Mama, we were hesitating. She, on the other hand, had gotten up and was starting to move toward the hill. Reverend Joy took note of it and quickly took her arm and led the way up. I don't know what he said to her as they walked away, but she thought it was funny. She giggled. I hadn't heard her do that in a long time. Actually, I hadn't never heard her do it quite like that, way a schoolgirl will do when she's playing some kind of game or the other.

When Mama and the Reverend Joy was a little ahead of us, I said to Jinx and Terry, "I'm not sure I like this."

"He might know we're on the run and is gonna turn us in," Jinx said.

"I doubt our pursuers have spread the word," Terry said. "They want to keep that money quiet. But he might have a car, and with him attracted to your mama, he may be generous enough to give us a ride to Gladewater and we won't need the raft. Come on, let's not let your mama out of our sight."

We gathered up our stuff, including the money and May Lynn's ashes, and followed Reverend Joy and Mama up and over the hill.

13

—⁓—

The Reverend Joy's house wasn't big, but it was solidly made of logs and had split shingles. It rose up higher than most single-floor houses. The shingles was coated over with a thin brushing of tar to keep out water, and I could see tar paper sticking out from under them at the edges. The roof was shiny in the sun. The front porch was tight, with firm steps, and had a rocking chair on it.

Out front of the house was a black car with a coating of dust and a front right tire and wheel missing. The axle on that side was up on some wood blocks and there was grass growing around the car like hair around a mole. A half dozen crows were camped on it and had speckled it like a hound pup with their white droppings; they gave us a beady look as we came up. With his car up on those wooden blocks, looked to me like we wouldn't be talking the reverend into taking us anywhere.

There was a well house out front, too. It was nicely built of seasoned lumber. It had a roof over it with a platform out to the side where you could step up and take hold of the rope and work the pulley to drop the bucket down the well. There was a pretty good-sized shed nearby, too. It was made of logs, like the house, and had the same kind of shingles. It had an open place with a roof over it and a long bench under it, and another section that was closed in by walls and a door. There was an outhouse not far away and it was painted blood red; it had been built recent, and a few spare two-by-fours and the like lay near it in the yard.

Only the garden looked out of step. It was a pretty big square with some buggy squash growing on top of badly hoed hills, and a line of beans that were yellowed and withering. The whole thing looked as if it was begging to be set on fire and plowed under, so as to be put out of its misery.

On a hill, not real far away, was a church. I figured that would be the reverend's church, and this would be the house the congregation provided.

Inside the house there was a window on every wall, two on each of the long walls. The windows was all lifted to let in air, and there was outside screens over the windows to keep out bugs. It was cooler inside than I would have thought, and that was probably on account of the tall ceiling. He had a new icebox in one corner and everything in the house was scattered about and old enough to have been found in a pyramid in Egypt. But there was plenty of it. We all took a seat at a big plank table in the center of the room. The reverend got some glasses out of a cabinet, went to the icebox, took an ice pick, and went to chopping us some chips. He put them in glasses, and from another part of the icebox he got out a pitcher of tea and poured tea into the glasses.

We sat and looked at each other and sipped our tea, which was made with lots of sugar; it was so sweet it made my head swim, but it was cold and wet and I was glad to have it.

The Reverend Joy lost interest in the rest of us and spent his time looking at Mama. It was the kind of sick look a calf has for its mama.

"You on some kind of picnic?" he asked her.

"A pilgrimage of sorts," Mama said. "We are off to see what we can see."

"Is that a fact?" he said.

"It is," Mama said.

"Well, I'm sure glad to have you in my house, and that God has brought us together," Reverend Joy said.

"Or the river," Jinx said.

"What's that?" he said.

"Maybe the river brought us together, and not God," Jinx said.

"Aren't they the same?" Reverend Joy said.

"They might be, but if they is the same," Jinx said, "that same river that will get you together for a glass of tea will drown you or get you snakebit."

The Reverend Joy grinned at Jinx. She looked a mess, as all of us was, except Mama. Then again, she hadn't dug up two bodies, burned up one in a brick factory, wrestled goods onto a boat, and poled and paddled down the river. That sort of thing had taken the freshness out of the rest of us. But Jinx, she was special messed up. She had bits of pine straw in her pigtails, and the sides of her pants showed damp dirt. I figured when she got up from that chair her butt would leave enough mud you could plant a fair stand of corn in it and have room left over for a hill or two of cucumbers.

"You don't sound like a strong believer in the Word or the Heart of the Lord," Reverend Joy said, never losing his smile.

"I got my own thoughts," Jinx said.

This was true, but I knew her well enough to know they weren't under lock and key and could come out and be seen with only the slightest bump of suggestion. I was hoping Reverend Joy would leave it there, but like the rest of his breed and politicians, he just couldn't.

"I suppose you're one of those wants to see a miracle before you'll believe," he said.

"That would be a good start," Jinx said. "I think that could get me in the boat right away."

The Reverend Joy chuckled a bit, like he was giggling over something silly a kitten had done, and maybe at the back of that giggle he was thinking about a sack to go with that kitten, along with some rocks and a trip to the river. "Miracles happen every day."

"You seen one?" Jinx said.

"The bluebird that sings in the morning," he said. "The sun that comes up. The——"

"What I want to see," Jinx said, "is something a little more surprising and less regular."

"Don't be rude, Jinx," Mama said.

After that remark the reverend lost his smile and it got so quiet in the room you could have heard a sparrow fart from the top of a tall pine tree. I was thinking that when I got the chance, I'd have to pull Jinx aside and explain to her how you just had to let religious folks run their thoughts out, because if you didn't believe what they did, they would keep coming back at you with it until you finally was a believer or lied or drowned yourself just to get some peace.

Finally a smile came back to visit the Reverend Joy's face. "I know a man that had a terrible accident. He got a wagon turned over on him and it crushed his chest. By the time they got him to the doctor he was dead. They laid him out and called the family, and when they come in to look at him, he woke up."

"He wasn't never dead, then," Jinx said. "The dead don't wake up."

"It was a miracle."

"Wasn't never dead," Jinx said again.

"Doctor said he was."

"Doctor was wrong," Jinx said.

"Now, you weren't there," Reverend Joy said.

"Was you?"

"Jinx," Mama said.

"No, but I got it on good word," the reverend said.

Jinx nodded and sipped her tea. "Did this man got a wagon rolled on him get up off the table and go on with things like nothing ever happened?"

"He did," the reverend said.

"Right then?"

"No. He had to recover. The ribs and chest had to heal."

"So," Jinx said, "it was a miracle that needed a doctor to look in on him, and he needed time to get over things, like that crushed chest and such."

"Yes, but God was watching."

"Uh-huh," Jinx said. "He might have been watching, but I can't see he did much. And where was he when that wagon rolled over on that fella? What was he doing then? And if that's a miracle, my ass is white."

"Jinx!" Mama said, but since Jinx didn't really know her that well, her complaint didn't carry much weight.

Jinx plowed ahead. "Always someone's got to tell me about miracles and how they happen now like in the Bible. Mama read that Bible to me when I was young, and it cured me of religion itself. That Old Testament is just chock-full of mean ol' men who killed whole tribes of people and was with other men's wives, and even their own children, and they're the heroes.

"Them other books, the New Testament about Jesus, they're better, but there ain't one miracle in that book like any miracle I've heard about that's happened now. That Lazarus, he didn't come back from the dead then need a week to rest before he could get out of bed. He come back all ready to go. And blind men and cripples Jesus was said to heal didn't have to have a doctor come help them out and cure them up after Jesus was said to put his word on them. They was in a miracle right then, not over a stretch of time. The cripples leaped up and walked, blind men took to seeing right away. Least, that's the stories. And it don't fit anything I've heard you talk about, no matter what you name it. Way I see it, if there's miracles, tell me how many folks done lost arms and legs and had them grow back. Got an eye poked out and had a new one pop back in their head. That happens now and then, I might go more in the direction of believing that hooey."

The Reverend Joy had been sitting there listening to Jinx politely, but his cheeks were red as fire and his smile had tumbled off. There was a feeling in the air like we had all just seen a cow drop a pile in the floor, but didn't none of us want to mention it.

The Reverend Joy sat staring at Jinx. Then slowly he found his smile again. It was a little crooked, but he had it back. "You know, baby girl, you have some real thoughts there on miracles. And maybe I've been too quick to call something that is explainable a miracle. But that doesn't mean there isn't a God and that he doesn't watch over us and there aren't miracles."

"I certainly believe he watches over us," Mama said.

"So do I," Terry said.

I decided to remain quiet and on the fence.

"You may not believe in him," Reverend Joy said, "but he believes in you. And he's up there watching and caring."

"Well, if he's up there and watching and caring," Jinx said, "he's sure one for making you earn your spot."

You'd think that stuff Jinx was talking about would have made the Reverend Joy sour on us right away, but it didn't. At first I think it crawled up under his skin like a dying animal, but the more he sat and thought on it, the more I think he liked it. I figure that was because he thought he might save Jinx and offer up her soul to Jesus, though most likely, like a lot of whites, he thought she'd end up in Nigger Heaven, which was separate of whites and would give the white folk someone to do their laundry and cooking during harp concerts and the like.

Anyway, they went at it, arguing religion. No matter how the reverend tried to give his ideas, he couldn't make headway. I could tell Jinx had become a challenge to him, his Wall of Jericho that needed tumbling down. This led to us staying for dinner, and having that ice cream—which was a little runny and not that cold—and then it led to the reverend sleeping in his car, and the rest of us sleeping in his house, though he made a few suggestions that indicated he might like Jinx out in the storage building.

That night, Mama slept in the bed in the other room, and the rest of us slept on pallets on the floor under the table. Terry went to sleep right away, but me and Jinx was awake. I could hear her tossing and turning.

I told Jinx, "If you don't get converted before supper tomorrow, we might have a whole day of something good to eat."

"I promise not to embrace Jesus before then."

"There may come a time, though," I said, "when he gets tired of the argument, and you might want to get converted so we can keep eating and having a roof over our heads. I think he likes trying to convert you right now, but later he may insist on it."

"What I was really thinking is we don't need no roof," Jinx said. "What we need is to get back on the river. We haven't gone that far, and here we sit."

"Mama's doing better," I said. "She even seems a little happy. Maybe she just needs some time."

"I had an uncle was a drunk, and that cure-all is the same kind of thing," Jinx said. "What happens is they quit a day or so, then they get to craving, and they get sick, then they get better if they don't go back to it. But the real bad time is coming yet, and you got to be ready for it."

"You don't know that," I said.

"I know it well enough," she said. "Same as I know that fried chicken tonight was too salty."

"You ain't against looking a gift horse in the mouth, are you?"

"Even if the horse is free, you ought to check its teeth now and again to make sure ain't none of them falling out," Jinx said. "Besides, I ain't the reason he wants us here. It ain't arguing religion he likes so much. He likes your mama."

"I see that," I said.

"He looks at her, it's like he's licking his lips over a pork chop."

"You think he's got bad intentions?" I asked.

"He's got regular man intentions, that's for sure."

That night rolled into a series of nights, and then I lost count. We got the river off our mind. The food was good and it was brought to the reverend free by his church members, though there was someone who always did overdo the salt.

It was a good life and easy, and I wasn't having to carry stove wood to bed with me. There wasn't any sudden outburst that ended in Mama holding her eye and limping off to the bedroom. The reverend had a good singing voice, and he sang spirituals and old songs, and he sang them well, like his voice was coming from down deep in a well.

This enjoyment didn't keep me from allowing the reverend to help us build that rudder he talked about for our raft. Then he built a kind of hut made of lumber and logs in the middle of it. It wasn't much of a hut, but it could hold all of us at one time if we didn't breathe heavy or think too hard. He even stocked the hut with a couple bags full of goods so that if we decided to leave, we'd have a few things with us.

But after it was built, we didn't leave. We was like flies stuck in sweet molasses. Things was so comfortable there, I was beginning to think we had gotten worked up for nothing, and no one was following us. A few miles down the river had given us a freedom. It had been at our fingertips and we hadn't even known it. I had hesitated about running away from home, but now realized just how much of a captive I had been. What really struck me was there hadn't been no walls or guards around me, yet I had stayed in my prison on a kind of honor system. I had been my own guard and prison wall, and hadn't even known it.

As I said, the reverend slept in his car, and now and again he would sit at the table in his house with a big pad and pencil, the Bible at his elbow, and would write out sermons. To see how they would go with his flock, he would try them out on us. We told him how it all hit us, and gave him a few tips on how it might sound better to his listeners. He didn't even mind that a nonbeliever like Jinx had some suggestions. He got so good at delivering them sermons, Jinx was damn near ready to get baptized.

While we was there, for our keep, we did chores. Mama hoed out the garden and showed Reverend Joy how to better take care of it. She even looked stronger, and the gardening gave her use of her muscles and some sunlight. But, as Jinx said it would, the cure-all came back on her. She had seemed clear of it, but then her need for it showed up. She did have a few days and nights where she got weak, yelled, and had some bad dreams—dreams about that black horse, and the other, winged now, and white as a cloud. We held her while she talked out of her head. The reverend didn't even ask her what was wrong. Just sat by her and put a damp rag on her head. It was clear to me he knew what was going on, but it was also clear to me he never intended to say a word. During the day Mama tossed and turned and the bed was wet with her sweat, which was thick as hog lard on the sheets.

After a few days of this, Jinx went off in the woods and got some roots and bark and such, brewed it all up together, put it in a cup, and gave it to Mama to sip. Jinx said it was what they had given her uncle that caused him to quit drinking. Mama tried to fight off drinking that stuff, but she was too weak. Jinx was able to slip it down her throat. From the smell of that mess, I figure Mama got better just to keep from having to drink any more of it. Jinx said it was because she wasn't a true-to-the-bone drunk, but was a drunk in her head, which meant she just didn't like her life and wanted to get away from it, and that the cure-all was the door out. Now that she had gotten off it, and things was good, she had lost the desire, and unlike most drunks, the worst of which would drink shoe polish or hair tonic if it had alcohol in it, Mama was most likely done with it. Or so we hoped.

It got so Mama washed the reverend's clothes, and ours, and while she did my overalls and shirt, I had to wear my good dress. This led to the reverend telling me how pretty I was, and it led to me believing it to such a point, next thing I knew I was up in church singing with the choir.

We all started going to church, and even Jinx got to come in, but she had to stay in the back and was told not to be too familiar with white people, and she wasn't supposed to discuss her views on religion, even if she was asked a direct question. That was okay with her. She mostly slept through the sermons.

Truth is, we was all pretty content.

Now, there did get to be some talk. Folks at the church started asking me about us, about where we had come from, how long we had been at the reverend's house, and exactly what was his and Mama's arrangement. They also wanted to know why was we staying around with a nigger, meaning Jinx, of course. I told them we was just folks he was helping out with good Christian charity, and that he was sleeping in the car and Mama in the house, and there wasn't nothing funny going on, and Jinx was a friend, which was a thing that kind of concerned them. They will tell you they got "good nigger friends," if you ask, but what they mean is they have colored folks who they know and nod at and hire for jobs wouldn't nobody do if they didn't need the quarter, which was a kind of standard payment for everything from cutting grass to chopping wood, even if it was done all day in the hot sun.

To sum it up, his flock started to talk bad about Reverend Joy after church, and fewer men shook hands with him at the door. Even the kids run by him like they was passing a wasp nest, and my guess is they didn't know sin from a pancake.

The women would stand out in the church lot and yak and think I wasn't hearing them, but I have good ears, and I'm nosy, too, so I heard a lot.

There was one woman about Mama's age, not bad-looking in a kind of long-nosed anteater way. She was always narrowing her eyes and smiling, but that smile reminded me of how a dog will do when it's trying to decide if it ought to snarl or not. She seemed to be the main source of the gossip, and reason for that was plain to me. She was the one Jinx identified as the Too Much Salt in the Fried Chicken Lady; the one that came around and smiled and brought food, and tried to peek about to see if Mama had her underwear hanging over the door or some such business. It was clear to me that she saw herself not so much as a protector against sin but as someone disappointed the sin she suspected wasn't hers, and that she wasn't going to be what she most wanted to be — the preacher's wife.

Anyway, she and them other women was talkers, standing around in their good-enough dresses and spit-shined shoes, their big church hats propped on their heads. It was the kind of talk that made me want to break off a limb and take to whacking her and that bunch of hypocrites across the back of the head.

I started to tell Mama and Reverend Joy about it, but figured if I did, then we'd have to leave, and we'd be on the river again in the Kingdom of the Snake. I thought about what it was we had planned to do, thought about May Lynn from time to time, about her being in a bag, and that she was still a long way from Hollywood. But the truth was, it wasn't at the front of my mind.

Terry, the one who most wanted to take her out there, had even settled down, though now and again he would take the bag with May Lynn in it and go out and set with it on the edge of the raft like they was spooning. I even heard him talking to her once when I come up behind them. I was on my way to sit on the edge of the raft and dunk my feet in the river, but when I heard him talking, I decided to turn around and go back up the hill and leave them to it. In time, he found a lard can to keep her in, like the money. I guess he figured that was safer, and it had a nifty handle for carrying.

Only Jinx wanted to move on, though I don't know how much May Lynn's ashes had to do with it. For all his kindness, the reverend still treated Jinx a bit like a stain. He had stopped trying to convert her, however, and said something about there being some souls that was bound on the Judgment Day train for hell and there was no way to stop it. He would bring this up now and again, and when he said it, he would look at Jinx, and she would go, "Choo-choo."

Anyway, we stuck, cause sometimes when you're happy, or at least reasonably content, you don't look up to see what's falling on you.

14

⎯⎯ɯ⎯⎯

More time passed, though I don't know exactly how long. I lost count of the days. When in church, I gradually noted that the number of people in the pews got smaller. It pretty much come down to Reverend Joy preaching to a smattering of hanger-ons and us, and we had heard it all before at the kitchen table and had even helped him fine-tune it. But we stuck out of loyalty, same as you would if a little kid wanted to read a poem to you they'd wrote and there wasn't any real good excuse to go somewhere, though next to offering my hand to a water moccasin to bite, listening to someone read a poem is high on my list of things I can't stand.

The women who had been bringing Reverend Joy food during the week, as it was customary to do for the preacher, stopped delivering it; that little perk we had been taking advantage of dried up like an old persimmon. Too Much Salt in the Fried Chicken Lady—or, as I sometimes thought of her, the Anteater—was the first to go.

After that, it was all downhill.

Her chatter, and that of her nest of hens, turned the flock so against the reverend, including that man we had seen him baptize, that some joined the Methodists, which was a low blow as far as Reverend Joy was concerned.

"They might as well be Catholics," he said.

The reverend's sadness began to rub off on us. Terry, who hadn't been in any hurry to go, had taken more frequent to carrying May Lynn's can of ashes and her diary to the raft. He'd sit there with the can by his side and the diary in his hands, reading. Jinx would sit on the raft with him, and do some fishing. Whatever she caught, she'd throw back. I had been wearing my good dress a lot even when I didn't need to, but now I put it away and went back to my overalls. It got so I dreaded Sunday church and Wednesday prayer meeting. Before, all I had to do was sit through it, but now, watching the reverend preach was painful. He seemed smaller in his clothes, like a dwarf that had put on a fat man's pants and jacket by mistake.

One Sunday evening there was only us and about five other people in the church. Four of them five was old folks who wouldn't have changed churches if it caught on fire, and one was the local drunk, who liked to come there to sleep sitting up in the back pew next to where Jinx liked to sleep, though now and again he wasn't above yelling out "Amen" or "Praise the Lord," which was more than Jinx was willing to do. But unlike Jinx, the drunk did some of his sleeping lying down in the pew, where our girl would kind of hood her eyes and nod sitting up.

Anyway, this Sunday I'm talking about, after the sermon, Reverend Joy was quick to get out from behind the pulpit and over to the door. He stopped and let Mama walk with him down the hill toward the house. Before, he always went to stand in the doorway to shake hands, and we'd go ahead and meet him later. But now, like a dog bored of a trick, he was done, partly because the five listeners was as eager to leave as he was, including the drunk.

Me and Terry and Jinx watched Reverend Joy and Mama walking down the hill toward the house. It was still bright out, it being sometime in early July now, and we stood in the lot, picking up gravel and tossing it at a sweet gum that grew near the church. It wasn't that we had anything against the sweet gum. It was just something to do.

"We ought to get on with it," Jinx said. "May Lynn ain't gonna go to Hollywood and scatter herself."

"I have been thinking the same thing," Terry said. "At first I found this comfortable, but less so now. I feel like we have been kidnapped by ourselves. That we are among the lotus-eaters."

"Who?" I asked.

"Something I read in a book once," he said. "Suffice to say that once you are in the clutches of the lotus-eaters, it isn't easy to depart from them. You eat of the lotus and are led to believe everything is pleasant even when it isn't. We had a plan, and we've laid it down. I suppose we should pick it up again. For me, the spell here is broken."

"I don't remember eating no lotus," Jinx said. "Whatever that is."

"It's a way of speaking," Terry said. "It represents a mood. A thought."

"Why don't you just say that?" Jinx said. "Why you got to represent it, or some such thing?"

"I'll work to improve," Terry said.

That night I lay on my pallet on the floor, dozing off and on, and then at some point I came wide awake. I felt like a hand had been laid on me and was shaking me, and when I woke, May Lynn was walking to the back of the cabin pointing in the direction of the river. She was wearing that same old dress she always wore. Her hair was wet and dripping and there was a sewing machine tied around her feet. She was dragging it behind her like a ball and chain, making no noise whatsoever. She was all swollen up like when we found her. When she got to the rear of the cabin, she turned and looked at me and frowned and jabbed one of her fat fingers at the back cabin wall, really hard. It was all so genuine I could smell the river on her.

Then I really woke up. I looked and there wasn't no ghost, but I sure felt like May Lynn had been in the room, urging me to get back on that raft and get on down to Gladewater and then Hollywood.

The whole thing made my stomach feel suddenly empty. I was also hot and sticky. I thought I might creep over and get myself some cool buttermilk from the icebox, but when I sat up, now that my eyes had become used to the dark, I noticed the door to the bedroom, where Mama slept, was open.

I got up and tippy-toed so as not to wake Terry, who was sleeping at the rear of the cabin, or Jinx, who slept near the front door. I went and looked in the bedroom. The bed was empty. I went back to the main room and over to the window by the front door. I hesitated a moment, listened to Jinx snore. She sounded like someone had stuffed one of her nostrils with a sock. I moved back the curtain. There was nothing out there to see but heat lightning dancing above the trees and a few fireflies fluttering about, bobbing back and forth like they were being bounced off an invisible wall.

I went back to my pallet and got my shoes I had set by it, put them on, then crept quietly out the front door and closed it gently. I stood there on the porch trying to decide if I should go through with what I was thinking. Finally I decided I was going to do just that, even if in the end it harelipped the pope.

I sidled over to the reverend's car and looked in the window. The reverend's blankets and pillow was in the front seat, but he wasn't with them, and Mama wasn't there, which was a relief, but it wasn't a deep kind of relief, because I still didn't know where neither one of them was. I don't exactly know why I was concerned about it, but I was. I didn't like to imagine Mama would be with Reverend Joy, at least in the way I was thinking. I guess she had the right to some kind of happiness, but it still bothered me, and I suppose it was because I was wanting her and my real father, Brian, to rekindle things, so we'd be some kind of family.

I decided it was best not to know what they was doing. I started back for the house. Then I heard talking. It was coming from the rear of the cabin, so I went carefully along the side of it. When I got to the edge of the back wall, I realized the sound was not as near as I thought, but because of the slope of the hill, and the way it had a horseshoe sort of bend in it, voices were coming up from down there. The words wasn't entirely clear, but I could tell the voices belonged to Mama and Reverend Joy.

I skulked down the hill, feeling like a thief with a baby under my arm and a hot pot of water and some salt and pepper waiting, and made my way through the cover of trees scattered here and there. I came to where the hill had a bit of a lift, and then another drop-off. I could really hear them good now. I sat down there on the edge of that drop-off because I could see them from there, too. It was just shapes I could see, but it was easy to recognize the shapes and voices. They was down by the water, sitting on the raft, talking. It was a rotten thing to do, but I sat down and listened.

It was just talk at first, and I don't remember much of the early stuff. Mostly it was the Reverend Joy doing the talking, about this and that, but there was something about his tone that made me feel like he had something wild caught inside his head and was trying to sneak up on it and let it loose without getting bit.

He said, "I don't know that I have actually been called to preach."

"God called you?" Mama said.

"I thought so. I really did. But now I'm less certain. I am beginning to think I called myself."

"You know why your church members are leaving, don't you?" Mama said.

"I do."

"And so do I. But instead of us leaving, instead of making it easy for you, we've stayed. We're at fault here. If we leave, things will go back the way they were."

"It's all right."

"No," Mama said. "No, it's not. Tomorrow we are going to load up and go on down the river."

"It's too late for that, Helen," he said. "What's done is done."

"Maybe not," she said.

I could see the reverend's arm move now and again, and then there would be a little plop in the water. I came to know he had a little pile of rocks with him, picked up on the way down, I figured, and he was chunking them into the water. He finished off the last of them and quit chunking. They both sat looking out at the dark river.

"You never told me why you were going down the river in the first place," he said.

Mama thought for a long time before she spoke. "I'm on the run from my husband, and the children are trying to get out to Hollywood."

"California?"

"Yes," she said, and then she told him the whole dang thing, except about the money and May Lynn being with us. She left that part out. I'm not sure why, but she did, and I was glad. But she told him near everything else. Even told him about Brian and her pregnancy, and how me and Don didn't get along, and how he hit her and me. She said some bad things about Gene, and so on. It surprised me she told him about the pregnancy part, marrying Don on the downslide, because she hadn't told me any of that until recent, and here she was sharing it with some fellow she had only known for a little while.

When she finished, she said, "And now you know what kind of woman I am."

"Before you start feeling bad about your existence, you should know something about mine," he said. "I am a murderer."

I was so startled I stood up, and then sat back down.

"Surely not," Mama said.

"Not by my own hand," he said. "But a murderer just the same. When I was a teenager I stole a man's rifle. It wasn't much of a rifle, but it was a theft. I was seen in the area where the rifle was stolen, and was questioned. I blamed it on a colored boy I knew. We had grown up fishing the river together, playing together. We had a big tree where we played, a great oak that overhung the river. We would go there to jump from limbs into the water and swim."

It was exactly the same thing me and Jinx and Terry and May Lynn used to do. It was odd to think he been a kid, just like us, doing the same thing we did for fun.

"One time," he continued, "the water was running swift from a big rain, and I jumped in and it was too strong for me. Jaren, that was his name, leaped in there after me, grabbed me, and fought that current. We both near drowned, but he stayed with it long after I had tuckered out. He pulled me out of the river. This very river. The Sabine. Saved my life. I told him then and there that I owed him my life, and that I would stand by him forever. And then this thing with the rifle came up.

"I had seen the old man prop it against his porch when I was walking by on my way to the fishing hole, where I was going to meet Jaren. Well, I can't explain it other than the devil was talking directly at me, but it came to me that I could just walk up on that empty porch, take hold of that rifle before he knew it was missing, and run off. And that's what I did. I took it home and hid it in our barn.

"Thing was, though, the old man noticed it missing immediately, and next thing I know the sheriff was at my door. The old man had seen me coming up the road, and he told the sheriff, and the sheriff asked me if I had stolen the rifle. I told him no. I told him I wouldn't steal, but I had seen Jaren going up that road ahead of me, and said he was known to be a thief, which wasn't true. But I told him that because the hot breath of the law was on my neck. They went and got Jaren, and even though they couldn't find the rifle, their blood was up. If it had been me they had, even if they had the rifle I stole, I'd have gone to court and maybe to jail. But Jaren, being colored, well, it was like a coon hunt.

"They got him and took him out in the woods, and they castrated him and chained him to a stump and poured pitch all over him and set him on fire. I heard them bragging about it down by the general store. They was bragging on how long he screamed and how loud, and how it all smelled. They was proud of themselves.

"I went out to where they said they had burned him. I could smell that cooked meat before I could see him. All that was left of him was a dark shape with bones sticking out of it. Animals had been at him. I was going to bury him, and had even brought a shovel with me, but I couldn't do it. I just couldn't stand it. I went over and lay down in the woods and just passed out asleep. Then I heard a noise and woke up. I looked out from the trees and saw a wagon pulled by a couple of mules. There was a man and a woman in the wagon, and I knew who they were right off. I had eaten dinner at their table more than once. It was Jaren's parents. And all the time they were there, his mother was moaning and crying and yelling to the sky. The man got out of the wagon with a blanket and laid it on the ground, and he got that body free and stretched it out on the blanket, and rolled the sides of the blanket over what was left of Jaren, and carried and put him in the back of the wagon. When Jaren's father finished, he and his clothes were covered in char from Jaren's body.

"Jaren's mama climbed back there with the body, and his daddy clucked the mules up, and they started off. I could hear his mama yelling and carrying on long after they were out of my sight. I got sick and threw up, and could hardly walk, but finally I went and got the rifle, determined I was going to tell the law I had taken it, but then I thought, what does it matter now? They've killed Jaren. And I'd be incarcerated. I was a coward. I took the rifle down to the river, by the oak tree where Jaren had saved me from drowning, and threw it in the water. I stayed quiet about what happened, and now and again I would hear those men laugh about the time they burned a nigger, and how they had shown that thief a thing or two. Jaren wasn't even a person to them. He was a thing. Castrating him wasn't any different to them than castrating a hog, and burning him wasn't any different than setting fire to a stump. I never told anyone until now what really happened. One day, that memory was haunting me like a ghost, and I came to the conclusion that God, to help me repent, had called upon me to spread his word. Now I think my own guilt might have been talking to me."

"Oh, Jack."

"Yes. Oh, Jack."

"How old were you when this happened?"

"I was thirteen, but age doesn't matter. I knew better. I sold him out for something he didn't do to keep from being tagged with the deed myself. They didn't question him. They didn't find the rifle on him. They just killed him. I always wondered if the last thing they told him was that they knew he had taken that rifle because I told them so."

"You poor man," Mama said.

"Me? Goodness, no. Me? Why, I'm the scum of the earth. I have murder on my hands, and I tried to absolve it by preaching. And now I know I wasn't even called. I called myself. And I'm not really any different, not at the core. That little colored girl, Jinx. She's just as smart and good as she can be, and I guess I thought I could make up for one evil deed by saving her soul so she wouldn't go to hell. But it's me that's going to hell, not her. It's me that belongs with the devil."

I understood then that what I thought was discomfort about Jinx being colored wasn't Reverend Joy's problem at all. He was toting around a sack of guilt, and in some way, she reminded him of it.

Frogs bleated. Something splashed out on the water.

"I told you my sins," Mama said. "I'm not clean, either."

"You haven't done anything of consequence but leave an abusive husband and strike out down the river with your child. My sin is heavy as the world and dark as the deepest shadow in hell."

It was a big statement from the reverend and sounded like a line out of a book, but it hit me like a fist between the eyes. Compared to him, Mama and me and my friends was all doing pretty good when it came to any kind of measurement of sin. What scared me then was what I figure makes some people religious. The sudden understanding that maybe there isn't any measurement, and that it's all up to us to decide. And no matter what you do, it only matters if you get caught, or you can live with yourself and the choices you make. It was a kind of revelation.

Thinking on that made me feel cold and empty and alone.

"You were a boy," Mama said to Reverend Joy. "You did something wrong. You stole and you told a horrible lie, but you were young and frightened. It's not an excuse, but it is a reason."

"Sounds like an excuse to me," he said. "I was evil."

"If that's true, you've shown the evil has been cleansed. You have been saved, Jack. You have saved others. You've been baptized, of course, and therefore you have been redeemed. You're a good preacher."

"Good or bad, I'm done now. There's nothing left for me here. I don't deserve to ask it, but I'm asking you. Can I go with you downriver? Away from here? I don't know where I'll go in the end, but away from here. Will you have me with you?"

"I suppose it's up to the children, at least to some extent," Mama said. "They will have to be asked. Frankly, I'm uncertain what it is I want to do next. But I suppose whatever it is I'll first have to go downriver."

"What about your first love—the man in Gladewater?"

"I don't know," Mama said. "That was a long time ago. The idea of him and what we had got me out of bed and on the raft, but I don't know it's such a good idea to dig up the past like an old grave. What's in it might stink."

I hadn't thought about that. Hadn't considered that Mama and Brian would meet and things wouldn't go back to where they were some seventeen years ago, that we wouldn't be just one big happy family. It was another one of those revelations, and I didn't like it. Basking in ignorance has much to be said for it.

"Will you have to tell the children what I have done?" he said. "Should I?"

"I suppose not," Mama said. "Another time, maybe, if you want to get it off your chest. But there isn't any going back in time, for me or for you. We got to wear our crowns of thorns. We can talk all we want, but we can't take them off."

"My thorns are sharper," he said, "but I suppose that is as it should be. I'm sick to death with the memory, and I wanted you to know. Somehow, telling you makes me feel better. Not about what I done, but it helps me bear it. I hope I haven't handed you a burden."

"Nothing I can't carry," Mama said.

"I appreciate that, Helen. I really do. Shall we leave tomorrow? I have to resign my church, which I might as well anyway. It doesn't mean I have to actually write out a resignation letter. I just need to go. It does no good to preach to the wind. I have to leave the cabin. It's given to the preacher to use, and I won't be the preacher anymore."

"All right, then," she said. "We can load the raft tomorrow morning. Then we can leave."

I saw Mama take the reverend's head in her hands, and their shadows mixed. I knew she was kissing him. More and more I realized I didn't know Mama at all.

They talked awhile, and held hands, and the Reverend Jack Joy even cried. She put her arms around him, and they leaned together and kissed again, and it was real kissing, what Jinx calls smackie-mouth.

I didn't want to see no more of it, so I got up and sneaked back into the house and onto my pallet, lay there with my mind full now of Jaren and his last moments, burning up, chained to a stump, all for a lie. And then I had to think about Mama, and how she was more than I knew as a person, and that she and the reverend was down there on the raft, kissing, and maybe more. I couldn't find any way to lose the thoughts, or to get hold of them.

Wasn't long after I laid down that the door opened, and I seen Mama's shape in the frame, and behind and above her, I seen more heat lightning dancing across the sky. Also behind her, I saw Reverend Joy heading toward his car. Then Mama eased the door closed and moved noiselessly to the bedroom.

In spite of all that was bothering me, I eventually nodded off.

My sleep was soon spoiled by the sound of lumber splitting. I sat bolt upright, and so did everyone else in the house, cause the door had been kicked back and broken apart; there was two hat-wearing shapes in the doorway. They brought with them the smell of liquor and sweat. One of them was holding a flashlight. It was shining across the room, right on my face, and it was blinding me. Jinx moved on the floor, said something in surprise, and one of the shapes kicked her hard enough she let out her air and was knocked tumbling. She twitched just enough that I knew she wasn't knocked out.

Mama came into the room instantly, and when she did, one of the shapes quick-stepped toward her. A hand struck out, and she went down with a scream.

"Stop it, damn it," I said, coming off my pallet and to my feet.

"Unladylike as always," said a familiar voice. "You best sit back down before I hit you, Sue Ellen."

The flashlight beam that was resting on me hopped around the room. I couldn't help but look where it went. It came to rest on Terry's pallet, where he was sitting up.

The voice said, "There's the sissy."

"Where's the damn preacher?" said the other man. I recognized that voice, too.

After a moment, both shapes moved deeper into the room. Then one of them spotted a lantern with the flashlight, and the lantern got lit. The lamp lighter was that one-eyed Constable Sy, and the other one, the kicker and hitter, was the man I had always known as Uncle Gene.

15

W ell, now," Uncle Gene said. "If it ain't my brother's wife, Helen, in another man's house, along with her sassy-ass daughter, the sissy, and a runaway nigger. Where's the preacher?"

It was easy to figure. They had been looking for us for some time now. All they had to do was ask along the river until they come to the right person, and someone who had seen us talked. With the reverend's congregation being on the outs with him, they had most likely been swift to say something, not realizing, of course, that the men looking for us was more than bill collectors. Course, I guess it could have been something they did by meaner purpose, and if that was the case, it wouldn't surprise me if it was the Fried Chicken with Too Much Salt Lady.

"I'm not going back," Mama said, coming off the floor and to her feet. She had a hand pressed against her face where she had been hit.

Gene took a seat by the table. "I know that, Helen. Where's the preacher?"

"He's gone off," I said. "They got rid of him at the church. Didn't like his living arrangements. He's gone off."

"That right?" Sy said. He had his hand on his holstered gun, letting it rest there like a bird that had lit on a post. Right then, I believed that story about what that holster was made out of. "Gene," he said, "go look in the back room, see if you can find a preacher. Bring him out, drawers or no drawers."

"You should be ashamed of yourself for thinking such a thing," Mama said.

"Now, don't get special on me, girl," Gene said. "You lowered your own drawers down before you took up with my brother. You done that, didn't you? It ain't like no one else has ever been under the bridge. Only thing I got to wonder is if you were charging a toll."

Even in the dark I could feel embarrassment come off Mama like heat off a fire. Gene went past her on his way to the room, paused to slap her on the butt. "You know," he said. "Always figured, you and me could have a good time, and I think we might still."

Mama wheeled and spit in his face.

Gene wiped the spit off with his sleeve and grinned at her. "Oh, your time is coming, honey. You can bet on that."

"Quit jawing and go look," Constable Sy said.

Gene went on. While he was in the bedroom looking around, Constable Sy said, "All of you might as well cooperate. I'm with the law."

"You're out of your formal jurisdiction," Terry said.

"You always was a smart little fruit," Constable Sy said. "But I figure you know jurisdiction doesn't really mean squat. It's not like I plan on taking that money back to the bank. It's not like I plan on running you folks in."

Gene came back. "No one in there."

"That surprises me," said Constable Sy, looking at Mama.

Gene went to the icebox, took out the fruit jar with buttermilk in it, screwed off the lid, and drank deep, spilling some of it on his chest. He burped and came to the table and took a chair. He sat the milk on the table at his elbow. The lantern lit one side of his face bright as day. The other side was dark as a hole in the ground.

"So you wasn't satisfying that preacher and he run off," Constable Sy said, looking at Mama. He was still standing, one leg cocked forward, his hand resting on his gun butt. "You look good, but I can bet you got a lot of the shrew about you."

"Come on over here and sit down," Gene said, motioning at Mama. "It's all right. Sit down. I ain't going to let anything happen to you."

Mama, one hand still on her jaw, went over and sat. She chose a chair far away from Gene.

Constable Sy took a chair on the opposite side, right across from her. He took the gun out of its holster and laid it on the table, kept his hand on top of it. "Like I said. You wasn't satisfying him, so he left you here. I figure he had to, as the folks we talked to said he wasn't living like a preacher, just talking like one, then coming back down here and snuggling up with you at night."

"He was letting us stay out of Christian generosity," Mama said. "That's all there was to it."

"Have it your way," Gene said. "Let's make this easy, then we'll leave you be. We want that money."

"Where's Cletus?" I asked.

"Cletus, he's got his own way of looking for you," Gene said. "He says he's going to hire that stinky nigger Skunk to come find you. Trying to get somebody knows Skunk that's willing to go look for him, like there really is a Skunk. But even if there is, he don't need to get him. We got you. He thought we wasn't never going to find you, but he was wrong."

"How's Don feel about all this?" Mama asked.

"Don looked for a few days then put himself in the house and hasn't come out, least not last I looked," Gene said. "You broke his heart. And I think that's a bad thing. Not that his heart is broke, but that he'd let it break over someone like you. You come to him with a baby in your belly and he took you in, and now here you are, out on the prowl." He looked at me. "You know Don ain't your daddy, don't you?"

"It's one of the great reliefs of my life," I said. "And that business about him having the Sight, that hasn't helped him none now, has it? It wasn't him found us."

"Ha," Gene said, and seemed to think that was genuinely funny.

"And I'm not on the prowl," Mama said. "I've just run away. That's all."

"I got a mind to see if you're worth what Don thought you was," Gene said. "Don said you could warm a cold night pretty good after you got liquored up."

"Hush up," Mama said. "There's children in the room."

Gene laughed and took another swig of buttermilk. "Now you got scruples. That's funny."

"Enough chitchat," said Constable Sy. "Here's how it's going to work. You give us that bag of money, and we'll go, and won't nothing happen to you. You don't, it's fixing to be a bad night for all of you. You going to wish you was dead and done gone to hell."

"I already wish that," I said.

Gene studied me for a while, said, "Sassy there, and the nigger gal, could be all right to keep us busy. And then we got Helen, too. It could be real good for us before it turns real bad for them. And we got the sissy, too. A sissy can be all right if you know how to use him."

"For God's sake, Sue Ellen's your niece," Mama said.

"Not by blood," Gene said. "And if she was, I don't know how much that would bother me. You might say since that money got stolen and you left, circumstances has changed in a big way."

"We lost the money," Terry said.

Constable Sy snapped his head toward Terry. "You're a liar. You're a damn liar, and that's the worst lie I've heard. You think we looked hard and long as we have to take a lie as the truth? You better have that money."

"The raft turned over and we lost it," Terry said.

Gene glanced at Constable Sy. "It could have happened," he said.

"If it did," Constable Sy said to Gene, "that's a real sad thing for everybody. But especially for them." Sy turned his attention back to us. "What we want to know, and all we want to know, is where the money is. You tell us that, we can all go our own way, without the messy part."

Gene reached in his pocket and took out a folding knife, flicked his wrist, and popped it open with a loud snap.

"You seen me gut fish and skin squirrels," Gene said, looking at me. "You know how I can work. You don't want me to start skinning, do you?"

"Leave her alone," Mama said.

"I would start at the toes and skin upward to the top of your head," he said. "I'd take your hide and hair right off. It wouldn't be any fun for anyone but me."

"We didn't take that money from you," Jinx said. "Wasn't your money."

"Damn, gal," Gene said. "I forgot your black ass was even here."

"You didn't take it from us," Constable Sy said. "But we're going to take it from you."

"What you going to tell Cletus?" I said.

"Thought we'd tell him you died," Gene said. "That we didn't find no money. And he wasted his fee on Skunk."

"There ain't no Skunk," Constable Sy said. "Cletus ought to know better. He might as well stick a dollar in his ass and wait for the leprechauns to leave him a note."

"All right, then," Gene said. "I've decided first thing I'm going to do is skin that little uppity darky."

Jinx was on her feet with her fists up. "You better brought you a bucket full of dinner, cause this fight here going to take all night."

Gene grinned at her and stood up. "That's all right," he said, waving the knife around. "I think I'm up to it."

A shadow fell across the open doorway. Reverend Joy came through it clutching a two-by-four. Gene and Constable Sy didn't see him, least not in time.

The board whistled and caught Gene upside the skull so hard it knocked his head around and made him look over his shoulder in a way a man can't do when his neck is on right. Before he hit the floor, Constable Sy, who was still sitting at the table, stood up as he grabbed his gun, but the board was there first. It caught him across the nose and knocked him back on the floor. He tried to sit up and Reverend Joy hit him again, right between the eyes. Constable Sy lay there not moving, but he was breathing loud, like a horse snorting water out of his nose.

"Come on," Reverend Joy said, tossing the board aside, picking up Constable Sy's pistol. "Come on."

The constable was almost to his feet when we ran outside. We ran past Constable Sy's truck in the yard, and started downhill toward the river. We was just following the Reverend Joy, like he knew something we didn't, but we all knew in the back of our minds where we was going. The raft. When we got to it, we loosened the rope, and pushed off with our poles. The water wasn't running fast, and we couldn't see good, but there was enough current to get us moving.

We hadn't gone far when something hit the raft. It hit and bounced off into the water. Looking back at the bank and up the hill, I saw Sy's big shape on the rise. He was bending down and coming up fast with small rocks, throwing them at us. One hit my foot hard enough it made me hop.

"You don't do this to me," he yelled. "You just don't do it. I'll catch you all. Every damn one of you."

"You couldn't catch a cold," I yelled back at him.

The rocks kept coming, and Constable Sy had a good arm. We was way out and still they was coming. Mama crawled into the hut Reverend Joy had built and hid out there, rocks clattering on top of it like hailstones.

Eventually the water was faster and we moved beyond his arm, sailing out of the little horseshoe spot where we had been and onto the main river. By that time, we couldn't see him anymore, though we could hear him running through the brush and trees and cussing his head off, trying to catch up.

Soon we couldn't hear him, either. We had a straight shot on the river now, and it was just a dark, wide line of water. There could have been sandbars or rocks or logs in our path and we wouldn't have seen them until we was right up on them. But we didn't have a choice. We used the poles to stay as straight as we could and let the water run us, Jinx doing her best with the rudder at the back.

Mama crawled out of the little hut and sat down in front of it. Reverend Joy, who had been standing on the raft like he was a rock target but hadn't so much as been grazed, looked at Mama and said, "I think I killed a man."

I was thinking: that makes two. But I didn't say anything. Jinx did, however.

"Hell, yeah, you killed him," she said. "You knocked his head all the way around on his neck. You hit him any harder, his brother, Don, would have died, too, and maybe them hogs they got in the yard would have keeled over. I ain't never seen nobody take a piece of wood like that."

"I didn't mean to hit him that hard," Reverend Joy said, and he sat down on the raft as if his legs had just melted. He still had the pistol in his hand, and the way he held it, loose and unconcerned, made me nervous. Mama scooted over beside him and put her arm around his shoulders.

"I don't know you didn't mean to," Jinx said. "I ain't never seen nobody get hit that hard that wasn't on purpose. I think you meant it."

"Jinx, hush," Terry said.

"I ain't got nothing for that Gene," Jinx said. "I hope he is dead."

"I think I heard something snap," Reverend Joy said.

"That was his neck," Jinx said.

"You did what you had to do," Mama said.

"Here's something I hate to bring up," Terry said. "The money is back at the cabin. And so are May Lynn's ashes."

"What money?" Reverend Joy said. "Whose ashes?"

These were the parts of the story Mama had left out when she told him why we was on the river. Now, as we floated on, she filled the Reverend Joy in on it. After she was done, he sat there taken aback, looking up at us with his mouth open. He had in one night lost his church, murdered a man, and discovered he had run off downriver with a bunch of thieves and grave robbers. It was a lot to take in. Right then his mind went somewhere we couldn't go, and it didn't try to come back, least not right away. He just turned around and, still clutching the pistol, crawled inside the hut, sticking his head in there and letting his feet hang out on the raft.

"Guess he didn't take none of that too well," Jinx said. "I was just trying to give him a compliment on his board slinging. It wasn't meant in a bad way." She studied his feet hanging out of the hut. "Even so, looks like he'd just go on and crawl the rest of the way in."

"I believe he has gone as far as his will allows," Terry said.

16

We drifted for a long time, me and Terry using the poles to keep the raft in the middle of the river. Jinx was still at the rudder, and she was beginning to get the hang of it. The reverend had done a fine job building the rudder, and it heaved easy and gave the raft better direction and kept us from swirling.

Reverend Joy hadn't moved from where he lay. Fact was, I thought he might have died, but Mama checked on him. She grabbed him by the feet and pulled him out of the hut. He drawed his knees up and put his hands under his chin, one of them still hanging on to the pistol, which was slightly unnerving. Mama sat by him, put a hand on his arm, but he didn't seem to notice.

"I feel certain we can navigate a good distance downriver," Terry said, poling the shallow bottom with his long pole. "Then we need to find a place to tie up, and go back for the money and May Lynn's ashes. Fact is, I think we could just take the ashes and leave the money. It's nothing but trouble."

"I don't like that," Jinx said, calling from her place at the rudder. "May Lynn's dead, but that money is still green as grass. I done ran off from home and been threatened with all kinds of mean things, and had rocks thrown at me, and now you're saying leave it. I ain't all that much for going back, but if we go back for May Lynn's burnt-up ass, I say we get that money."

"We could take enough to continue our trip and leave the rest," Terry said. "Maybe if we do that, Constable Sy will be satisfied with the bulk of the money. We could just leave it on the table. He may decide to stop bothering us, especially if we are far away and are not causing him concern."

"There's still Cletus and Skunk," Jinx said. "And maybe Don."

"There isn't anyone called Skunk," Terry said. "He's nothing more than a story people tell to scare their children."

"He's a story that will chop off hands, you can bet on that," Jinx said. "I come out of this, I'd just as soon not have to ask someone else to pick my nose and wipe my butt."

"If he's real, you'll not only be missing hands," I said. "You'll be dead."

"I take to that even less," Jinx said.

"I tell you again," Terry said. "There is no Skunk."

"There are a lot of folks who believe in Skunk," Mama said. "I've heard about him all my life."

"Have you seen him, Mrs. Wilson?" Terry asked.

"Well, no. But I know people who say they have."

"There are people who have told me with considerable conviction that they've seen snakes that can grab their tails with their teeth and roll downhill like a hoop, or snakes that can suck a milk cow dry, but with all due respect, ma'am, I don't believe it."

"I ain't no believer in snakes can do that," Jinx said. "But I believe in Skunk."

"Here's the thing," I said. "Skunk or no Skunk, we got to go back for the money and the ashes. There's a man been killed over that money and tucked in a shallow grave, and there's another dead one back there in the reverend's house. We've come this far, I say we need that money and we owe May Lynn a little something for drawing that map we found, and for being our friend."

"I don't know that I want you children to do that," Mama said.

"No offense again, Mrs. Wilson, but you really don't have a say in this," Terry said. "You haven't said boo to Sue Ellen all this time, and now you want to tell her how to do things? I'm glad you're back from where you went, but these decisions are now ours."

"He's right, Mama," I said, before she could say anything back. "You don't have a say in this. You came with us, not the other way around."

"I suppose that's true," she said. She sounded the way she did when she had been in bed sucking cure-all. I hated that. I liked her better a little on the feisty side. But that still didn't change the fact that Terry was right. This wasn't her decision.

I peeked at Reverend Joy. He appeared to be asleep.

"All right, then," I said. "We go back for the money and the ashes. But I'll tell you this, we ought not all go. Someone needs to stay with the raft, and the other thing is I don't want to drag all of us through the woods. And the reverend there, we'd have to carry him, or pull him behind us on a rope, so that won't work. We're going to do this, we're going to have to sneak."

"You done talked me into it," Jinx called from the back. "I'll stay. Anybody else can go that wants to. Me and your mama and the reverend, we'll hold down the raft and you and Terry go."

It wasn't long before the water got deep and the poles were useless. What we had was the rudder, and me and Terry squatting on either side of the raft, using the boat paddles. The raft went fast, and we didn't see a good place to stop for a long time. Finally we could barely make out a sandbar that jutted out into the river. We let the force of the water ride the raft up on it.

Terry took one of the paddles and put the narrow end in the soft, damp sand, pushed it down tight, and tied the docking rope off to it. Reverend Joy was still out of it, Mama sitting by him with her arm draped over his shoulders, him still with the pistol. For all he knew he was someplace on Mars having his hair combed by a nine-eyed octopus.

"Let me have the pistol," I said to him.

I had to say it several times before he looked up at me.

"You got Constable Sy's pistol," I said. "I might need it."

Reverend Joy came hurtling back from Mars, but his voice seemed to come from far away. "Haven't we done enough?"

"It's all right, Jack," Mama said. "Give her the pistol. Just for protection."

The reverend was slow to realize he had hold of the pistol, and he was even slower to give it up, but in time he handed it to me. It was a small pistol, and I put it in the deep pocket of my overalls. Reverend Joy dipped his head as if the weight was just too much. "May the good Lord be with you," he said.

"It's a good walk back," I said. "Lot longer walking than it was riding the river. It'll be daylight before we get turned around good. We'll try and bring some food if we can get it. All you got to do is wait. Jinx, we don't come back by the end of next day, you need to push off and go."

"All right," Jinx said.

"You could have at least hesitated a little," Terry said.

"I know a good plan when I hear it," Jinx said.

"We can't just push off without you," Mama said.

"I think we can," Jinx said. "It don't take but two of us to handle the raft, Mrs. Wilson."

"That's not what I meant," Mama said. "I meant we can't go off without them if they're late."

"I know what you meant," Jinx said. "And I meant what I

meant. We can, and will. Waiting here for One-Eyed Sy to catch up with us won't do nobody no good."

"Me and Terry will be back," I said to Mama. "So don't worry. And even if you go on without us, that don't mean we ain't coming. We'll just have to find another way and meet up with you in Gladewater."

"Maybe I should go with you," she said.

"We need you here," I said. "And though you're doing better, you ain't doing so good you'd have the energy to go the way we're going. Me and Terry can travel quicker without you."

When the reverend built the hut on the raft, we had stashed a few of our things inside of it, in case we had to leave in a hurry. That had turned out to be a smart move. One of those things was a flashlight. There was also twine and rags, matches, tow sacks, a pocketknife, and a few tins of sardines, which we opened right then and ate with our fingers. We took the flashlight and started off.

We walked along the sandbar on up to the bank, and it was a slog. We had to use damp roots to hang on to and climb up. On the shore there was lots of trees, and it wasn't as starlit as it was out on the river cause the tree trunks was so close together. The woods was hard to work past, but we kept threading our way until it broke out into a marshy run of land that went on for quite a few miles. Without so many trees it was clear, and there was some light, but it was uncomfortable going. To our left was a line of woods that looked like a wall of shadow. To our right was another line, but it thinned in spots and sloped off toward the water in such a way there wasn't any good place to stand, let alone walk. We was close enough for a while to hear the river run and smell it, but because of the way the marsh was, we had to go wide away from it and head toward the far line of trees. Our feet sunk deep in the muck. Pulling them out and dropping them back down made a sound like a giant baby struggling to suck on an empty tit, and it wore us slap out.

We was able to find the right stars to figure on how to go, which wasn't a real chore anyway, as all we had to do was follow the river back and we'd come to the cabin. But it wasn't all a straight shot, not with the way the brush and brambles grew up in spots in the marsh. You could easily get off the path and not realize you was far from the river, or you could get turned around and not know it until it was too late. So when we could look at the stars, we did. Just to make sure we was going the true direction.

After what seemed a long time, we came to a little tree all grown up by itself in the middle of the marsh. It was big enough to lean against and rest, so we did. While we leaned, we kicked our heels into the tree and shook the mud off our shoes.

"I lied to you," Terry said.

"About what?"

"About how I'm not a sissy. I tried to say that May Lynn naked did something for me, but it didn't. I didn't want to lie to you, but I didn't want you to think I'm the way I am. As a friend, however, I have to admit it to you."

"Terry, I don't care."

"Really?"

"I know how you've been to me, and that's good. I see how you are with Jinx, and how you've been the one most concerned about May Lynn's Hollywood dream, which ain't something me and Jinx have been as rich about. I'm proud of you and happy to call you a friend. You and Jinx are my best friends."

"A colored girl and a queer," he said. "You sure have chosen some strange company."

"Only thing strange about it is the people that might think it's strange."

"So you don't think less of me for lying about that, telling you I had an interest in May Lynn?"

"No. I will say, had you not been someone who likes boys, I would find it hard not to like you, you know, in the boy-girl way. You are about the best-looking and nicest thing I've ever seen."

"Well, if I were not how I am, I am certain I would have been interested in you as well, in a boy-and-girl way." He paused, and when he spoke again, he sounded serious as a heart attack. "As for nice, well, don't think I'm all that nice. I'm not."

"That's sweet," I said. "And you are nice. If it matters any, you ain't sissy. You might like boys, but you ain't sissy. You're tough enough. You're tough as you have to be. You're plenty tough."

"Thanks," he said, and he looked away from me, out toward the outer dark. "There's lots of things I might tell you in time."

I didn't know what that meant, and considering we had things to do, I didn't push it. We needed to get moving. Lightning started to pop in the sky, and way in the distance we heard thunder. That got us going again, but it turned out to just be a night of dry lightning and dull rumbling.

Near morning a fog rose up. It was white as cotton and thick as a winter cloud. The flashlight bounced off the fog, and the fog rolled around us, head-high. There was no noise from frogs or crickets, which was kind of odd, and except for our feet stomping in the deep muck, it was quiet and lonely-feeling out there.

On we went, and then there was a lightening in the east, pink as a rose petal where it was low to the ground, bright and golden at the top. We could see it above the fog, and some of the morning light was so bright we could see right through the fog. Then the day's heat started up, and the fog melted like ice cream. Terry turned off the flashlight and put it away in a tow sack.

It was solid light when a five-foot-long rat snake wriggled through the grass in front of us. We stopped and watched it slither by, then started again. Big white birds flew up from the river, and one flew high over our heads with a fish in its mouth. Terry said, "Maybe that's some kind of good omen."

"Unless you're considering from the fish's point of view," I said.

By the time the sun was high and hot, we still hadn't recognized anything. It was hard to tell just how far we had come, not knowing what time it was when we started out, but we guessed something like four hours, maybe five. Had we been on flat, dry land, we'd have already covered the necessary distance, but the muck slowed us and wore us out, so it was pleasing to reach a stretch of pines and get out of that mess.

The pines was a thin stand. Looking through them, on the far side, I spotted the church where the reverend had been minister. We had come out on higher ground than I expected. It had gone up so gradual, I hadn't realized we was climbing. We was well above the reverend's house.

We went to the church. The front door was thrown open; inside, some of the Christians had written on the walls. ADULTEROR was painted in big black letters in two places, and in another spot was a longer sentence that declared something Reverend Joy did with donkeys, which I knew was a lie. We hadn't seen a donkey once since we'd been there.

"They ain't much on spelling, are they?" Terry said.

We came out of the church and halted just below it and looked down the trail at the cabin. The front door was still thrown open and there was lantern light inside. Constable Sy's truck hadn't moved.

"You think he's waiting inside?" Terry asked.

"Don't know. Seems funny he'd stay there. Maybe he's looking for the money."

"He won't find it," Terry said.

"If it's still in your sack on the floor, it won't take a prize bloodhound to sniff it out," I said.

"I moved it."

"Out of the house?"

"It's in the toolshed."

"Reverend keeps that locked," I said.

"I know where he hides the key. That's how I got it moved in there in the first place."

"And pray tell, where does he hide the key?"

"That's the drawback," Terry said. "The money and May Lynn are no longer in the house, but the key is still there, shoved into a crack in the front-door frame, along the side. I saw him stick it there once. When he was gone, I borrowed it and used it to take a peek in the shed. I wanted to see what was in there. Way he locked it up, I thought he might have something in there we needed to know about. What he had was lumber and some nice tools and finally, for me, a good hiding place for the money and the ashes."

"So we still have to go down there in broad daylight. We might as well strip off and paint ourselves barn-red and run down yelling at the top of our lungs."

"It does present a challenge," Terry said. "Where can we find the paint?"

"Ha."

We went wide and came down near the side of the house, and hid up in the tree line. We stood in the trees and looked around. It was as quiet as a deaf-mute taking a nap down there. The morning light was spreading.

"What's that on the porch?" Terry said.

I looked at what he was talking about for a long time. I said, "It looks like spilled black paint."

"Why would there be black paint on the front porch?" he said.

"Someone had black paint up at the church," I said. "Maybe they brought it down here to write on things."

"I doubt that," Terry said.

"Yeah," I said. "Me, too."

I don't know how long we stood there, listening and watching, but after a while curiosity got the best of us. I pulled the pistol from my overalls and we sneaked down there and slipped up on the porch. About where the doorway started there was the black mess, and now that we was close, I could see it wasn't paint—it was blood that had dried dark. There was lots of it.

I cocked the revolver, and we eased along to the window and looked in. I could see Uncle Gene lying on the floor on his stomach. His head was still turned around on his shoulder and his face was looking right at me, his eyes as dull as if they had been worked over with sandpaper. Jinx was right. That had been some lick Reverend Joy had given him.

On the table, on his back, stretched out and tied down with rope, was Constable Sy. Blood had dripped off the table, and the floor must have sloped slightly because the blood had ran toward the wall and out the door. I had no idea there was that much blood in a person, even a big man like Constable Sy.

"What in hell happened here?" Terry said.

I suppose the thing for us to have done was to have lit out for the raft, but we didn't. What we had seen through the window yanked us forward as surely as if we was on a rope.

Over by the door we was careful to try and not step in the blood, but it wasn't any use. We couldn't help it. It was everywhere. As we went inside, our shoes, already mud-coated and sticky, stuck to the floor like flies to molasses. The inside smelled bad, really bad, and not just because of the blood. The air was rank, like body odor on top of dead things on top of old river mud on top of what was left in the outhouse.

I stood at Uncle Gene. His death didn't heat up much sympathy. What occurred to me was that he wouldn't leap up suddenly and hit his wife anymore. When she found out he was dead, I wondered if she would feel like a bird that had just figured out the cage door had been left open. I hoped so. I liked to imagine her burning his clothes and dancing around the fire and taking a piss on the whole mess after it had gone black and cold.

But that broken neck wasn't all that was horrible about his body. There was something else. His hands was cut off at the wrist from jagged strikes. It was the same for Constable Sy, who had been bound to the table with wraps of rope. The lantern had been placed by his head so whoever had done him in would have a close light to work by. The jar with the buttermilk was empty, and the jar itself had bloody fingerprints on it. Whoever had done this had paused in his work to refresh himself.

The picture of an animal of some kind had been carved into Constable Sy's forehead; a duck with a ruler and a pocketknife could have made pretty much the same mark.

If Constable Sy had lived, he'd have needed two patches, cause his other eye had been scooped out, and flies was crawling around inside his head. There was a spoon lying on the table, and it was bloody, and I had a pretty good idea how the eye had been taken out.

Constable Sy had been cut and stabbed in a lot of places. You could see where his wrists had been placed on the table and struck. There was deep chop marks in the wood. His head was thrown back and his mouth was open and his tongue was torn out. His shoes was off and his toes had been whittled down to nubs so there was only the bones left, poking out like little wet sticks. The badge he always wore on his shirt pocket was missing.

I felt sick. I carefully set the hammer on the pistol down and put the gun back in my overalls pocket.

"What sort of design is that etched into his head?" Terry asked, leaning over Constable Sy. "Is that representative of some breed of cat?"

I looked at Terry, sniffed the foul air loudly so as to add to what I was about to say. "I wouldn't hold it up as an example of much, but it looks like a skunk to me."

"Oh," he said.

It was spine-chilling to think we might have just missed Skunk catching up to us, or that he was out there now looking for us. I guess he saw Uncle Gene and Constable Sy as standing in the way of his progress, trying to do what he had been hired to do, so he had taken them out. Or maybe he thought they had the money, or knew where it was. Whatever the reason, if we had been here when he came, we'd have been tortured, and no doubt we'd have given up the goods, as well as our lives. Course, if he hadn't come, and the reverend hadn't showed up with that board, the same thing could have come about with Constable Sy and Gene before he got there. I wondered by how many minutes we had missed Skunk showing up.

A short time before, I was mostly sure there was no Skunk; now there was no way I could doubt him. No way I couldn't fear him. He was out there, and his stinky self was looking for us.

We each took one of the tow sacks that Terry had brought from the raft and gathered up the rest of our goods, including a few tins of food and a bit of bread. Then Terry scratched around for the key he said was hidden in the door frame. He found it right off. Outside the house, standing on the end of the porch, I put my sack aside and leaned over and vomited. When I did, and Terry smelled it, it was just one stink too much. He leaned over and tossed up his insides, too.

When we was finished doing that, we scratched our feet in the dirt to get the blood off our shoes, then went out to the well and pulled up the bucket. There was a dipper hanging there on a stout cord, and we dipped water from the bucket and took turns drinking.

As we did, I looked over and seen the front door of Reverend Joy's car was slightly open. I nudged Terry, and he saw what I was talking about right away. Hefting the flashlight, he started over there. I pulled the pistol and followed.

At the car, Terry looked through the windshield, then back at me. He shook his head, opened the front door so we could see inside clearly. The reverend's blanket and pillow was in there. They was pushed around, not neat like he usually left them. There was blood smears from fingers all over the dash and all over the pillow and the back of the car seat. I noticed then that there was blood on the inside and outside door handle. That same smell from the house came rolling out of there like a speeding truck. It hit us hard enough we had to back up. I thought for a moment I was going to throw up again.

"He slept in the car," Terry said. "Skunk. He killed Constable Sy, chopped him and Gene up, came out here, and spent the night in the car. That's some guts."

"That's some crazy," I said.

Terry looked down at his hand, lifted it, and showed it to me. Where he had taken hold of the car door he had gotten blood on himself. We went back to the well. I poured water over his hand and rinsed it away.

"Let's get the money and ashes and leave," I said.

"Gladly," Terry said.

"You think this Skunk fellow has given up on us?" I said.

Terry shrugged. "How can we know? I doubt it. I think he likes what he does. I didn't even consider there really could be a Skunk, but now I'm scared to death there is. I owe Jinx an apology."

"If he was following us, after taking a sleep, he might be going along the river now," I said. "Mama and Jinx are on that sandbar waiting on us. If he gets there first—"

I let that hang.

Terry hustled over to the work shed and unlocked it. It was tight in there with lumber from the reverend's projects. There was a birdhouse in the corner, almost finished. Terry moved toward the back, bent down by the wall, and pulled at one of the boards. It creaked and the nails slipped out. There was a surprising lot of room between that board and the outside boards. Inside was two good-sized lard buckets.

Terry pulled them out by their wire handles and set them on top of the lumber. He found a screwdriver, used that to pry open the lids. Inside the cans was something wrapped in old hand towels. He took out first one, then the other, unwrapped them. There was a fruit jar wrapped up in each hand towel. One held the ashes, the other had the money.

"I wanted you to see how I arranged the money and what's left of May Lynn," he said. "I preferred you to know what was what."

"Now I know," I said. "Close them up, and let's get."

We gathered up our tow sacks. I put one can—I don't even know which one—in my bag, and Terry put the other in his. I shoved the pistol in my overalls and we got out of there.

17

We figured since Skunk must have a bit of squirrel blood in him from living in the woods, he would take the shorter, surer route of moving close to the river. The way things grew along the river from the reverend's house to the raft was thick, and we thought for us the better choice would be to do as we had done before. Go wide. Maybe that way we could stay away from Skunk.

Skunk. It was so hard to get the idea of him being real wrapped around my mind. Finding out he was real was like finding out the Billy Goats Gruff was real and didn't like you personally.

In the daytime it wasn't so scary traveling through the marshes, and at first we was making good time. We saw lots of snakes as we went, even a spreading adder, which isn't all that common. They ain't poisonous, but they can give a person quite a start, rising up like they do with their head fanning out like they're a cobra.

We also saw what the snakes was looking for—mice and rats. There was one spot we come to where they ran through the marsh grass thick as fleas on a mangy dog's hide. There was lots of crows cawing, and we could see where wild hogs had torn up the land. The heat from the day made the marsh heat up and smell bad, but compared to what we had smelled in the cabin, it was like French perfume. That thunder we heard the night before we could hear again, and there were new flashes of lightning in the daylight sky.

"That rain seems determined to come," I said. "But it keeps taking a rest."

"I can't say that I blame it," Terry said. "A rest would be nice."

He was right about that. After trudging through the mud the night before and after seeing what we had seen, we got so tired that when we came to a run of shady cottonwoods, we stopped under them without even discussing it. We tossed our bags aside and sat down and leaned against the trunk of one of the trees and closed our eyes to rest. And though they say there's no rest for the wicked and the good don't need any, exhaustion caught up with us like a train and run us over.

I dreamed of Hollywood again, and it was the same dream as before, with us on the raft with May Lynn's ashes, but this time, as we sailed, no one waved as we went past. All the pretty people looked fine, but they stunk bad enough to gag a maggot. It was a stink that brought me awake.

When I opened my eyes, it was almost dark. I thought I had been asleep only a few minutes, but we had slept most of the day away. I sniffed the stinking air and glanced at Terry beside me. He was awake. I started to say something, but he reached out and touched me gently, said, "Shh." He pointed. I looked.

Way down in the direction of the river, running through the dying light, was a man shape. The shape was dark and wore a derby hat; something bright was pinned to it. The shape's hair was long and kinky and it stuck out from under the hat on the sides and rolled down the man's neck like a large wad of copper wire.

Something flopped along the side of his head as he ran. His face in the twilight looked like polished mahogany washed in blood. He had a walking stick with him, and as his feet lifted I saw they was way long and wide. I thought for a moment that whoever this was wasn't human. Course, the smell told me who it was. It was Skunk. But maybe Skunk wasn't human.

We watched until Skunk was way beyond us and was swallowed up by where the ground sloped toward the Sabine. After a while, I said, "Some master tracker. Here we was, and he didn't see us asleep under a tree."

"We were in a fortunate spot," Terry said. "We were hard to see here in the shadows. I speculate that after he abandoned the car, he found someplace to sleep more comfortably out here in the open. It's more his natural way of doing things. Had we not taken to the higher ground, birds would be pecking our remains right now. What I presume he's doing is following what Constable Sy told him when he was tortured. That we had taken to the river. He isn't actually following a sign because he believes we're downriver on the raft, so he doesn't need to look for any indication we're on land."

"But isn't there a place where he'll cross our sign from this morning?" I said.

"If he does, he'll know where we came from and where the raft is, or he'll turn and come back for us. Or he'll do one first and then the other."

"Then we need to get to the raft first," I said.

"So we're going to fly over his head?"

"No," I said. "We're going to sail under his feet."

"You mean the river?"

"Of course I mean the river," I said.

"And how are we going to do that? Swim for miles? Ride a fish?"

"One thing for sure is we need to get down to the water, and we need to get there fast, and we need to do it well behind Skunk's trail . . . Good grief, did you see his feet?"

"I did, and it couldn't have been feet."

"Oversized shoes?" I said.

"Like snowshoes. You know what those are?"

I shook my head.

"They're made long and wide to walk on snow. Those shoes he had on were made to walk on the marsh and move quickly and not bog down. He would know that from being on wet ground so much."

"Come on. I got an idea, but we have to hurry."

We jumped up and grabbed our bags and started toward the river, crossing Skunk's trail as we went. The riverbank was full of trees, and there was underbrush and blackberry vines to contend with, too. Close to the river the bank was falling off from being washed by rain. Roots from trees stuck out all over. Below them was a thin line of damp sand and gravel. We swung off some of the roots and dropped onto the wet sand, went along close to the river for a good long ways. I looked around and around, but didn't see what I needed. Terry and me kept going, and finally, I saw a dead tree above us, sticking out of the bank. It was short— ten feet long—and thick. The limbs had mostly dropped off of it from rot. The top of it had long ago come loose and fallen away and been washed downriver. Its weight was causing the rest of it to lean out toward the water and its roots was springing out of the ground.

I laid aside my bag, scuttled up to the high ground, and crawled out onto the tree. "Come on," I said. "Help me."

Terry was looking at me as if I had suddenly lost my senses. But he put his bag down and climbed up and behind me on the dead tree.

"Bounce," I said, and began bumping my butt up and down.

Terry followed the plan, and we bounced for quite some time before I heard the roots slipping completely loose of the bank. The dead tree fell.

It struck the ground below, throwing us off it. When we looked up, we saw that it had broken nearly in half. We had to stand on it and bounce with our feet until the pieces were free of one another.

I opened my bag, looked inside, grabbed a ball of twine, and slung the bag over my shoulder. I used twine to tie the bag to my overalls strap, and then I wrapped a couple runs of twine around it and my waist, so that it fastened to my back. I cut the twine loose with my pocketknife, cut another run of it, tied a loop of it to the handle of Constable Sy's pistol, then made a loose necklace of it; the gun hung around my neck and down on my chest. After that, I helped Terry tie up his bag in a similar fashion, though he didn't have an overalls strap to help him out like I did.

I put the knife away, said, "Come on. Push."

We shoved the log out into the water, and I practically leaped at it like a lizard. Terry followed suit, and away we went, down the river. The log tried to turn loose of us at first, but we found places on either side where we could hang, and that balanced it out.

By this time twilight was gone and night had dropped down on us like a croaker sack. But the black was lit now and then by lightning. It was sizzling across the sky in bright runs, and thunder was banging out like someone striking a number ten washtub with an ax handle.

The water was cool and it was hard to hang on to the log, especially now that we was in a wider and swifter part of the river. It started raining hard enough it was like bullets slamming onto our heads; it made the river run even faster. To make matters worse, the old tree was loosing bark, and it was chock-full of ants that bit me and made my skin feel like hot tacks were being knocked into it.

The log kept dipping, though, and pretty soon there were no more ants. There was just us and that log, the rainstorm, and the dark water. The lightning flashed and lit up the sky in such a way that the riverbank was clear and bright for a moment—and I saw Skunk squatting on the side of the bank between two trees. He was sitting there like a statue, watching us rush by.

I could see he had the mud shoes strapped on his back, because they was poking up over his derby. The water ran along the rim of his hat and leaped off at the front. The badge he had taken from Constable Sy was pinned to his derby. What I had seen flopping along the side of his face was a dead bird, dangling head-down on a cord fastened up in his copper hair. Jinx had said it was a seasoned bluebird, but it didn't look all that seasoned to me, and I couldn't have told you in that glimpse if it was blue or black or plaid, but it was a bird. I spied a hatchet hanging off his belt, and a big cane knife in a sheath, near big as a sword. He clutched his gnarly walking stick in the middle. I could see his face in the flash. It was reddish, like an old penny, and squashed into shape, like a gourd that had grown funny. He seemed about as interested in us as a fly was in arithmetic.

Then we sailed on, and the long run of lightning was gone. I had to yell over the roar of the river, "Did you see that?"

"See what?"

"It was Skunk. He must have crossed our trail below, cut back, and made for the river, found our new trail."

"That's not good news," Terry said.

There was another flash of lightning. I glanced toward the bank, and there was Skunk, running along, dodging through low-hanging limbs and jumping over bushes like a rabbit.

"Worse news," I said.

"I see him," Terry said.

And then we didn't see him. The flash was gone and the thunder boomed and the river churned on.

The water carried us along and the rain picked up and the lightning kept flashing, more often now, and the thunder came up behind it quick-like; it was so loud it made the water in the river shake, and it made me shake, too.

I don't know how long we sped on like that, but in time the river began to narrow again, which is the way the Sabine does, and we was coming to a place where we could see a sandbar poking out into the water from the shore. I immediately thought that would be Skunk's moment to reach us.

Way the lightning was coming now, our wet path was lit up every few seconds. I used the flashes to look toward the bank, then toward the sandbar, but I didn't see Skunk. Maybe the rapid river had carried us so far beyond he couldn't catch up.

It was so damn miserable being out there in the water on that fraying log, I was thinking maybe we could get off of it at the sandbar, go through the woods the rest of the way. If we were ahead of Skunk, maybe we could stay ahead.

Whatever the good or the bad of that plan, the idea got dropped, cause there was a long lightning flash, and I saw Skunk running above on the bank. He would be coming up on the sandbar about the same time as we was, though it lay below where he was on the bank by a good twenty feet.

"Paddle wide," I said.

We each had just one arm to spare on either side of the log, and our legs to kick with, but we went at it, thrashing around like a monstrous catfish. The log veered, but Skunk jumped. I saw him do it in one long flash of the lightning. He looked for a moment like he was pinned in midair. The tree limbs in the background looked like bony fingers clutching at him. Then he came unstuck and landed on the sandbar as gentle as a cat. The lightning went away, and it was so dark you couldn't see your hand in front of your face.

"Kick," I screamed above the growl of the river. And kick we did, thrashing our legs in the water and pulling with our free arms.

When the lightning flashed again, there was Skunk, running out to the tip of the sandbar just as we were about to sail around it. He wasn't no more than ten feet away when I grabbed that pistol on the cord around my neck, swiveled it toward Skunk, and told Terry, "Duck."

Terry bobbed his head down and I fired. I didn't even know if that pistol would work, cause it had gotten some water, that's for sure, but the shells was tight, and it fired. There was a brief, bright blast, and I saw the bird under his hat cut loose and fly away. Skunk startled and stopped, and then there wasn't any light, though I could tell even in the dark that Skunk had moved his arm real quick, and then I heard Terry scream.

PART THREE

SKUNK

18

‒‒‒ɱ‒‒‒

We sailed around the tip of that sandbar even as Skunk was running down it trying to reach us. Terry was taking on something terrible, yelling out loud, and in another flash of lightning I saw why that was. That hatchet Skunk had been carrying was now sticking in our log, right near his hand. It was just a glimpse in that brief light, but I saw right away that the tip of Terry's finger on the hand clutching the log was chopped off clean and spurting blood. That damn Skunk had thrown the hatchet at him.

There wasn't no time to worry about such things, though, and we kept kicking and waving in the water with our free arms. When I glanced back, I saw Skunk going into the water. His head bobbed like a big fishing cork. That derby hat seemed stuck to his head; a birthmark couldn't have been on him any tighter.

Water got deeper and wider and swifter, and pretty soon we were really moving along—so fast I thought I was going to lose my grip. Finally I had to use both hands to clutch the log, and so did Terry. We were still kicking at the water, but mostly now the river and rain was hauling us along lickety-split.

I peeked back, expecting to see Skunk right behind me, but I couldn't see him anymore. I didn't know if the water had taken him under or if he had given up and swam for shore. Maybe he was out there and I just couldn't see him, because there was not only the dark but there was all manner of limbs and logs and such blasting along on the river's swift current.

I kept hoping the rain would quit, but it didn't. It wasn't a running rain by any measure; it was what Mama always called a deluge and what Jinx described as being like a cow pissing on a flat rock.

The lightning kept on sizzling across the sky, and there was a time when it shot a bolt out of the blackness and hit a tree by the riverbank, blazed it up like a torch. The light from it threw itself across the water and made the current look like a river of blood. I could feel the heat from the fire all the way out to where we was. I could also see something else. A hump in the water near the shore, and then the hump come up, and went back down, diving and fighting the current, and then I saw that hump reach the bank and glide up it, and flow into the woods like a shadow. I couldn't make it out good, but I figured it was Skunk. How he had swum in that swirling mess and been able to make it to shore was beyond me. I thought maybe my eyes was playing tricks on me and what I had seen was a beaver, made to look larger by the licking flames of the lightning-lit tree.

The river carried us on. The bag strapped on my back was heavy with water. If I could have taken the time to let loose of the log with my other hand, I might well have got my pocketknife from my overalls and cut myself free of it. That wet bag was like someone was riding on my back, tugging me down.

Finally the storm slowed enough and cleared enough that there was a little heavenly light, and I recognized that we had been in that place before, and that the raft should be parked up on a sandbar not too far away.

Sure enough, we hadn't gone along much further when I saw it. It wasn't in the same place exactly, as the water had gotten high enough to have pressed it off the bar and against the bank. In fact, the sandbar wasn't there no more. It was either washed away or underwater, or a little of both.

Terry and me quit drifting with the flow of the river, and started kicking and flailing our free arms. It was a hell of a battle, and we couldn't make our log do what we wanted. We sailed right on by the raft. There wasn't anyone standing or sitting on it, and I hoped they was inside the hut, which was a reasonable thought. But it also occurred to me they could have been washed off and drowned. Then I told myself if that was true, how come the raft was tied to a big tree root at the bank? Someone had to do that, and that meant someone had to be alive when the raft was banged up to shore. But that didn't mean they couldn't have been carried off later by a rush of water. All these thoughts was pounding around in my head like they was wearing army boots. I was trying to sort them out when we finally got the log veered and was close enough to shore to let loose of it and swim for it. The last I seen of our log and the hatchet stuck up in it, it was sailing away, blending with the rest of the branches and twigs that had come loose and were floating in the water.

The bag had been heavy before, but now, without the log for support, it almost dragged me under. Once again, I wanted to be shed of it, but swimming for my life didn't allow it.

Eventually we got to a spot on the bank where it wasn't high, and we got hold of some roots sticking out, and just clung there for a time trying to get our breath and strength back. Right then I felt like a horse that had been rode hard and put up wet without its oats.

After a time, I crawled up on the bank, the wet bag damn near pulling me back in the water. When I got up there, I stuck out a hand and helped Terry up. The hand he gave me was the cut one, and I could feel his warm blood on my flesh as I yanked him onto shore. We both lay there on our backs with the rain coming down on us, not moving, not able to think for a long while. Eventually, we got up and I found my pocketknife and cut the bags off of us. We paused to get the flashlight out of Terry's bag. It was wet, but by unscrewing it and taking out the batteries and shaking out the water, putting it together again, we was able to make it work. We used it to check the contents of our haul. Everything in the way of food I had in the bag, except the canned goods, was ruined. The lard bucket looked to be sealed as tight as before. I took it out and used my knife to pry off the lid. It was dry inside, and the jar was still intact, wrapped as it was in an old hand towel. I got it out and held it up and looked at it. It was May Lynn's ashes, and I felt then that the weight that had been on my back might well have been her ghost, if a ghost could be heavy as a crate of bricks.

Terry checked his can, and the money was safe inside the jar. We put the jars back in the cans and sealed them. I had a sudden thought, and checked for the pistol around my neck, but it was gone. It had come loose and was now at the bottom of the river.

We shouldn't have done it, but I guess we was worn out from lugging those wet sacks, so we carried our cans by their handles and went back along the bank to find the raft, and find it we did. The bank was a little higher up than where we had come ashore, but it wasn't so high we couldn't drop down on the raft from above.

When we did, Jinx come out of the hut on all fours with a boat paddle in her hands. She started yelling about how she was going to come upside our head with that thing. Then she saw it was us.

"Dang it," she said. "You dropping down on the raft like that, I thought you was Constable Sy. I damn near browned my pants."

"He ain't going to be coming," I said.

"Dead," Terry said, with his wounded hand clutched up against his chest.

"How'd he get dead?" Jinx said.

Before we could answer, I saw Mama poke her head out of the hut.

"I been worried sick," she said.

"We're all right," I said.

"Did you say Constable Sy was dead?" Mama asked, keeping herself mostly inside the hut, away from the rain.

"He is," I said. "But we didn't do it. And we got to heave off and go, cause someone's coming after us that might be worse than Constable Sy."

"Who's coming?" Jinx said.

"Skunk," Terry said. "You were correct in your assumptions about him being real. He's not only real, we've seen him and he's seen us, and——"

Terry held out his hand.

"What in the world?" Mama said from the confines of the hut.

"He chopped off my finger with a throw of a hatchet," Terry said. "Had I not chosen in that moment to turn my head and adjust my body slightly, I would have taken that hatchet to the skull."

Then Terry went to his knees, settled there for a moment, carefully placing his lard can full of money beside him, and then he fell flat on his face.

"Well," Jinx said, looking down at Terry. "I had this whole brave story I was going to tell. About how the rain come and washed away the boat paddle that was stuck up in the sandbar, then washed away the bar. How we nearly got swamped, and fought the rain to get tied off. But with there being a Skunk, as I said there was, and you two done seen him, and Terry coming in here with part of his finger chopped off, falling out like that, it sort of takes away from it. I'll just say we had a hard time of it."

Mama had come out of the hut now, and she and me rolled Terry over and looked at his finger. It was just the tip of it cut off, but he had lost some blood, and that combined with the savage nature of our adventure had worn him out.

I didn't feel so spry myself. I put my can down, and Mama and Jinx and me got Terry pulled inside the hut. It was tight in there, and we didn't go in with him, just sort of pushed him inside, next to the reverend, who I could see was stretched out on his back, not moving.

I said, "Is he dead?"

"No," Mama said. "He's where the dead go before they let go of their body."

Mama crawled inside the hut and got some rags out of one of the bags that was up in there, and went to tying off Terry's finger. Terry was awake now, but he wasn't frisky.

I got the cans and took those and put them inside the hut, back behind the reverend. Mama was still tying up Terry's hand. She looked at the cans, said, "I suppose that's May Lynn and the money."

"Yep," I said. "And so far we've made sure not to mix them."

I crawled out then, and me and Jinx got the raft untied from the bank. Jinx had been smart enough to tie the rafting poles down with twine on the side of the raft, and now we cut them loose and took them and pushed off into the river.

The rain was still coming, but it was coming less and less now. The river was not near as brisk as it was before. When we got pushed off good, Jinx took to the rudder and I walked from side to side on the raft, poling it as much as I could until the pole didn't touch bottom. It was hard to see what was coming, but we went along well until light came. I first saw it through the trees, a sweet pink glow, and then a bright-red warm apple swelling up to fill the sky.

It was a good thing to see, that light, cause things look and seem better in the light, even if that ain't always the truth. But, like Jinx once said to me, "At least when it ain't dark you got a better chance of seeing what's sneaking up on you."

The sky may have been lighter, but the river was near dark as sin and stuffed with limbs and leaves. I saw a dead possum float by, and a snake that had somehow died in the storm. The air smelled full of the earth. Eventually the sun was up high enough that the water seemed less coffeelike and more like milk with chocolate in it. Birds started chirping and flying between trees. The day warmed and mostly dried my damp clothes.

I took my turn at the rudder, and Jinx came to sit up front, waiting for when she might need to use the pole or the paddle to guide the raft. Mama came out of the hut with her bag and pulled it open and took out some dried meat I hadn't known was in there. She gave us some of it. The meat was damp where the sack had got wet and the moisture had bled through; it was pretty swell nonetheless. We didn't have any fresh water, though, and right then I would have kicked a bear in the teeth for some.

Terry finally crawled out of the hut and came over and had some of the dried meat.

"You all right?" I said.

"I am tolerable," he said, holding up his bandaged hand.

"The reverend moving in there?" I asked.

"He farted once," Terry said, "but except for that physical exclamation, he's as quiet as the grave."

"I fear he won't live," Mama said.

"He ain't had it no worse than the rest of us," Jinx said.

I, of course, knew what had happened to the reverend, and knew all that had happened since then had happened on top of how he felt about himself. It was too much for him. It was like one too many bricks had been piled on him and that last one had broken him down. I didn't mention this, because nobody knew I had overheard his business, and I didn't think it was time to bring it up.

The river was still flowing well, and the sun was drying my clothes. I was beginning to feel right positive. I had begun to think things were going to shake out all right, and that we were away from Skunk and would soon be someplace where he couldn't follow.

I was starting to think about the money again, and what I could do with it. I thought about May Lynn's ashes as well, though there was a part of me that was still mad because I felt those damn ashes in that can had tried to drown me, and I think I was jealous of her, even in death.

Now the river tapered, and I began to hear this rumbling noise. It was so loud I thought maybe it was thunder again, and that we were in for another rain. But when I looked at the sky it was bright and blue as could be, and the only clouds up there were fluffy white, without so much as a shadow of rain.

"What's that?" I asked Terry, who was standing next to me.

"I don't know," he said.

"It's the river," Jinx called from her place at the rudder.

We was in a very narrow stretch now, but the water was really moving, the way the last bit of something will race through the bottom of a funnel. There was a wider spot beyond, and it had about a ten-foot drop-off that hit right where the water was swirling around and around like someone using a spoon to mix something up in a bowl. It roared like it was angry.

"Whirlpool," Terry said.

Now, I didn't know a lot about whirlpools, but I had heard a story Don told about a boy he used to swim with that had got caught up in one and sucked down, and had drowned before anyone could get to him. Wasn't no one could swim down in that whirlpool after him, cause if they did, they wouldn't come up. Don said they had to wait for the water to spit him out, which it eventually did, dead as last year's news.

"There ain't no way around it," I said. "We got to go into it."

On either side of the whirlpool the bank was not soft, like it usually was, but there was big flat rocks that looked like they was stacked on one another, pancake-style. I was trying to figure the best thing to do when Mama came out of the hut, wobbling from side to side. "We're gonna capsize," she said.

This wasn't information we needed. It was pretty clear that if things didn't change, this was indeed what was going to happen. And since the only thing that could change our situation was a miracle from God—a real one, where the raft was picked up and carried over the whirlpool and set down in calm water—things looked grim.

We was short on miracles that day, but we wasn't short on water. The raft went over that drop-off and we sailed out in the air with a lot of force, like a dried cow patty being tossed. The raft came down on the water hard. I heard the hut groan. I heard the reverend's body smack around inside of it. Logs creaked and heaved, and then we was swirling around and around, fast as if we was inside a rolling car tire. Once I looked out to see that Jinx was in the water, having been thrown free, and she still had the rudder handle in her hand where it had broken off. Next thing I knew the raft was going down and the water was rising up on the sides of it. I had somehow ended up on my belly, clutching at the lumber that was nailed to the logs.

The raft rose up, and for a second there I thought I was going to get my miracle, but it was just the way the water spun. It spurted the raft skyward, out of the whirlpool. But now it was heading into those pancake rocks. Actually, it was more like those rocks were coming to the raft; they clashed against one side, then the raft went the other way and caught the rocks on the other side. I clung to the raft best I could, and after a while I realized the hut was gone and half the raft was missing. I was clinging to a piece of it, and a piece was about all that was left.

The piece I was hanging on to slammed up against the rocks and it come apart, and a chunk of it went one way and a chunk went the other. I tried to go both ways, clinging to different sections as one part went east and one went west.

My arms wasn't long enough, however, and pretty soon I wasn't holding on to anything. I was in the water and I was going down and then back up. When I came up, I tried to gulp air, but the water took me down again.

Finally I decided that the Sabine was out to drown me, and that's all there was to it. That point of view lasted about the time it takes to bat an eye, and then my inborn stubbornness took over.

Can't say how it happened, but the next thing I knew I had a knee on the edge of the bank, and there was rocks poking me. I wilted there for a moment, then got to my feet and staggered along, off the bank and onto a run of green grass. I was on the opposite side of the bank than the one Skunk had been on, and that gave me a bit of relief, even if it didn't really amount to all that much.

I didn't stumble far before I fell down. I lay there for a moment, and eventually, after a long time, got up and tried to walk again. That lasted until I got to some shade trees. I tumbled down beneath them and lay still. I knew there was a lot of things at risk, including Mama, Reverend Joy, and my friends, but it felt like I didn't have any bones in my legs and my head was stuffed with mud. I couldn't think and I couldn't move.

Reckon I lay there a long time, because the day got long and the sun got hotter and I passed out. Eventually, I opened my eyes, realizing I had passed out. It was some squirrels that got me focused, being in the trees above me, chattering like a couple of old biddies over a fence line. I managed to sit up and look around. From where I lay I could see the river, but I couldn't see Mama or anybody else.

It took me about the time it takes a baby to be born and to learn to walk before I could get to my feet and go down to the shoreline for a look, fearing all the while what I might see. There was good reason for that worry, because what I did see made my heart sink like a lead boat.

It was the reverend.

The river was calmer beyond the falls and the rocks, and where it went off to the right there was a narrow split in some boulders and the river ran through it; the reverend was hung there between the boulders. He was lodged in tight as a pig in a jug. A big piece of the raft had broken off and stuck through his stomach. I scrambled along the bank and climbed over some smaller rocks, and swam out to the center, where he was. It was much easier than before. The rain was gone and the river was slower. There were plenty of rocks to climb on till I could get to one of the boulders.

When I got out to where he was jammed up, I inched along the top of the boulder until I was just above the reverend. I called out his name.

It was a long time in coming, but he finally said, "And now I'm called home."

"Sounds like you're still here," I said, hoping that would cheer him up, but it was a silly thought. The raft piece was sticking out of his lower back and blood was leaking around the wooden ram in little driblets. It was stuck so tight I figured it was all that was holding him together.

I noodled around on the rocks until I could get down on another one that was lower, and could see the reverend's face. It wasn't a pretty sight. His skin was white, his lips were dark, and blood was bubbling out of his nose and mouth. He lifted his eyes, as he was too weak to lift his head, and said, "You are an angel."

I knew then he was really bad off. "No. It's me, Sue Ellen," I said.

"I see now I'm forgiven, or you wouldn't be here," he said.

I started to correct him, tell him again who I was, but right then I knew there wasn't any use, and it was best to let him think I was holding open the door to heaven so he could fall through.

He dropped his eyes. His chest, which had been heaving hard, quit moving. It was as if he got heavier. The big piece of wood sticking through him shifted and he eased down lower, his ankles going into the water. Then he was still again, hanging there like a big piece of fruit.

I didn't like it none, but I left him where he was. I didn't have the strength or the will to try and drag him loose, especially with that big piece of wood in him. There wasn't anything else I could do for him. I wanted to find Mama and my friends, though I feared what it was I would come up on. I climbed back on top the boulder and looked out over the river. I could see there was a limb sticking out from a tree by the bank. The limb had been underwater a short time ago, but now the water was low again, and it was out. There was something hanging from it.

I swam back toward shore, started walking toward where that something was hanging. My heart was beating fast and I was having trouble breathing. When I got to the limb, I saw what was hanging was one of the bags me and Terry had taken from the reverend's shed. I eased up against the trunk of the tree, then out on the limb, and got the bag. It was work, but I tugged it back to shore. I pulled the bow that tied it off at the top, and even wet it come loose easy. I looked inside. Everything in there was pretty much ruined, but there was one of the lard cans and the lid was still tight. I hadn't lost my pocketknife, so I got it out of my sticky-wet pocket, opened it, and used it to prize up the can lid. The jar was unbroken and the padding inside was dry. It was full of May Lynn's ashes.

I put things back how they was, and, carrying the bag with the can in it, went walking again. Then I saw Terry. He was standing up, leaning against a tree, reaching across with his right hand and holding his left elbow. The other bag was at his feet.

I ran over to him, and he let go of his arm and hugged me.

"I thought you had gone under," he said.

"I thought you had," I said.

"This bag washed up on shore," he said, "and I rescued it and was leaning against this tree thinking everybody else was drowned. I hurt my arm a little, nothing bad, but a little. It doesn't hurt near as much as my finger."

He held up his hand. The bandage had washed off. His hand was swollen all the way from where the hatchet had cut off the tip of his finger to his wrist; it looked like a ham hock.

"It hurts," he said, "and when I look at it, it hurts more. You okay?"

"I feel like I been beat with a bag full of hammers," I said.

I told him what had happened to Reverend Joy.

"May God have mercy on his soul," he said. "He was all right to us, and I think his heart was good."

"The rare true Christian," I said.

We said nothing for a moment, and I guess that was a kind of unspoken moment of silence for the reverend. But our circumstances didn't allow us too much time for being sentimental or sad.

Terry said, "I don't know what's in my bag. The money or May Lynn."

"The money," I said. "I have May Lynn, and she's high and dry."

"Wonder how the money is," Terry said.

"What I'm worried about is Mama and Jinx," I said, but that didn't keep me from pulling the bow loose on his bag. We got the can out and pried it open and looked inside the padded jar. Just like the jar in my can, it wasn't broken. It was in fine shape, and so was the money. Everything else in the bag was ruined. I tried the flashlight, but the water had messed it up. I took the lard cans out of each of the bags while Terry leaned against the tree. I figured those lard cans was all that was worth carrying.

Then we heard Jinx yell. We looked up and our hearts soared, cause there she and Mama came, dripping wet, walking along the bank toward where we was standing. We hurried to meet them, went about hugging each other, and then we found a place on the shore where the sun was bright and all of us just sat there, numb, with the sun beating down on us, drying us out.

I told them about the reverend, and when I did Mama burst out crying. I had to hold her. In time she stopped, and we all lay down on the ground in the hot sunlight and fell asleep from exhaustion.

19

When I woke up, it was fresh dark, but not so much I couldn't see good. Terry and Jinx was still asleep. Mama was down by the edge of the river, squatting on her haunches, looking out at the river. I went and sat down by her.

"I walked down to find Jack," she said. "He was hung up good. I could see that from the shore. I wanted to swim out there and free him, but I didn't. I'm not that good a swimmer and I'm bone-tired. It was luck and nothing else that allowed me and Jinx to survive. We clung to a piece of the raft and it washed up against the shore and got hung up in some roots, and we were able to get onto land. We were lucky, and Jack, a man of the Word, one of God's chosen, was killed. I don't understand it."

"I don't think there's any understanding to it," I said.

"What are we gonna do now, Sue Ellen?"

All of a sudden, I felt like the mother and like Mama was the child.

"I don't know just yet," I said.

"While I was sleeping, I had the dream about the black horse again, and the white one, but this time the white horse not only had wings but he was flying up and away, fast. I was running and jumping like a kid, hopping up trying to grab onto his hind legs, or his tail. I kept jumping even though he was long gone from me. And that black horse, he came closer, and I forgot about the white horse, and I started to run. The black horse came on behind me, snorting fire out of its nostrils and mouth. He came closer and closer, and I couldn't run any faster. He was right on me, and then . . . I woke up."

"It's just a dream, Mama. Ain't no horses after you. Why would a horse be after you?"

She shook her head. "I think it may be some kind of sign. Some kind of warning. I feel it means something."

"It means you need some rest, Mama. That's what it means."

We went back to where Jinx and Terry was. Jinx was up now and she was on her knees beside Terry. She said, "He ain't looking so good."

He wasn't. Even by starlight I could see his hand was swole up a lot bigger than before.

"I reckon we'll have to walk out, find some people," I said.

"We're wanted," Jinx said.

"Just by Don and Cletus," I said. "They ain't going to tell no law about that money. They're as big a crook as we are, worse."

"There's Skunk," Jinx said. "He could have been out there watching us sleep, for all we know. They say he's like that. That he does things on his own time, that it's all just a game to him."

"Let's hope they're wrong," I said.

"We could end up dead on a big nest of hope," Jinx said.

And then something hit me. "You know, there is another problem."

"And what's that?" Mama asked.

"Gene and Constable Sy," I said. "We was the last ones anyone knew to be in that house. I got to reckon we're going to be the ones most likely figured for the killing."

"I hadn't thought of that," Jinx said. "So maybe we're wanted after all, and in a big way." After a moment, she said, "Course, Reverend Joy, he did the killing of Gene with that board. He's dead, so we could lay both of them killings on him."

"That isn't right," Mama said.

"It ain't right," Jinx said. "But it sure is workable."

"No," I said. "We won't do that. He tried to help us."

"I know that," Jinx said, her voice deep. "I was trying it on for size. But it didn't fit. I guess you got to walk out and take the chance. Maybe we all got to walk out. Jail is bound to be better than Skunk."

"I'm not sure Terry can walk out," Mama said. "And what about the reverend?"

"He damn sure ain't walking nowhere," Jinx said.

"That's not what I meant," Mama said.

"If we pull him loose," I said, "we got no way to bury him proper. So I don't think there's a good way to go when it comes to him."

"We can't just leave him hanging there," Mama said.

"I ain't as bothered by it as you two," Jinx said.

I looked down at Terry. "We can talk about it till the blood poison kills Terry, or while he might have a bit of strength, we can try to get going. Way I see it, night is Skunk's time, and we keep standing here chatting, he's gonna solve all our problems for us, and not in a way we're gonna like."

"All right, then," Mama said. "But how do we go?"

I thought on that a moment. "We could walk toward the tree line, see if there's a road somewhere, but probably the best thing is to stay along the river. The river always leads to a town or somebody."

We talked about it some more, and finally come to the conclusion it was best to stick together. Might have a chance that way, but if we split up, we was sure as hell going to be killed if Skunk was out there. Three of us could fight him better than one or two. Of course, there was Terry, but in his condition our best bet was to grab him by the ankles and sling him about, use him as a weapon.

Terry made it to his feet with some coaxing, and was able to walk with one arm over my shoulder, the other over Jinx's. But he was out of it, jabbering about this and that: "It was an accident," he said over and over.

"What's that?" I said. "What was an accident?"

"The water," he said.

"It wasn't your fault," I said. "A storm does what it does."

We kept walking, his arm over our shoulders, carrying our lard cans, me with May Lynn in mine, and Mama carrying the one with the money in it.

We stayed close to the river as we could, but sometimes the growth around it got wild, and we had to go wider, come back closer to it when the stuff thinned. I don't know how long we walked, but we finally came to a place where there was a big burned patch with a chimney sticking up. It had happened a long time off, because the rain from the night before hadn't stirred the char up, and there wasn't any burned smell about it. Up against the shore I could see a boat chained to a big oak that had died and fallen into the water.

We stopped and laid Terry out on the dirt and set our lard cans down. Mama sat beside him, and me and Jinx went down to the boat. The chain ran through a hole in the front of the boat and was wrapped around the log and fastened back to the boat with a padlock. The way it was looped under the log, I figured someone had to have gone to a lot of trouble to get in the water and under the log to wrap the chain. It couldn't be pulled off either end. One end of the log went out in the water. The other end had a bunch of dead limbs on it, and you couldn't pull the chain over them. If we had an ax, then we could have chopped the limbs off and pulled the chain free. But no ax appeared.

We looked around for a rock, something, anything, to bang that padlock off, but all there was in that way was the bricks in the chimney, and they was caulked tight. We couldn't find any means to work one loose.

I kept looking around for Skunk, but I figured by the time I saw him come up, it would be too late. Besides, we was all so tired we could hardly move. I went over and sat down by Mama while Jinx went off in the woods to take care of nature's business.

"Sorry you came now?" I said.

"I don't think I am," Mama said. "It would have been nice had things worked out a bit smoother, but I'm not sorry. I'm sorry for the reverend, and even Gene and Constable Sy, I guess."

"Constable Sy got it pretty bad," I said. "Skunk did some things to him for fun."

Mama nodded. "I'm still glad I came."

"Even if you dream scary dreams of horses?"

"Even if I do."

About that time Jinx came out of the woods, hurrying along so fast I was afraid she might have come up on Skunk.

"There's lights on the other side of them trees," she said.

"Skunk?"

"I don't know it ain't Skunk," she said. "But I figure he's a whole lot sneakier than to go out there and light a fire, and him trying to creep up on us."

"You stay here with Terry," I said to Mama, and me and Jinx hustled into the woods. This wasn't the smartest thing in the world, to leave them by themselves, but it seemed at this point less smart to have them approach a fire with us. It could be Skunk, and he might not even care to put a sneak on. For that matter, whoever it was might not be friendly. It was better two young girls who could run like deer went to see what was what, instead of a tired woman and a boy we'd have to drag around by the arm.

We hadn't gone far when I could see the same light Jinx had seen. It was definitely firelight, and we could faintly hear someone talking. Easing closer, we could make out the fire was in a big clearing, and beyond the clearing was some trees. We squatted down and looked out at the fire and listened as best we could to the voices, but there wasn't much that could be made out. There was some laughing, and I could tell one of the voices was a man, and the others was a woman and child, and there was some other voices, too, that might have been older children. It was hard to tell.

Jinx and I didn't even discuss it; we just got up and walked out of the woods where we was hiding and started toward the fire. I called out, "Hallo, the fire."

The voices stopped, and I seen then that there was two men, because they both stood up and looked in our direction. We kept walking.

One of the men said, "Who's out there?"

"Some near-drowned people," I said.

There was some hesitation, but one of the men called out, "Come on up," and that's what we did.

When we got closer we could feel the heat of the fire. Though it was a warm night, we were still a bit damp, and it felt good. I sniffed something cooking, and the smell made my stomach hurt like it was going through a washer wringer. Where the smell came from was a big lard can setting on some logs in the fire. It was full of something and that something was bubbling.

I looked around at the others. The fire flickered over their faces. There was three young people, one maybe six, and the other two was a boy and a girl in their early teens. The woman was about Mama's age, and she looked like she would have been pretty in daylight with a good dress on and her hair done right. Both men had on worn-out clothes and hats. I figured the one that was about the woman's age was her husband, and the other man, though older, looked enough like the younger man I reckoned it was his father. They both had on old suit coats, which wasn't the best thing for the weather, but I reasoned out they thought they might need them when the weather changed, and wearing them was the best way to keep up with their goods. They wore ragged hats and had some bundles bound up and lying near the fire. It didn't take much thinking to know they was on the scout, trying to survive with what they had, same as us.

"We had an accident on the river," I said. "Our raft got torn apart in the rainstorm, and we near drowned. We got an injured boy back there with part of his finger chopped off and his hand all swole up."

"Chopped off?" the woman said.

"Yes, ma'am, he got it caught up in something when the raft broke up, and it come off. We been walking, trying to find our way out."

It was a lie, but I figured I might not want to point out we had been chased by a crazy man with a hatchet, since he was most likely still out there.

"We come here by train," said the older man. "Not to this spot, but back there"—he pointed—"where there's a higher grade. The train slowed down and we could jump. We was tired of riding in the boxcar. You ride long enough, and you jump off, you feel like you're still riding. I just now got over it. Thing is, though, I ain't so sure jumping off was the smart idea. We're just out here in the woods now. I was fed up plenty with that train then, but now I'm wishing we was back on it."

"We've walked awhile," said the woman.

"We're thinking we ought to catch the next train coming through," said the older man, "though this ain't a good spot for it."

I looked out beyond them, knew then that the rail line run right past us, not more than a hundred feet away.

"When's that next train come through?" I said.

"We ain't got no schedule," said the younger man. "We're new to this hoboing. We wasn't born to it. We never had so much to begin with, but then it got so there wasn't any work, and what work there was had fifty men after the job."

"Jud," the wife said. "She's just asking a question, not our life stories."

"No problem, ma'am," I said.

"We was in the Dust Bowl up in Oklahoma," the older man said. "Day that first dust storm come in. We hadn't never seen nothing like it."

"I don't know there's ever been anything like it," Jud said.

"Naw," said the old man. "Nothing like it."

"These girls don't want to hear all that," said the woman, but that didn't slow the old man down.

"At first," he said, "out there on the horizon, it looked like a rain cloud, but the color was wrong, and it was too low to the ground. It got closer, and I thought, twister. But it wasn't that. It was like big balls of dirty cotton being pushed along by the wind, balls higher than a house and wider than a town. It was sand. The birds was flying in front of it fast as they could go. And then it come. It hit the house and knocked out the windows, throwed glass and dirt every which way. It ripped the curtains to shreds. Everything turned dark, so goddamn dark we couldn't see each other in it. It come and it come. We lay on the floor coughing. Then, when it was gone, we went out and looked at the fields. There wasn't even a sprig of grass out there. It was like the storm had pulled everything up from the ground, including the ground. All the good planting soil was gone, taken off to God knows where. But them storms wasn't done. They just kept coming. One after another. We fixed windows and we put wet rags around the cracks. We even sealed some with flour paste. But them storms, they didn't make no never mind. I thought it was like in the Bible for a time. I thought it was the end times. And later, I sort of wished it had been, cause there wasn't nothing left for nobody to eat that was worth eating. Oh, there was the rabbits at first. They was starving just like we was, and they was everywhere. Them rabbits was so poor, you had to eat three to get a meal for one person. And even cleaned and cooked they tasted like grit. Then if that wasn't enough of a rock to tote up the mountain, along come a tornado and blowed our house all over Oklahoma. We got what was left and piled it in our truck, which by the grace of God didn't get blowed away with the house. It got turned over two or three times and righted, but we was lucky there. It ran, even if it did have an engine full of sand.

"We went out to California to pick oranges, and that wasn't no good. Everyone in the whole damn world seemed to be there. You could work all day and not make enough to buy a sack of flour. We come back this direction for no good reason at all. It's greener than Oklahoma, but there ain't nothing here for nobody to do. We're on our way somewhere else."

"Where?" I said.

"Just somewhere else," he said.

"You went on and told our life story anyhow," the woman said to the old man.

"I reckon I did," he said, slumping his shoulders. "Reckon I did. It was just all balled up inside me."

"It got out," she said, then looked at Jinx. "The boy. Can he walk?"

"I don't know," I said.

"If we could get him here by the fire, I might could look at his hand. I've done some patching up in my time."

"We can try and cart him over here," I said.

"Jud and Boone here can help you, you need it," she said. "We can give you a bite to eat."

"We ain't got that much to share," Jud said. "Some beans is all, and not enough for any more mouths."

"Hush, Jud," the woman said. "We'll make do, if we all just get a spoonful."

Jud looked at the woman, then looked back at the fire. From experience, he knew he wasn't going to win any kind of a battle over sharing beans, or much of anything else.

"There's also another person," I said. "My mother."

"Bring them both here," she said.

Jud nodded toward the can on the fire. "You ain't got nothing to add to the fixings, do you?"

"No, sir," I said. "Sorry. Everything we had is at the bottom of the river, except for a couple of nonfood items."

"All right," Jud said, and then sighed. "Let's go see we can get this friend of yours. But I ought to tell you, I got a gun."

To prove that, he pulled a pistol out of his coat pocket. It was a very small pistol. It had an over-and-under barrel that rattled a little in its groove. Most likely, he shot it at you, you'd have to lean into the gun to get hit—provided it didn't explode in his face.

"We ain't aiming to get shot," Jinx said. They all looked at her kind of startled. She had been so quiet up until now they may have figured her for a deaf-mute.

"Ain't no shooting going on," Jud said.

He put the gun back in his coat, and we started out with them toward the river.

20

It was a real job, but we finally got Terry to the fire.

We sat there while the woman—who, we learned, was named Clementine—looked at Terry's hand. By firelight it looked bad as bad could be. It was swollen big and had gone purple and there was some dark lines moving up the wrist toward the elbow. You could smell the wound, like meat going to rot.

The men both stared at Mama. I don't think they meant to be rude, but it isn't every day you see someone looked like her out in the woods wandering around. Even damp as a pissed-on hen, she was still something special, and I couldn't help but envy her. I guess I looked all right, but there wasn't any way I was ever going to look like her.

"What's in them buckets?" said Jud.

We had carried our lard cans with us, and I was sitting on mine, and Jinx on hers.

"It's a friend of ours got burned up in a fire in a house," I said. I didn't feel too bad telling that lie, as part of it was true.

"What?" said Boone.

"She was a big friend, and she's packed in both buckets," I said.

"You scooped her out of a fire?" Jud said.

"What was left of her."

I got off the lard can and used my pocketknife to open it up. I put the knife away and took out the jar and showed it to them by holding it close to the fire. It was dark with ashes.

"What in hell are you doing with her burned up like that?" said Jud.

"We're taking what's left to her relatives, to let them decide where she ought to be buried. We figured we ought not just let her ashes lie around and dry out and get blown away by the wind."

"That's something," Boone said, trying to wrap his head around that.

"I guess that's the Christian thing to do," Clementine said.

"You ought to have just kicked some dirt over that ash," Boone said. "I don't know it's so Christian to carry her around in a bucket. That don't seem right, keeping a woman in a bucket, even if she is dead and burned to ash."

"How do you know what ash is hers and what ash is the house?" Jud said.

"I reckon God can sort that out," I said.

This seemed to end any interest in the buckets, and Jinx didn't have to open the other, cause if they had seen that money, desperate circumstances might have changed their character.

"It's bad infected," said Clementine after she had checked over Terry's hand. "There ain't nothing for it but to let some of the poison out. I can do it, but I can't make no promises."

"Then you better do it," Jinx said. She was near Terry and she was looking at his hand lying across his chest.

"It's going to wake him up, when I do what I got to do," said Clementine, "and it's going to hurt like the fires of hell for a moment, but if we can let the poison out, he'll do better, at least until you can find a doctor."

"My Clementine was a nurse," said Jud.

"Not official," she said. "I just helped the doctor out until this Depression come down. He called me a nurse, but all the training I got I picked up from doing. Jud, I'm going to need your knife."

Jud gave her a large pocketknife, and Clementine opened it up and poked the blade in the fire and held it there. She held it there a long time. We sat and watched. When the blade started to glow red, she said, "He's going to need holding down."

Jinx got his arm, the one that didn't have a hand on it the color of an eggplant, and held it down. Jud came and straddled Terry and sat on his legs. I got hold of his other arm, the one with the injured hand, and held it out on a rag Clementine had spread on the ground.

Clementine wrapped a rag around her hand and pulled the knife out of the fire. I seen a whiff of smoke come off the knife, and then she went straight to Terry's hand and poked it into his wound. Terry screamed. When she poked that knife in his hand, the pus all bound up in it from finger to wrist leaped out of the cut and hit me in the face like it was coming from a hose. It was such a surprise I almost let go of his arm.

"You got to hold him," Clementine said.

I pulled myself together, held him tight. She cut him again, and more pus come out, but not in quite the leap as before. It was dark stuff, and thick. Terry had quit screaming, but he was whimpering like a wet kitten.

Clementine laid the knife aside. She took up Terry's hand and stroked it with her thumb, bringing more pus out of the cuts. This caused Terry to go back to making serious noise. She kept at it until the wound was flat. Already it was less dark, having let out a lot of its coloring through the cuts she had made.

"Boone," Clementine said, "I'm going to have to have some of your shine."

"How much?" Boone said.

"Whatever I need," she said. "Now get it."

Boone grumbled a bit, went over to one of the packs, tore it open. He come back with something small wrapped in cloth. Clementine opened the bundle. Inside of it was a little jar of what I suspected was homemade hooch. She unscrewed the jar lid and poured the stuff on Terry's hand. It made him jump. She poured more of it, and he didn't jump this time, but lay there breathing easy.

She lifted up the jar and took a swig of it. She offered us all a sip, but we turned it down, though I saw Mama lick her lips a little. That alcohol smell was the same you could smell in that cure-all, and I know it tempted her, but she shook her head.

Clementine set the shine down on the ground. Boone came over and put the lid on it and wrapped it up again and put it back in his bundle. Clementine bound up Terry's hand gently with some torn white cloth.

Mama said, "Is he going to be better?"

"He could only have got worse," Clementine said. "I think he will get better, but he won't get well unless he gets to a doctor. He needs some real attention. He won't get it out here from me. All this dirt and such. It'll get in the wound, and there ain't no way around it."

"Thank you," Mama said, and me and Jinx chimed in with the same words.

Jinx pulled a handkerchief out of her overalls and used it to wipe the pus off my face, and then she put the rag in the fire.

You'd think after that we'd have all lost our appetite, but we hadn't. Jud had some empty cans in his pack, cans that had once had something or another in them but had lost their labeling. He gave me and Jinx one to share. They gave the older kids one to share, another for the mother and the little girl to have. In the end, everyone had a can or a can to share with someone else. None of those kids said a thing through all this, not to us or their family. They didn't act like kids ought to. It was like all their juice had been let out, and it hurt me to see it.

We all ate our bit of beans, and when that was done, we went looking for dead wood to keep the fire going, even if it was a warm night. The fire gave a bit of light, and there was a comfort in it.

Everyone stretched out on the ground to rest. I tried to, but couldn't. I was thinking about Skunk. Jinx came over close to me. She was thinking about Skunk, too. She leaned into my ear. "We ought to be ready if Skunk shows up."

I showed her that I had my pocketknife open and by my side.

"You might as well try to poke a bull to death with a needle," she said.

"At least maybe I can give him something to remember me by."

"He won't need those pokes," she said. "He'll have your hands to remember you by."

It don't seem natural to be that scared and still tired, but me not being able to sleep only lasted awhile, then I felt like I was falling from a high tree, floating down like a single pine straw. I all of a sudden couldn't keep my eyes open, and when daylight come and I woke up with both my hands not chopped off, I breathed a sigh of relief.

I looked over at Jinx. She was sitting by the fire. She had her elbows on her knees and her head in her hands. At first I thought she was awake, but then I saw she had fallen asleep that way.

I got up and walked off in the woods, and took care of some business, and then I walked down to the river. The water had calmed considerable, and looking out at it, I wished for our stolen raft.

I walked around down there, hungry for breakfast. I came up on the spot where we had thrown away the bags the buckets had been in. I thought maybe I ought to look through them again, to see if any of the dried meat had survived.

The meat in the bags stunk bad as Terry's wound. I emptied the bags out on the ground, but there wasn't nothing there of any use. I walked back the way we had before, and came to where the reverend was. He had buzzards on him and they had plucked away his eyes and torn at his nose and lips. I picked up a rock and threw it at them and shooed at them until they flew off.

I thought maybe I should tell the folks back at the fire, see if they could help me get him out of them rocks and bury him, but I also feared they might think we had killed him.

I don't know why I did it, but I went and looked for a stout stick, and found one. I swam out to him, which was easier now that I had rested and the water wasn't so angry. I climbed on the rocks to where I could touch him with the stick. He was near blue and had swollen up like a dog tick. I went to poking at him with that stick until he finally come loose and fell down in the water. The water picked him up, and the piece of the raft sticking through him made him float as easy as a paper boat; the water toted him along until he was out of sight. I sat on those rocks for a long time, just feeling the warm sun and looking in the direction he had gone. I didn't know how to feel about what I had done, but somehow I couldn't just let those buzzards at him, and I wasn't able to haul him out of the rocks and onto shore.

I tossed the stick away, and when I felt up to it, swam back to shore. I walked back the way I had come. When I got to those two empty bags lying on the ground where me and Terry had left them, I looked down at them, and then a thing that had been in the back of my mind connected up with some other things, and in that moment I was sick to my stomach. I put my hands against a sappy pine and leaned into it and threw up on the bark.

I knew something in that moment just as sure as it had been explained to me by words coming out of someone's mouth. It had been hung up in front of me clear as the sun, and I hadn't understood it till right then.

It took a while, but when I got myself together, I decided it wasn't the time to mention what I had figured out. I walked back to where the others were. And when I got there, everyone was up except Terry, who still looked like death warmed over.

"I was worried about you," Mama said.

The little girl, who had yet to speak, surprised me when she said, "We been told not to run off. We'd done that, Daddy would have tanned our hide."

"She ain't no little girl," Jud said. He was stirring the fire apart with a stick. "And she ain't no business of ours. She can do what she wants. You hold your mouth, child."

The little girl went silent and pouty. I tried to smile at her and cheer her up, but she wasn't having any of that. She looked away and went about her business, which was helping her family get its goods together. She and her family had all their stuff bundled up and the fire out within minutes.

"We're going to go now," said Clementine, boosting a bundle over her shoulder. "We wish y'all well, but we got to go on our own. We don't want to be rude, and not be good Christians, but there isn't any more we can do for you. Got to take care of our own. I can only tell you what I already have. You need to get that young fellow to a doctor, or that hand and arm are going to go bad. May life turn around for you."

"Same for you," Mama said.

With that, Clementine, who looked much older in daylight, like she had been wet down and beat out on rocks and hung up to dry in the noonday sun, nodded at us, and started out after her family, who had already began to walk away. We stayed where we was and watched them wander alongside the railroad tracks. It would stand to reason that that was the way we ought to go, too, but our problem was Terry. We would have to carry him, and we didn't have a way to do that and be able to toss him on a train. The only thing left for us to do was figure out how to get that boat off the chain and get Terry into it and float down the river.

Terry had still to come around. I looked down at him, and even sick like he was, his face all sweaty, his hair wet with it, he was still a pretty boy. He and May Lynn were two of a type, and looked as if they would have belonged together. Jinx was sitting by him on the ground, staring down at him. The look on her face was soft and sweet, not something that was normal to Jinx. She often had a way of looking as if she had been carved out of licorice with a dull knife, but when she relaxed her face, she was very pretty and her eyes was like a doe's. She reached out and pushed Terry's damp hair back.

Mama got up and glanced after the family going along the railroad tracks. She took me aside and said, "I almost tore open their bundle last night to get at that liquor. I was fine until I smelled it last night, and then I was ready to have me some if I had to jump that poor woman and fight her for it, fight the whole bunch of them. And then I got hold of myself, but it wasn't easy. It was like trying to pull a team of wild horses back to keep them from running over a cliff."

Mama seemed to have horses on the brain. I said, "Longer you stay away from it, easier it'll be."

"I'm not so sure," Mama said. "What about Terry?"

"I figure I got to get that boat loose," I said. "We all get in it, it'll be a tight fit, but I don't think we got a choice. Why don't you stay here with Terry, and me and Jinx will see what we can find?"

It was that problem about leaving them alone again, but it still seemed worse to drag him down to the boat and us turn out not to be able to work it loose. And there needed to be someone there with him.

Me and Jinx went down by the river looking again for a rock heavy enough that we might strike the padlock off the chain. Taking the boat was stealing again, and it made me to think if I wasn't careful I could be a career criminal. Criminal business was steady work, and sometimes there was money in it, but there was that whole prison thing, too, and that didn't appeal to me much. But bad times bred bad intentions, and right now surviving was more important than anything.

"You think Terry's going to be okay?" Jinx asked me. We was prowling around near the shoreline, farther up from where we had looked before, trying to come across a solid enough rock. Most of them was weak and came apart after they had been tested with a few strikes to the ground.

"I don't know," I said. "I guess it depends on if we can get him to a doctor."

"He sure is pretty," she said.

I stopped and looked at her. "He is, but how come you're just now noticing it?"

"I've always noticed it," she said. "I'd have to be blind not to. It's just that . . . Well . . ."

"He's white," I said.

"Yeah. That kind of thing don't work in these parts, and I know he's my friend and all, but I sometimes think of him in ways I shouldn't, him being sissy and all."

"I didn't know you was attached like that."

"I didn't neither until I thought he might die. I guess I figured since we were going out to California there might be a little different outlook there. That he might be interested if I cleaned myself up some and learned how to talk right."

"You know he's a sissy, right?"

"It ain't nothing but dreaming nohow, and I wish I hadn't told you."

"It's all right," I said. "I've thought the same thing about him."

"Yeah, but you ain't colored," she said.

"It wouldn't matter," I said. "He ain't got the desire for neither of us. If he didn't have the desire for May Lynn, he damn sure don't have it for us."

Jinx went quiet when I said that, and there wasn't any more talking to her about it or anything else. She trudged along and made some space between us for a while, and we went back to searching for that rock we needed.

Finally we come across one that was heavy and solid, but easy enough for one person to handle if they meant business. Me and Jinx took turns carrying it back to the boat, and when we got there, I took the first crack at it by climbing in the boat and striking the lock. The boat moved when I struck it and the chain rattled, but the only thing I managed to do to the lock was scratch it up some.

"Let me have that goddamn rock," Jinx said. She climbed in the boat as I climbed out. She picked it up and lifted it high above her head. Her mouth twisted up, and then she brought that rock down with a good lick. The padlock leaped open, as if on command.

"Now," she said, "let's go up there and get Terry."

We left the loose padlock poking through the chain, got the paddles out of the boat, put them on shore, then went back to where Terry lay. We folded his bad arm across his chest. It had already swole up again, and there were red lines moving up to his elbow. I knew what that was. Blood poisoning.

I got his feet and Mama and Jinx got him under the shoulders. We struggled with him across the clearing and went into the woods, only banging his head into a tree a couple of times before we got down to the boat and managed to stretch him out in the bottom of it. Then we loosed the chain from the padlock, got in the boat, and pushed off.

I didn't feel any real relief until we was out in the center of the river and the water was carrying us along. Jinx was in the back paddling, with Mama having to sit up so close to her they was near like one person. I was in the front, and I found I was hitting the water with the paddle hard, thinking on what I thought I knew now and feeling really angry about it and at the same time sad and confused. I knew there wasn't no need dwelling on it, not right then, even though it was bothering me something furious. I wanted to tell someone, but didn't know how. I guess I knew, too, that no matter how certain I felt about what I was thinking, it was just a guess.

Skunk was a bigger worry, and that's where I put my mind and let it rest. I had come to think that he was in fact playing with us, and on more than one occasion when we was on land the hair on the back of my neck had stood up, and when I had turned there was nothing. I didn't mention this to the others, because I didn't know if there was something real to it or it was just me imagining.

My thought was if we could stay in the middle of the river all the way to Gladewater, providing I'd even know when we got there, we might have a chance. But there was another thing. I was bad hungry and my stomach was growling like a dog. It wasn't until we come to a spot in the river where the shore was cleared of trees, and we could see a house set back a ways from the river with some chickens in the yard, that I finally couldn't stand it anymore. Those darn chickens running around out there made me lick my lips.

I looked back at Jinx, and she didn't say nothing, but it was like she knew what I was thinking, cause she just nodded at me.

I paddled the boat toward land and she paddled with me. Me and Jinx and Mama tugged the boat on shore about halfway, and then I said, "Me and Jinx are gonna see we can get some food. Mama, you stay with Terry. Something goes wrong up there, or there's a ruckus, or you even think you see Skunk, or if you don't hear from us after too long, you push off and paddle like you're rowing across the Jordan for the Promised Land."

"Be careful," she said, and with that me and Jinx started up to the house.

The place was on a rise in the land. The grass was tall in the yard and green, but not from any kind of cultivating; it was naturally that way. Some quail flew up as we come along, and there wasn't no chickens after all. Me and Jinx was both surprised to see they was just big water birds pecking around for bugs. They took to the air as we got closer to them. Off in the distance I could see an old pen with the slats broken down, a well that had a near-fallen-down board curbing, and an outhouse that had a slat missing on the side.

Me and Jinx talked stuff over as we went, and we come to the decision that the thing to do was just to be straight up about it, and depend on the kindness of strangers, ask them to give us something to eat. Right then I was so hungry I'd have settled for a fistful of raw beans.

Since Jinx was colored, she knew she had to linger back and let me do the talking, in case it turned out to be white folks who lived there. If they was colored, then she could come up and talk. It was best to start out expecting someone white, as they could get real upset about a colored on their stoop.

I stepped up to the door and knocked briskly and stepped back. There was stirring in the house, like a rat crawling out from under newspapers, and soon the door opened. Standing there was an old woman, thin as a broomstick and bent over like a horseshoe. She wore a long faded blue gingham dress and a filthy white bonnet with straps that was tied off under her chin. Some white hair had escaped out from under it in spots, and one greasy strand was stuck to her face; at first glance it looked like a scar. Her face itself was dark as old leather and had about as much charm as a stomped-in mud hole.

"Ma'am," I said. "Me and this little girl would love to eat almost anything, if you got it to spare. We could gather some wood for you, jobs like that and such. We're terrible hungry."

I thought it best not to mention Mama and Terry just yet.

The old woman studied us. "How about dirt?" she said.

"Ma'am?"

"Would you eat dirt?"

I glanced back at Jinx.

Jinx said, "We got to draw the line at dirt."

"Then you ain't that terrible hungry," said the old woman. "You was hungry, you'd eat dirt."

"Yes, ma'am," I said. "Well, we want to thank you for your time and wish you a good day."

I started to turn, but the door opened wider, and I saw then she had a big pistol in her hand. My first thought was if she pulled the trigger the firing of the gun would knock her down. She lifted it and held it at us with both hands. She held it steady, considering the size of her, and there was about her a kind of hard knowledge that changed my mind. Right then I decided she could not only shoot that pistol and not be knocked down but she could probably hit what she was aiming at.

"I ain't got no one to chop wood," she said. "I reckon you can chop wood."

"We can do that," I said, looking at the pistol.

"I wouldn't mind servants," she said.

She waved the pistol at us, had us come inside. The place was a wreck. Chairs was turned this way and that, a table was on its side, the legs poking out like a dead animal's legs. There was all manner of junk in there, and it smelled kind of ripe, like old food.

"I ain't straightened the place up lately," she said.

Since the dawn of creation, I thought.

"Before you chop wood, I thought you ought to help me set things right in here. After you're done, I'll see I can feed you."

"Set things right?" Jinx said.

The old woman studied Jinx. "When I was a child, my family had its own niggers. They gave me one to play with. You remind me of her."

"How old was you then, about a hundred?" Jinx said.

"I was four or five," the old woman said. "I've lost some count on my age. But I'm near eighty. And you want to sass, you ought to know that little girl they gave me got to thinking she was going to be one with the Lincoln thinkers. Me and her got into a tussle, and my daddy sold her to a traveling house of sin."

"A what?" Jinx said.

"They made her a whore," said the old woman.

"She was probably relieved," Jinx said.

"Just start cleaning," said the old woman.

21

Just as we started cleaning, the old woman sat in a rocking chair and let the pistol rest in her lap. She was far enough away from us she could bring it up fast.

"You don't want to throw out nothing precious," said the old woman.

"And what would that be?" Jinx said. She seemed determined to get shot.

"That would be anything precious, you little smart mouth," said the old woman.

"Jinx, help me set the table up," I said, hoping to take the conversation on a different journey.

We set the table up, straightened the chairs, got a broom, and swept up broken plates. Everything was covered in dust, and there was enough of it you could have easily copied out the King James Bible with a finger and some dedicated intention.

I reckoned there had been a fight in there, and whoever it was that was fighting had been serious about it. Stuff was slung everywhere, and there was even some dried turds on the floor. From the heavy coating of dust, and the dryness of the turds, it was easy to figure that the fight had taken place a long time before and things had been left as they were.

There was a shelf dangling by one nail over the fireplace mantel. A hatchet and an ax was leaning up against the wall near the hearth. There was a metal rod in the fireplace, and it went from one side of it to the other, and had a big black pot hanging on it. There was a little fire under the pot. I could see where the old woman had chopped up some furniture for firewood.

While we cleaned, I watched the old woman out of the corner of one eye, and I watched that ax and hatchet with the other. I didn't want to add murder to my criminal activities, but more than that, I didn't want to be murdered, which was a thing I thought might be in the planning.

The old woman pointed out a broom to Jinx, and Jinx took it and went to sweeping. The old woman opened the door so she could sweep the dust and such out. It was an old broom, handmade from a slightly crooked stick, some twine, and straw. I figured she probably rode it around the room on full-moon nights.

This went on for some time, this cleaning. I was wondering how it was with Mama and Terry, and this wondering got answered for me about the time we had the place mostly straightened up.

Mama, having not listened to me about staying where she was, or going on without us, come up to the open door just as Jinx was sweeping out some dirt. Mama stuck her pretty head inside. When she did, the old woman pressed the pistol to her nose and without so much as a howdy-do said, "Come on in. There's plenty of work."

Mama looked at the gun and the old woman behind it, then she looked at Jinx holding the broom, and then at me. I had just finished righting all the chairs and was standing there with my face hanging out.

"You didn't stay so good, did you?" I said.

"I got worried," Mama said.

"And I got the gun," said the old woman. "Come in this house."

Mama came in and went right to work. The old woman went back to the rocker and rocked back and forth, pointing the pistol at us.

I managed to get close to Mama and say, "Where's Terry?"

"Down by the river," she said. "I thought he'd be fine until I found you."

"I told you to go on," I said.

"You can tell me as you choose," she said. "And I can do as I choose."

"Y'all shut up," said the old woman.

We washed dishes and straightened up both rooms of the house. Then the old woman guided us outside with the pistol at our backs, and we came to a woodpile. There was an ax with a rusty blade sticking up in a log. There was some pieces of kindling lying around. Some of it was cut in two, but most of it was big stuff with little limbs still on it. You could see where it had been whittled at now and again. There was a wooden wheelbarrow next to the log, and there was grass grown up around it.

"It takes me too long to get anything done anymore," she said. "Used to I could cut down a whole tree and turn it into boards, or firewood, or shingles, or a box of toothpicks. I ain't got the strength no more to push the wheelbarrow, let alone cut wood."

She had Jinx take the ax and start chopping. She made me and Mama gather up firewood and stack it in the wheelbarrow. She was wily enough not to get too close to any of us, especially Jinx, who was swinging the ax with an enthusiasm that had little to do with splitting wood. Every time Jinx brought the ax down, you could imagine her splitting that old woman's head from crown to jaw.

While we worked, the old woman kept looking at me and Mama, and eventually she said, "You two some kind of kin?"

"Mother and daughter," Mama said.

"You look alike plenty in the face, except the girl's got a stouter jaw," the old woman said.

I can't say as any of this was meant as a compliment, but I was surprised to have any part of Mama recognized in myself, and it made me feel kind of good, even if I had a stout jaw. That said, the whole thing with Terry lying down there by the river was starting to get to me, and I decided I had to say something about it, take a chance, because if we didn't get him away from there before long, he might be dead. Or Skunk might come up and finish him off.

I put a piece of wood in the wheelbarrow, looked over at the old woman and her gun. Out in the sunlight, I could see the whites of her eyes was weepy and red, and the eyes themselves was dark as wet pecan shells. She didn't have but a few rotting teeth in her mouth.

"Listen, ma'am, I have to tell you there's a wounded boy down there by the river. He traveled here with us. We just wanted some food, and had to leave him there for a while. My mama was supposed to be watching him, but she abandoned ship."

"I was worried about you," Mama said.

I plowed on. "We don't want no trouble. We've cleaned your house, and gathered up wood. We been here for hours, and he's been down there, hurt. I ain't asking to get shot, but I got to go down there and get him. That's all there is to it. Fact is it will probably take two of us to bring him back."

The old woman pursed her dry lips and narrowed her weepy eyes. "I tell you what. I'll keep this mother of yours, and you and this girl go down there and get him. I'll take a look at him. You don't come back right smart, I'm going to shoot your mama in the head."

"All right," I said. "But you got to give us time to get down there and get hold of him and bring him back. He's a good-sized boy and he can't walk at all, so we got to tote him."

"Just get on with it."

We went down there, and Terry was still lying in the boat. Me and Jinx tugged him out of it, being careful as we could, and laid him gently on the ground. Then we pulled the boat all the way on shore, dragged it under a tree. There wasn't no time to waste, so we didn't try to hide it, just left it. I took our two lard buckets out of it, carried them over to where a bunch of blackberry vines grew, and pushed the cans down in them. It wasn't a great hiding place, but it was something.

Terry was out of it, and he had a fever hot as the devil's ass. I got him by the legs and Jinx got his arms, and we managed our way up the riverbank and onto the grass field. We had to put him down a few times and regroup, but we stayed with it.

It had already been getting late when we went down there, and now the sun was angling off behind some trees in a big red glow. Within half an hour, it would be dark.

We got Terry up to the house, and when we did, the old woman was standing there in the doorway with her pistol. She waved the pistol at us, and we carried him inside. She had us lay him out on an old woven rug that might have been some color or another once. Mama was sitting in a chair, her hands in her lap. Near the fireplace was all the wood we had gathered up. The wheelbarrow was by the fireplace.

"I know we ain't a concern of yours," I said. "But he sure needs help. If you could just let me attend to him best I can."

"You go over there and stand by your mama," she said, then swung the pistol at Jinx. "You too, girl."

Me and Jinx went to opposite sides of the chair where Mama was and sat down on the floor. I had made up my mind that soon as the chance opened up, I was going to jump that old bat, take my odds with gunfire. I was fed up. My take was if I could get my hands on her, them old bones would get snapped like dry kindling.

The old woman bent down on her knees, the way a horse will do when it goes to settle down before it falls on its side. She did a bit of that until she was off her knees and on her butt. She laid the pistol on the rug beside Terry, reached out, and felt his forehead.

She glanced up at us. "There's a well out to the side. One of you girls, but not both, go out there and crank up a bucket of water and bring it back."

I went out and did that. When I came back and sat the bucket down, the old woman wasn't paying me a lot of mind. The gun was lying on that dusty rug within easy reach. But I hesitated. She was looking at Terry's hand, and there was something about the way she did it made me think she might even know what she was doing. I went over and sat down on the floor again.

"That hand ain't no good," said the old woman. "You there," she said to Jinx. "Go over there to that trunk, open it up, and bring me that long wooden box out of it."

Jinx brought the box. This time the old woman had hold of the gun. I guess all that business she had said about having a slave when she was a child and selling it off made her realize Jinx might be in a bad mood. Anyway, Jinx put the box down, and the old woman had me roll over a log of firewood. I couldn't figure what that was about, but when I was done with that, I went back and sat down on the floor again.

The old woman rolled up the sleeve of the injured arm, and when she did, I let out a gasp. Not only was the hand looking dark and full of sin, so was the arm, near up to the elbow. She put her bony fingers on the side of his neck.

"He ain't got much pulse," she said. "He ain't gonna last no time at all with that arm on him. He may not last long with it off."

"Say what?" I said.

"You get that bucket of water I had you bring up, and pour it in that pot by the fire. Take down the pot hanging there, stoke up the fire, and put the water on to heat. I'm going to have to take that arm."

"Take it?" Jinx said.

"It's got to come off," said the old woman.

"The hell it does," Jinx said.

"It ain't no skin off my nose neither way," said the old woman. "But it needs to come off, and I know how to do it."

"You could let us go and we could take him to the doctor," I said.

"I could, but I ain't going to," said the old woman. "Besides, I ain't got no car, and I ate my plow mule, which is why the house was a mess. I went out and shot him and it didn't kill him, and he run in here through the open door and we had a hell of a fight. I bet I shot him four times. He was kicking and bucking and throwing turds. He made quite a mess of the place. Even when he went down, I had to reload and shoot him another couple of times. I was right fond of that mule. I point that out to let you understand that you people I don't even know. So don't try to get feisty.

"What I'm telling you gals is, by the time you've toted him out, even if I was to let you go, he'll be deader than a dirt clod. Even with his arm off he don't have a big chance. He's gotten bad off."

We just sat there stunned, trying to take in all she was saying.

The old woman patted the wooden box.

"This here is a surgeon's box," she said. "My daddy was a surgeon in the Civil War, and after the war he was a doctor way out on the far side of Texas, near a town called Mason. When I was just twelve or so, I helped him nurse folks. I know how this is done. I helped him do it a few times, and I even done it a couple times myself when he was older and sick and took to the bottle. Didn't no one know I did it, as the patients was under ether. But I knew the way to go about it from watching Daddy. I'll have to cut through quick, lay out a flap of skin, and saw through the bone. I can do that before you could wipe your ass."

"You can't do that to him," Jinx said, her eyes wet with tears. "He's too pretty to lose an arm."

"Everyone is prettier today than they will be tomorrow," the old woman said. "But dead ain't pretty at all."

"I ought to grab up a piece of firewood and stove your head in," Jinx said.

"You could try that," the old woman said. "But I know how to give him a chance. I can't do that with my head stove in. And this here pistol is known to my hand. It was my daddy's, and he killed Yankees with it. It's been converted to cartridges, and it's got six in it. I'm a good shot. I've killed plenty of game and a crazy mule, and when I was young and pretty as your mama there I once shot a suitor who didn't know where to keep his hands. After he was dead, my daddy and brothers hung him to a tree and rode past him on horses and hit him with clubs until you wouldn't have known if he was a man or a side of beef. So I got the stomach for it."

"Why would you help us?" I asked.

"I don't rightly know," the old woman said.

Mama said, "His arm is bad, kids. It's real bad. He's getting worse by the moment."

"You mean we ought to cut it off?" I said.

The old woman spoke before Mama could. "You don't, I got some shovels tucked up under the back of the house there. They'll fit you girls' hands good enough to dig a grave."

I looked at Terry. He hardly seemed to be breathing.

"Go ahead and do it," Mama said.

"What?" I said. "How come you get to choose?"

"Someone's got to."

"She's just a mean old woman wants to cut something off, anything, and on anybody," Jinx said. "You don't get to say nothing. He's our friend, not yours."

"I can do it or I can't," the old woman said.

Jinx said, "Can we get a close look at him?"

The old woman picked up the pistol and scooted back on her butt a ways, said, "Gander all you want, but come at me, and I'll shoot."

Jinx moved over first, and I went right behind her. She leaned down, her eyes right close. "Terry," she said.

He didn't say nothing back. His eyes was rolled up in his head, white as fresh chicken eggs.

She touched his sweaty forehead. "He's so hot, Sue Ellen."

I touched him, too, and I was quick in agreement. "It's like there's a brush fire burning inside of him."

We looked at his arm. It was mostly black now, and swollen up about the size of a plumped-up ham. There was red streaks above the black part, and meat was starting to peel off the arm. It smelled strong of rot. It was oozing pus, and flies had laid maggots in it.

"I don't think there's no choice," I said, looking at Jinx.

"I don't want to make that call," she said.

"Ain't there a doctor somewhere near?" I said to the old woman.

"You could take him by boat, if I was to let you leave, and I won't do that. I need you people to help me out. I'm old. I ain't got nobody else."

"Only friends you can have is the ones you keep at the end of a gun barrel," Jinx said.

"I reckon that's true," the old woman said. "And I can live with that."

I looked to Mama. I had learned to take my own advice over the years, but now I wanted some.

"What do we do, Mama?"

"A doctor would be best," Mama said. "But even a doctor couldn't save that arm. It's already lost. The only thing now is to not lose Terry. It's better to lose a piece of him than all of him."

"Listen to her," said the old woman.

"We should have took him right away to a doctor," Jinx said. "When he first got hurt."

"Shoulda, woulda, coulda," the old woman said.

"Cut it off, you old bat," I said, tears in my eyes. "And do it right. Do it right, or gun or no gun, so help me, I'll kill you and hang you in a tree and beat you with a stick like your father and brothers did that poor man."

"Once you're dead it don't matter," the old woman said. "Nothing matters then."

"Do it, then!" Jinx said. "Do it! Do it and get it over with, you old witch!"

"Y'all push back there, and I'm going to need you, woman," she said, nodding at Mama. "And you two are going to have to do what I say when I call on you. Make sure that water's hot."

The old woman opened the wooden box. There was a leather strap in there, and she took it out and fastened it on Terry's arm above the elbow and tightened it off with a metal screw from the box. She got out a little bottle and put it on the floor.

"That would have been ether," she said, "but I ain't got no more of it. He'll have to do without it."

"What is it for?" Jinx said.

"It puts a person under, makes them loopy," she said. "They don't feel so much pain."

"So what's Terry got for pain?" Jinx asked.

"He ain't got nothing but me quick at work," she said. "He

might come out of his doze, and if he does, you got to hold him down. You got to hold his head, arms, and legs. You may have to put your butt on him, but you got to hold him down." She laced her old, gnarly fingers together and cracked them gently. "Let's get started."

22

The old woman fastened the leather strap and twisted the screw. Pus oozed out all over Terry's hand, wrist, and forearm.

"I'm going to cut beneath the elbow, down as far as seems smart. I'm going to cut a lot of bone and keep as much skin as I can, but a lot of it's rotten. I may not get to flap it after all. I might have to nub it at the bone, which ain't as good. But we got what we got."

The old woman looked at us. "I'm going to push this pistol aside now, and you can wrestle it away if you have a mind to. I ain't so strong anymore. But you do, this boy won't get the surgery. If you nab it after the surgery, I may decide not to close it up right. You got to leave the gun to me. I see in your eyes you got plans, but I'm telling you, when he's cut and sawed and sewed, you're going to need me to make sure he don't go under. He might anyway. But you got to leave me be, cause if he's got any kind of chance, that chance is me."

There were saws and an assortment of blades in the box. The

old woman picked out what she needed, had us take them and dump them in the pot of water, which was now boiling something fierce. She cranked the screw some more, tightened the strap on his arm. Terry groaned once, and then lay silent and still.

There were tongs in the box, and she had us dunk those in the water and use them to get hold of the instruments, lift them out of the water, and place them across the box. I figured if she was trying to be clean, there was a chance the box wasn't all that sanitary, but we was beyond that moment. This was as good as it was going to get, and I knew it.

When the instruments was cooled a mite, she clicked them into the saw handles with her hands, which didn't look all that clean themselves, said, "Now you better hold him."

It was as bad as you might think. She went with the knife first, and she cut into the meat, and deep, and when she did, Terry started to scream. He tried to sit up, but Jinx sat on his head, like an elephant on a stool. I had hold of his legs, Mama his good arm, and the old witch had the other arm by the oozing wrist. She cut around that arm like she was notching an arrow, and then she chunked the knife aside and grabbed a saw and went at it. She sawed fast. When the bone was near cut through, she stopped and sat back and sweated and breathed heavy.

Terry was screaming loud enough to wake the dead, and considering Jinx had her butt square on his head, it was quite a feat. He tried to get loose of us, but we held him down.

"I ain't as young as I used to be," said the old woman. "I'm tuckered out, but I ain't through the bone yet. And the saw's done got dull."

Without a word, Mama grabbed up another blade, fastened it in the old blade's place. She got to work, finishing up the job in a few seconds. When she had it done, the old woman, who had cut the arm in such a way as to leave a good-sized flap of good skin hanging, folded it over, got a needle and stout thread from the box, and went to sewing.

Somewhere during all this, Terry quit screaming or moving, and for a moment, I thought Jinx had smothered him with her butt. But when she got off of him I saw right off he was breathing. He was passed out.

The old woman was breathing heavily, and I thought I could hear her heart knocking against her chest like a moth beating its wings inside a jar.

Jinx got the pistol off the floor. "Now that he's sewed up," she said, cocking it, "I figure I can just go on and put a bullet through your head."

The old woman looked at her with the same excitement you show for a salad.

I got to say this for Jinx, she's one of them can do what she says she's going to do, cause she pulled the trigger. There was a snapping sound. She cocked and pulled it again, and nothing happened. She glanced down at the pistol.

The old woman scratched her chin, said, "It's got shells in it, but ain't none of them got loads in them. I screwed them loose and poured out the powder. I used that powder to burn out a wound I got on my knee one time. Works pretty good you know what you're doing and can take the pain, and don't use so much you catch on fire or blow your ass in the wind."

Jinx lifted the pistol as if to hit the old woman. Mama caught her hand. "She's bad; we don't have to be."

"I ain't that bad," said the old lady, looking truly surprised, her face drooping like wax melting off a candle. "I done saved that boy's life. I'm just here alone and ain't no one left to take care of me."

"Ain't nobody wants to," Jinx said, jerking her hand free. "Why would they?"

"Everybody needs someone to help," said the old woman. "Everyone's got to have somebody."

"They don't always get it," Jinx said.

"You have a point," the old woman said, and tried to get off the floor, but couldn't make it.

"I say we take her out and hang her from a tree and beat her head in with a stick," Jinx said. "The way Sue Ellen said we ought to, the way this old witch said her daddy done that fella."

"We won't do that," Mama said.

"You ain't got no say in this thing," Jinx said, but she didn't get no farther. Mama reached out and snatched the pistol from Jinx's hand and tossed it away, banging it up against the wall, causing some dusty knickknack of some kind to fall off a shelf and explode.

"I don't want to hear that again," Mama said. "I do have a say. I might not have at first, but there's nothing you've been through that I haven't. I say what I want, and if you think you can do what you want with her, then you got to start with me. We aren't those kind of people. You had shot her, you would have regretted it. You don't want to be that way. You aren't that way."

"I might be," Jinx said.

"She's right, Jinx," I said. "We ain't like that. We don't want to be same as her."

Jinx looked at the floor and Terry's blood that had pooled there. She looked at the old woman, who was trying to appear pitiful. A dog with a thorn in its paw couldn't have looked as miserable as she did.

Mama helped the old woman up, guided her to the rocking chair. Once in the rocker, the old woman rocked gently, glaring at us with her watery eyes, breathing heavily.

"You need to clean that blood off my floor," she said between breaths. "I done your boy a favor, now do me one. You owe me."

"You are something," Mama said, and shook her head.

I looked at Terry, then at the old woman. "We're going to put him in your bed, and that's where he's going to stay until he gets well enough we can haul him out. You'll just have to sleep in that chair for a few days. I just hope him nesting in your bed won't get him some kind of disease, or that some of your meanness is under the covers and crawls all over him."

The old woman wrinkled her nose, closed her eyes, leaned back in the chair, and started rocking furiously.

We went out to the well and got some water to clean up with. There was blood all over the floor, and we was all covered in it, too. Mama heated up some water and washed our clothes while we all stood around with the old woman's blankets wrapped around us. Mama even helped the old woman change her clothes and wiped her down a bit, all of this done in privacy in the bedroom. We wiped up the blood on the floor and rolled up the bloody rug where Terry had been operated on and put it aside at the far side of the room.

We found some whiskey and poured that on Terry's nub to keep out infection. The old woman had some aspirin, so we gave him a couple of those. He was still mostly out of it, and I doubt he remembered chewing them or sipping water. When Mama had him dressed in his freshly washed and dried clothes, we carried him to the bedroom and put him in the bed with a prop of pillows and a thin blanket over him.

I got a rag and went back to the other room and picked up Terry's cut-off arm and put it in the box with the saws, then closed it up. I put it on the mantel over the fireplace. I didn't know what else to do with it.

I went in and looked at Terry, sat in a chair by the bed for a while, then Jinx took over for a stretch.

Out in the other room the old woman was still in her rocker. Mama put some pillows in the chair to make her more comfortable, got a blanket to drape over her knees. The old woman was cleaned up now, but she still had on that stupid bonnet, and there were drops of Terry's blood on it where the wound had spewed when she first cut through the arm. She rocked and looked at the fire in the fireplace.

Mama was using the fire and one of the big black pots to cook up some dandelion greens she had gathered near the front door of the house. She found a bottle of vinegar, and some salt and black pepper, and done as much as she could with it.

While it cooked, night fell solid. I went over and made sure the door lock was thrown. There was little wooden doors that closed from inside over the windows. I closed them all and threw the latches on them.

"There's screens over a couple of them windows," the old woman said. "You could leave them shutters open. It'll be cooler."

I didn't answer her. I would have preferred cool air, but I was thinking about Skunk. I had let thought of him slip away for a while, but now he was back on my mind.

I took Jinx a bowl of greens, came back, and got my own. I sat on the floor near Mama and the old woman, who smacked over those cooked weeds with her gummy mouth so loud a hog would have left the room in embarrassment. But we couldn't leave; we had to bear it. So we sat and ate. It tasted good, though anything would have tasted good about then that wouldn't break a tooth off.

When the old woman was finished, she gave me her bowl to put aside, leaned back, and rested her hands on her belly. "I ain't always lived like this. We was cotton money. Had slaves. I remember it. I was, let me see . . . ten years old when the War Between the States come to its unfortunate end. We went to growing corn when the cotton was played out, and we did all right for a time.

Then this and that happened, a few hot years with not enough rain, and we was in a hole we couldn't never get out of again. Daddy eventually had enough of it and shot himself. Mama run off with someone, and my sister got married and moved up north. Married a damn Yankee, can you imagine? And him a former solider against the South. I had just as soon seen her take up with a horse thief.

"Anyway, cause of that, we didn't never speak again, never exchanged a letter. My brother went off to the war and didn't come back. He might have got killed, or he might have stayed over there. Ain't nobody knows. Wasn't never heard of again. I eventually had to sell the house and the land. I kept this piece on the back end of it, had a house built, been here for years. Them that owned the land that had been mine gave up and moved on, and the woods claimed it. So I guess it's same as if it all still belonged to me. Married once, but Hiram liked to mess with other women. I shot the son of a bitch, told everyone he run off."

"You killed him?"

"Deader than a doornail," she said. "Ain't nobody knows but me and ya'll. I've kept it to myself, for reasons I figure are clear. Now, though, at my age, what's it matter who knows what? He was buried out near where the woods start to grow up some thirty-five years ago. About five years ago I found a skull out in the yard, dug up and gnawed on by a coyote from the looks of it. I'm pretty sure it was Hiram. I broke it up with the ax. I was still strong enough then to do it. Lately, I've got down in my back some. Ain't got the energy to get nothing done. Last thing I done was kill that mule and skin it up and eat it. I wouldn't have done it, except I couldn't feed it no more, and I was hungry myself. It was a good old mule, and me and him done a lot of plowing in our time. I figured if he could have figured out some way to kill me and eat me for corn, he would have. I reckon I just got to him first."

I grinned in spite of myself.

"Killing that mule tuckered me out such, I ain't never come back to myself. That's why I was glad to see ya'll."

"We could have cleaned the place for a meal," I said. "You didn't need to threaten us with a pistol."

"The gun was empty."

"We didn't know that."

"I wanted to keep you around. I guess at the bottom of it, I knew it wouldn't work out. But it seemed like a good idea at the time."

In that moment, I surprised myself by feeling sorry for her.

"What are all of you afraid of?" she said. "What are you running from?"

"Who says we're running or afraid?" Mama said.

"Your eyes," said the old woman. "Way you look around. Check the door and the windows."

"Why would it matter to you?" I said.

"It don't, except if they come for you, they might come for me," the old woman said. "I figure I got a right to know on account of that."

"You lost your rights to much of anything when you held us prisoner," I said.

"Maybe she ought to know," Mama said. "Maybe she's earned that by saving Terry."

"She just wanted to see she could still cut someone's arm off," I said.

"Me and your mama together did a good job, didn't we?" the old woman said. "Me and her saved that boy."

"I still hate you," Jinx called from the other room.

"All right, here's the short version," I said. "We made some people mad. We're on our way to California, and they got a man named Skunk on our tail. That's as much as you need to know."

"Skunk?" the old woman said, and I swear, even there in the near dark, the room lit only by the fire in the fireplace, I was sure I could see her turn pale.

"You know of him?" I asked.

She nodded. "If that hellhound is on your trail, then you're already dead and just walking around."

"I don't plan to just roll over and let him have me," I said.

"It don't matter," said the old woman.

"It matters to me," I said.

"What you need to do is go in the bedroom there, look in the chifforobe and get the pistol shells, and load up that pistol. Then you ought to get the shotgun out of the closet. It's loaded and there's a box of shells in there for it. I was going to try and get to it later and blow your head off, but I don't think I can get out of this chair again, and I doubt you'll help me over there so I can take hold of it."

"You got that right," Jinx called out.

I went and got the shells for the pistol, pulled the shotgun and shells for it from the closet. I gave the pistol to Jinx and she loaded it while I went back in the main room with the shotgun. It was a double-barrel. A twelve-gauge. I had the box of shells for it with me, and I sat down on the floor and laid the shotgun across my legs and set the box of shells nearby.

"Surely," Mama said, "he's given up by now."

"He don't give up," the old woman said. "He might take a break, get bored, or decide to go off and look at something he ain't seen for a day or two, but he'll come back."

"You're just going on old stories," I said.

She shook her head. She licked her lips, said, "I heard tell my mama and daddy knew Skunk's mama. That after the slaves was freed, she used to work for our family, doing laundry and stuff, cooking. She lived in a shack on the back end of her former master's property, Eval Turpin. The master was long dead, but his grandson, Justin, lived there without no living kin. But them that had been slaves he let live on the farm, let their children and their children's children live there, too. He didn't hire them or pay them nothing, cause he didn't have nothing himself. Like my family, when cotton wasn't king no more, his family went broke, and stayed that way.

"One of the women living there was named Mary, and she got with baby by a half-Comanche nigger, and had a child. She called him Absalom. He wasn't never right, would stir the ground with a stick, killing ants, just grinning. That's what Daddy said. Said he talked all the time, but a lot of it was nonsense. He was even suspected of killing one of Daddy's prize coonhounds by feeding it meat with broken glass in it. Daddy said he never knew for sure, but suspected it. Said that old dog was just as good a dog as there was, and followed Absalom around like he was the boy's pet, and then the boy did that to him. Probably just to see him suffer.

"When Absalom was little, his daddy, the half-breed, got tired of hearing his babble, and held him down and pulled out his tongue with a pair of pliers, and run off, and wasn't never seen again. Wasn't but a few years later, when the boy was ten or so, his mama got scared of him. Said she'd wake up at night and he'd be standing over her, just looking down at her the way he looked at those ants. One morning she gathered him up and took him out in a boat. It was the boy's birthday, and she later said she thought that was about the right time to do it. She told him they was going fishing, but what she did was she shoved him out of the boat, and pushed him in the water, leaned out of the boat and held him under.

"My daddy said she done it and didn't feel bad about it, because she thought there was something in that child that was wrong, and that she was doing what she ought to do. What God would have wanted her to do. She said she could see that boy's eyes looking up at her from beneath the water, looking up through the cracks of her fingers as she held him down. She said his eyes was cold as marbles. He didn't drown, though. She took a boat paddle to him and hit him some licks with it, and he floated off. She thought he was dead. But he ended up on shore, and he lived. Stayed out in the woods like a wild animal. He lived in such a wild way he got a stink about him, and that's how he come to be called Skunk."

"I done told them this story," Jinx said.

"Well, then," the old woman said, "if you told it like I told it, then you told it true."

"The pliers part was new," Jinx said.

"That's the little detail that matters," said the old woman.

"You didn't mention about how he lives in places where he hangs up bones and such, and they rattle in the wind."

"I ain't never heard that part," said the old woman.

"You didn't tell nothing but a story most everyone tells," Jinx said. "I don't believe your daddy knew Skunk or his mama. I think you're just yarning."

"I'm telling it like it was told to me," she said. "From white men, reliable and truthful."

"Ha," Jinx said.

"Now, here's some more details," said the old woman. "After Skunk was grown, after everyone thought he was dead and rotted away in the woods, he come back. He was a young man by then, and somehow he had survived. Daddy said one morning Justin Turpin went down to Mary's shack cause he was starting to take up with her in secret, but when he got there she was skinned and nailed to the side of the shack like a deer hide. She was just a head and a skin, and he had put a boat paddle between her teeth. He hadn't never forgot, and that's how everyone knew who it was. What had been inside her was outside of her, piled up on a chopping block in the yard, and it was still warm. Turpin had missed Skunk by just a few minutes. Her hands was gone. Chopped off. They say he does that now all the time, when he kills someone, on account of his mama's hands holding him under that water, and him trying to come up, and those hands holding him down. I can't vouch that's the reason, but that's how folks guess at it. He don't like the thought of hands because a pair almost drowned him.

"Anyway, in time he got to be known about, and it got known, too, that he was a tracker and a killer if you paid him with the things he wanted. I thought by now he might really be dead, but if you're telling your story true, I reckon he ain't."

"No," I said. "He ain't. But we haven't seen him in days."

"He's like the heat, wind, rain, and the earth," the old woman said. "Days to him ain't nothing. He ain't one for time. He does what he does cause he's been asked, and he's getting something out of it. Shoes, or food, or hats and such. Or at least that's his reasons if you look at the surface of the thing, but you scratch them reasons a little, it's got more to do with him doing it because he likes it. He got him a taste of killing, and for him, it was sweet. Once he sets out on the job, he's going to finish it, come hell or high water, even if he takes his time about it. And now you done brought this stone killer to my door."

"Thought you wanted company," Jinx said.

The old woman shook her head. "I figure it don't matter. The hand of fate is already laid upon me. I'm going to die soon."

"You old fool," Jinx said. "You're near three hundred years old. Of course you're going to die soon, and should have been dead already."

"Let's be quiet before we wake Terry up," Mama said. "Let's let him rest."

23

It was early morning, the sun leaking light through the edges of the shutters like river water, but that wasn't what brought me awake. It was the screaming.

I sprung to my feet, holding the shotgun. The screaming was coming from the bedroom. The door was still open and I could see Terry, awake and aware now. Feeling pain and knowing he had lost an arm and hadn't had a say in the matter. He was sitting up, trying to throw a foot out of bed.

Jinx was on the bed with him, holding him back by his good arm. But he was showing some serious strength for a worn-out, one-armed fella.

Me and Mama rushed in there, tried to comfort him, but it wasn't no use. He went on like that, screaming and yelling about his arm, struggling. It took all three of us to pin him to the mattress. Finally he was just so weak from all that had gone on, he fell back on the bed unconscious.

The three of us was shaken bad. We made sure he was all right, not bleeding from the stump, then went out and closed the door.

"He woke up screaming for me to put his arm back on," Jinx said. "I tried to tell him we had to do it. I hope I was telling him right."

The old woman in her rocker, her back to us, hadn't stirred through any of this. That infuriated Jinx.

"You don't care about him or nobody," Jinx said to the old woman's back. "You could hear him scream all night, and it wouldn't be anything to you."

The old woman didn't respond, just sat still in her rocker.

Jinx was really mad. She went around front of the rocker, started to say something to her, and stopped. The look on Jinx's face made us come around to look at her. We looked closer at the old woman, seen her mouth was hanging open. Her eyes looked like they was filmed over with candle wax. She was dead.

"That figures." Jinx put her hands on her hips. "She didn't die bad at all. She just went in her sleep after three hundred and fifty million years of meanness."

"Poor thing," Mama said.

Jinx looked at Mama with a look of confusion, shook her head. "You white people are something."

"Don't make us a pair," I said. "I can't feel no sympathy for her, neither."

"She's still a human being," Mama said. "God makes all human beings, no matter who they are."

"Well, he needs him a better mold," Jinx said, "cause some of these he's making ain't worth the waste of material."

Now, I ain't proud of this next part, but we wasn't sure what to do with the old woman. We didn't even know her name, and really didn't want to. We was also scared right then of going outside after all that talk about Skunk, and though we knew we'd have to in time, we decided it was more than we was ready to handle right then. So what we done was we took that bloody rug we had rolled up and laid aside, unrolled it, and wrapped her up in it. We done it so good you couldn't see nothing left of her but the bottoms of her shoes on one end and the top of her cotton bonnet on the other. Then we put her and the rug in the closet and shut the door. It seemed like a good idea at the time.

So now the day wore on, and we looked around the house for some food and found some dried-out biscuits in the stove warmer. If there had been enough of them, we could have used them to build a wall around the house — and it would have been solid, too. We soaked the biscuits in water till they wouldn't break your teeth off, and ate what we could of them.

I took some of the wet bread into Terry, who was starting to stir. He was covered in sweat, but then again, it wasn't just his condition. We all were sweating. It was summer hot and the house was closed up tight as an old maid's purse. The idea of opening some windows was mentioned, but no one wanted to be the one that let Skunk in, so we just grinned and stood it.

By the time I come into Terry's room with the biscuits, Mama and Jinx had stretched out on some pallets in the living room, cause it was my time with him, and as that was the case, and as he was awake and needed to be fed, I closed the door and sat down in the chair next to the bed.

I tried to give him some of them softened biscuits, but he wouldn't have none of it. He pushed the tin plate to the other side of the bed. He said, "You shouldn't have allowed my arm to be removed."

"There wasn't no choice. You had been out of it for some time, and was sick and feverish, and that arm of yours was black as a hole in the ground, and juicy-like with pus."

He sat there for a while, said, "What did you do with it?"

"We put it in a box," I said.

"Where is it now?"

"It's in the other room on a shelf."

"On a shelf?"

"We hadn't been wanting to go outside no more because of Skunk. The old lady knew about him." I told Terry all she had said. I finished with: "The old lady is dead and rolled up in a rug and stuck in the closet."

"What happened to the money and May Lynn?"

"Down by the river pushed up under some blackberry bushes."

"You sure there wasn't another alternative when it came to my arm?" Terry asked.

"If that means another choice, I don't think so."

"May I see it?"

"Your arm?"

"Yes."

"What for?"

"I want to see the shape it was in."

"It's been cut off all day and it's warm," I said.

"I understand that," he said.

"All right," I said, and went quietly out the door and got the box. I went back to the bedroom, closed the door again, and set the box on the bed, opened it up. Stink came out of it like a dead fish. Terry wrinkled his nose, looked in.

"Close it up, Sue Ellen."

I did.

"You did right," he said. "It had progressed to an irreparable stage."

"It would have killed you," I said. "Old woman who kept us here was as rotten as they come, rotten as that arm, but she knew how to cut it off, though Mama had to finish up the job."

"There's an old woman wrapped in a rug?"

"In the closet."

"After all we have been through," Terry said, "something like that shouldn't astonish me."

"Terry, I got to ask you about something I think I've figured out, and I wish I hadn't."

He looked at me while I tried to find the words. I couldn't find them, least not right away.

"I thought you might have something on your mind," he said. "Way you're staring at me, I doubt it's just because I am a cripple."

"It ain't that at all."

"Then let loose with it."

"May Lynn, when we found her body, it had a sewing machine wired to it, tied off in a bow. Later, when I was down by the river, I came upon a bag you had tied. I had seen it before, the way you tied it off, but it didn't hit me because I couldn't believe such a thing. But it struck me then, way that bow looked. It wasn't wire, but it had the same look about it that wire bow had. It got me to thinking. You was sure all fired up about burning her to ash and taking her off to Hollywood. Also, your mama, she was a seamstress, and your stepdaddy made her get rid of her stuff, and then it all come together."

Terry looked at the wall the way you would if you could see enemy soldiers marching toward you.

"I don't know why you done it, Terry," I said. "That's what's been hard for me to cipher, but I think you done it. I feel bad for thinking that way, but it sure looks like——"

"I did it," he said. "I am responsible."

Even though I figured as much, hearing him say it made it feel like someone had ripped the bottom out of the world.

"Why?" I said.

"It isn't what you might conjecture," he said.

"Then what kind of 'jecture is it?"

Terry leaned back heavily against the pillows. The air in the room was as stuffy as if we was in a tow sack with a bunch of chicken feathers.

"We have all been so close for years," he said, "and now it's come to this."

"How did it happen?" I said. "And why?"

"Me and her had begun to talk privately. I had come to the conclusion that she was on her way to Hollywood. I was glad for her, really, and even then I thought I might go with her. She confided in me about a lot of things, and one of those things was she was certain that she could cure me."

"Cure you?"

"Of being a sissy."

"Oh."

"I believed my life would be enhanced if I could be attracted to girls. I knew from the way men acted around her that if I could be attracted to anyone, it should be her. But it wasn't that way. Well, not the way it should be, boy and girl, that sort of thing. We were out at the swimming hole, at night, up in the old oak over the river, out on the big limb. It was night and she was stripped off, and so was I, like we had done many times before, and she stood up on the limb, and positioned herself on it with a knee forward, her hands on her hips, said to me, 'Terry, how do you like my body?'

"I wasn't entirely sure how to respond to that question, so I said something like: 'It's excellent. Very nice.' This just made her mad. I didn't know what I was supposed to say. She said, 'You can't look at me and want me the way a man wants a woman?'

"I said, 'I guess not,' and May Lynn, she says, 'Everyone wants me, and if you don't, then you are a queer and you'll stay that way,' or words to that effect. She said that very mean, and I was so upset with her I pushed her. I didn't mean to do it, or rather I didn't even know I was doing it until she went backward off the limb and fell in the water."

"She's jumped out of that tree plenty," I said. "How'd that kill her?"

"It didn't," Terry said. "I looked down at her, and she looked up and laughed. Not in a fun way, like we'd had a bit of a disagreement, but like she knew why I had done it. That I was in fact a sissy, and couldn't live up to what she thought a man ought to be. The worst part was she saw all that as something funny and pathetic. I was so irate I leaped off that limb at her, gathered my feet beneath me cannonball-style. And I hit her, too. I remember looking down just in time to see her face look up at me, and I observed her expression change. It went from humor to fear, and I have to admit that in that brief moment, it pleased me. I hit on top of her. It was a hard hit. It drove both of us down deep in the water.

"When I floated up, I wasn't angry anymore, just frightened. I knew how hard I had dropped on her. I searched for her, but she wasn't anywhere to be seen. Then I saw her pop up in the moonlight like a cork. I think she shook her head a little, like there were cobwebs in her brain. She was drifting downriver, and I started swimming for her, hard as I could, but it seemed like the harder I tried, the more rapidly she was swept away. I couldn't catch up. She tried to swim, but she couldn't swim fast enough to defeat the current. She screamed, Sue Ellen. She screamed, and she called my name, and then she went under.

"I was at the end of my strength. I didn't leap after her. I knew if I did, I would drown as well. I struck out for shore. It didn't seem to me I was going to make it. Part of me didn't want to, but the other part of me, the cowardly part that wanted to live, just kept swimming. Next thing I knew I was on the shore. I looked out over the water, to see if I could find her, but I couldn't. She had gone under, and as far as I could tell, she hadn't come up."

"Jesus, Terry."

"That isn't the worst of it. I ran along the shore, calling her name, but nothing. And then I came to a place where the river turned, and there she was. She had washed up in a bend and was banging up against the shore. I grabbed her and tugged on her until I managed to haul her from the river. I don't know how far I pulled her, but when I looked back at the river it was a far distance from me. I laid her out in the grass. I talked to her. I yelled at her. I sat her up, bent her over, thinking some of the water would come out of her, but she was gone.

"I didn't know what to do. I panicked. I started wandering around aimlessly. I finally walked back and got my clothes and got dressed. I got her dress because I couldn't stand for her to be naked like that. I pulled it on her body as best I could and left her there, decided to go home. It made sense all of a sudden. I would just go home. I was almost home and I thought: I left my friend lying back there dead in the grass and I didn't plan to tell anyone. I can't explain it. I thought if I tried to tell someone what had occurred, they might think I murdered her . . . Which I guess I did. Before I got home, I veered back to the place on the river where my stepfather had deposited all my mama's sewing materials. He had become angry, and didn't merely demand she quit, he made me help him load all her equipment, everything that had to do with her sewing business, in the back of his truck. We drove down to the river, backed to where it sloped off, and I had to get in the truck bed with him and help him toss everything out. He thought he'd shove the sewing machine out and it would slide into the river. It didn't make it all the way. It ended up partially in the river, partially on land.

"I remembered that event walking back home, and at the time, I thought it best to hide May Lynn's body. It doesn't seem smart at the moment, but back then the idea arrived in such a fashion I convinced myself it was a stroke of genius.

"There was some wire with the sewing machine. It had come out of the pickup. It was wire for binding bricks into piles, and it had been in the back of the truck. Some of it came out when we pushed Mama's equipment out. I got the wire and coiled it up and tried to carry the sewing machine.

"The machine was heavy. It took me hours to move it, having to stop and put it down and rest, dragging it most of the time. But I managed to get it to where her body lay. I carried her down to the river, went back and tugged the machine to her, fastened it to her with the wire. I pushed it off in the water, and she went with it. I got down in the water then, and ducked under and held my breath. I tugged on that sewing machine until I arrived at a drop-off I knew was there because I had fished the area before. Then I swam out and went home. I snuck in. I had snuck out to see May Lynn earlier. I had been gone so long I thought for sure I'd end up being discovered. Maybe I wanted to be. But everyone was sound asleep. I lay down and tried to sleep, but couldn't. A few days later you asked me to go fishing. When you told me where, I knew it was the spot where I had pulled her off into the water. I kept thinking she would be deep enough it wouldn't matter. I also knew if she was found, that would throw suspicion off of me. On top of that, I couldn't believe it had happened. It seemed like a horrible dream. And then we pulled her up. I knew when we were tugging on that line what it was. Knew as sure as I know I now have one arm. I should have confessed, but...I couldn't. I just couldn't.

"After that, all I could think about was getting her out to Hollywood. Before we had gotten into that spat, that's what she had talked about. She said she was going. I didn't know about the money. Not then. But now, thinking back on it, I understand that she had the money and she had the plan. And that night, in a moment of stupidity, I changed those plans. I killed her."

I considered on this a long time. "It was an accident, Terry. If it happened the way you said. It was an accident."

"It happened how I said. I jumped on top of her. I meant to

do it. But I didn't mean for that to happen. You have to believe me."

"I do," I said.

"Accident or not, it doesn't make me innocent," he said. "But I want you to know I didn't mean for her to die."

The door opened. Jinx came in; she lay across the bed and put her arm across Terry's chest. "I heard all that. I can't believe you didn't tell me, too. Instead I had to lean up against the door like a thief."

"I would have told you," Terry said. "She asked, so I told her. I had plans to reveal the same thing to you."

I glanced through the open doorway. Unlike Jinx, Mama hadn't heard a thing. I could hear her gently snoring. I think you could have set a firecracker off and she wouldn't have heard it.

I closed the door silently. Jinx kept hugging Terry. He patted her arm with his good hand.

"She shouldn't have teased you," Jinx said.

"That's no excuse," he said.

"Well, it wasn't right," Jinx said. "You are how you are, and May Lynn could think pretty high and mighty of herself at times. You ain't got no need to get cured of nothing. I'll tell you this, if it'll make you feel any better. I tried to kill the old woman here, and on purpose, not by any accident. But the gun didn't have no good bullets in it. It just clicked, and then she died on her own."

"That's best," Terry said.

"I consider it a disappointment," Jinx said.

24

It was decided not to tell Mama about what Terry had told us, least not right away, and that if it was told, we'd leave it to him to do it. I can't say it felt good to find out how May Lynn had died, but I believed Terry's story, and it made me feel some better to know he hadn't just outright murdered her.

We was locked up in that house for a day without much water, and with no real good food to eat, just the last of those greens Mama had cooked up, and they had soured. It finally got to where it was go out and get something to eat or just get in the closet with the old woman and wait for death. I wasn't certain Skunk was still out there anywhere, but if the stories about Skunk was true, then he could be. But my fear of Skunk couldn't feed us. I had to get some kind of groceries pulled into the house, even if they was blackberries and frog legs.

There was also the matter of the old woman in the closet. She had already started to stink. She had to be taken out and buried, if for no other reason than so we could stay in that cabin in peace.

I was thinking on all this, bored, prowling around the house, looking for food goods—dried beans or peas, or a very large mouse—and I come upon an old tin box. I opened it. There was some faded blue ribbons inside, a bit of string and such, and there was some old photographs. They was of a young girl and an older man. He was standing with his hand on the girl's shoulder. He had an expression like something inside him had backed up and stoppered and had turned rotten. The little girl had to be the old woman many years back. I could see something about that face that made me think it was her, but she looked happy. I wondered if she had been happy a lot when she was young. It was hard to imagine, but I reckoned it was true. The man in the picture had the same disappointed and bitter face the old woman had had; she had grown up to be him.

I slipped the photographs back in the tin and put it back where I had found it.

The food hunt being a failure, it was decided someone was going to have to stay with Terry, and someone was going to have to go out there in the big wide world and find something to eat, get the cans with the money and May Lynn. After that, it was all a crapshoot, because there wasn't no way Terry was well enough for being laid down in the bottom of a boat and floated down to Gladewater.

We had to come up with a plan, and we did. It wasn't the kind of plan that was going to be taught in military handbooks, but it was something, and it was this: me and Jinx would take the pistol and go and get water and find something to eat and get the cans. Mama would stay with Terry and keep the shotgun. But first we had to get a shovel and bury the old woman and Terry's sawed-off arm. The idea of the body and arm in the house with us, and the smell they was starting to make, led us to want to get rid of them right away.

Like I said, none of this was anything that would have given Robert E. Lee pause, but it's what we had.

We had Mama, against her disapproval, lock me and Jinx outside. Jinx carried the pistol, which was now loaded with real bullets, and me and her walked out back and found a shovel shoved up under the house, right where the old woman said it would be. We found some soft dirt that was far away from the well, and we took turns digging and holding the pistol. It took about two hours to get the grave dug deep and wide and long enough. When it was done, we went back to the house and called out to Mama and she let us in. Me and Jinx took the old woman out of the closet. We carried her outside and had Mama lock us out again. Jinx laid the pistol on top of the rolled rug, and with one of us carrying the head end, the other the feet, we toted her to the hole and laid her on the ground. Jinx set the pistol aside. We picked up the old woman again and dropped her in the hole. I ain't going to lie. It wasn't done gentle, and there wasn't no ceremony to it. We started covering her up right away, trying to keep an eye peeled for Skunk. Skunk didn't appear, and when we finally had her good and buried, Jinx took the shovel and patted the ground solid.

"Should we say some words?" I said.

"How about 'I'm glad you're dead, you old bitch'?"

"I was thinking of something nicer. Like she saved Terry's life by cutting off his arm."

"Well, then," Jinx said, "there, you said it."

Back at the house, we got the box of sawing tools with Terry's arm in it, and we took it out to a spot by the woods and dug a hole there and buried it.

Next we went down to the river to check on the lard cans and to look for food. I didn't see sign of Skunk nowhere, but I had this uncomfortable feeling that someone was watching us. I hadn't had it when we was digging the holes, but now I did, and it was a feeling strong as lye soap. It could have been Skunk, a nest of birds, or just my imagination, but whatever it was made my skin crawl like a snake.

When we got down to the river we seen there was big fresh boot prints in the mud by the water, and the boat we had pulled up under the tree had the bottom hacked out of it. When I saw that, the hair on the back of my neck stuck up like porcupine quills. I looked ever which way, and Jinx did, too, turning with that big horse pistol in her hands, but we didn't see no one. I sniffed the air. There seemed to be a faint stink hanging about, but it was possible I imagined it.

While Jinx watched, I went to where I had stuffed the cans under the berry vines. They was both there. I got hold of them, and we stood there for a moment trying to decide what to do.

"He's done hacked the boat up to keep us from leaving," Jinx said.

"We don't have to go by river," I said.

"No," Jinx said. "But it's harder for him to get us on the river. We walk out, we might as well just go on and hack off our own hands and cut our own throats now."

"We're out of choices."

"We still got the cabin, that's something," Jinx said.

"But no food," I said.

"We got to take care of that."

For a couple of scroungers, we didn't have nothing to carry anything with, so we decided to walk back to the cabin and leave the buckets and try and find a sack to gather up food. Like I said, we wasn't planners of the first order.

As we went back, that feeling of someone watching grew. I even heard movement off to our right. Jinx did, too, cause she turned the pistol in that direction. But there wasn't nothing to be seen other than a briar patch, and a mystifying briar patch it was. There was an opening in it here and there, but it was the largest, most twisted-up mess of briars I have ever seen; the whole thing was higher than a tall man's head. It curled and twined its way from where we was all the way back into the depths of the woods, down to the river.

It was a patch of vines and briars I figured had been there for darn near as long as there had been woods. The patch was more open near where we was, but looking back into it, it got wider and deeper and darker. The vines was big around as my thumb in lots of places, and bigger in others, and the thorns, which looked as sharp and vicious as barbed wire, grew close together in a way that reminded me of those nets you make that are thin at one end and wide at the other. A fish will swim through the neck into the bigger part, and then it's too dumb to get turned around and swim out.

When we got to the house, and Mama let us in, we put the buckets on the floor near the fireplace. We didn't tell Mama about the tracks and the boat. She was scared enough with us out there, and we still had to have food.

Outside again, Jinx with the pistol, me tugging a tow sack and a shovel, we went along near the woods and found some wild onions and more dandelion greens. We even dug up some sassafras bushes, got the roots for tea. Meat would have been nice, but there wasn't any that we could get unless we shot it, and neither me nor Jinx felt we was a good enough shot with a pistol to hit anything that we couldn't beat to death better with the barrel.

Finally we got our courage up and went back down by the river to where the berry vines were. We picked some berries and put them in the bag, though they got a mite mashed up with everything else in there. Jinx found a dead fish washed up on the bank next to a good-sized log. She picked the fish up and smelled it.

"It ain't been dead long," she said. "Pretty good-sized bass."

"What killed it?"

"Since it didn't leave a note," she said, "I'm going to figure it just died."

Jinx gave me the fish, and I put it in the bag.

It was late afternoon by the time we was back at the house with our fattened sack. Terry was sleeping, and Mama was sitting in the middle of the room in the old woman's rocking chair, holding the shotgun. The air was stiff as wire and sticky warm.

"We didn't even know her name," Mama said. "You buried her, and we don't even know what to call her."

"I knew what to call her," Jinx said.

Mama started to say something, realized it was useless. Nobody was on her side.

I cleaned the fish and put the guts and the head in the fireplace and burned them up. I got a frying pan that looked pretty clean, wiped it out with some rags, and used a bit of lard the old lady had to fry up the fish. Mama cooked the greens and the mashed berries up together in another pot. It was really hot with that fire going in that closed-up house, but we had to eat. When the fish and the greens and berries was cooked up, Mama skinned some of the sassafras root and boiled up some tea from it. We wiped some plates down to where they were serviceable and laid out our supper. Jinx took Terry his, sat on the bed by him and fed him a bite of his, and then ate a bite of hers. We could see them through the open door. Jinx was being so sweet I almost thought she had been stolen away and replaced by someone that looked like her.

Mama sat in the rocking chair with her plate. I sat on the floor with mine, and we ate using our fingers, cause the forks and such looked a lot nastier than the plates. The greens mixed with the berries tasted better than I would have figured, and the fish was fresh dead like Jinx said, and tasted as good as if we had caught it on a hook within the hour.

When we was finished eating, Jinx came out of the bedroom and closed the door on a well-fed and now sleeping Terry. The water in the pot with the sassafras roots was boiling. We poured it in cups and sipped. We took our time about it, sweating in front of the fire. It would have tasted better with some sugar or honey.

Finally I got up, stirred the fire around, broke it down until it wasn't blazing and wasn't so hot.

"I've been thinking, Sue Ellen," Mama said, "and I don't see any other way for it. You and Jinx have to take the boat and go to Gladewater, find some way to come back for Terry and myself."

"Yeah, well," I said. "That plan's good enough if we had a boat."

"What?"

I told her what we had seen. She let out her breath, leaned out of the rocker, and put the cup on the floor. "He can't still be after us," she said.

"You've heard all the stories we have," I said. "Someone darn sure wrecked the boat and left boot prints down by the river."

"It could have been anyone," Mama said. "Mischievous kids."

"Kids don't have feet big as that," Jinx said.

We sat tight after that, sat there until the room was full of shadow and we heard the wind pick up, followed by rain.

Why couldn't the damn weather make up its mind? Why couldn't Skunk just come on and try and get us? This was my thinking, and it just went around and around in a circle. The rain kept building, and pretty soon we could hear lightning crackling and thunder banging around like a drunk in a store full of pots and pans. The storm raged like it did that night on the river, except inside the house we was high and dry. Or was until the roof started to leak. It wasn't much of a leak, and was near a window, but it made me feel all the more dreary.

Terry woke up a few times in pain, and we gave him some more of the home brew that was there. I hadn't never wanted to drink, but right then I was thinking of a snort. I didn't do it, though, if for no other reason than it might give Mama liberty to do the same. Besides, Terry needed it more than any of us.

When Terry finally got back to sleep, I sat by his bed and looked through the open door at Mama rocking slowly in her chair. Rain was coming down the chimney. I could hear what was left of the fire in the fireplace hissing, and there was a bit of smoke. The wind was howling and carrying on and there was sizzling lightning and clattering thunder.

The roof banged loudly. I looked up. It was like a tree limb had fallen on it, but there wasn't no trees near the house. Maybe one had blown out of the woods and onto the roof.

The sound came again, a heavy sound, along with a creaking, and I knew then what it was.

I glanced through the open doorway at Mama and Jinx. They was looking up, too. That's because they figured what I had figured.

Someone was on the roof.

25

There's no describing how I felt then, because I knew not only that someone was on the roof but that—of course—it was Skunk. I couldn't figure why he would choose to do that, out there in the rain, and in such a way we could all hear him and know where he was, but then it come to me. He knew how fearful we would be, and he was someone who sucked off misery.

I got up and wandered into the big room. Mama glanced at me. I couldn't see her face there in the dark, but I knew she was scared, like me. Jinx was walking around the room, following the sound of Skunk on the roof. She held the pistol and looked at the ceiling. The board roof heaved a bit in one spot. Jinx snapped up the gun and fired. It was loud as the crack of doom, and my ears rang. Sawdust drifted down from the ceiling. I heard footsteps moving quickly across the roof, and then they ceased.

"I think he jumped off," Jinx said.

"You think you hit him?" Mama asked.

"If I did, he was mighty spry afterwards," Jinx said.

We stayed right where we was, waiting to hear him climbing back on the roof, but that didn't happen. Instead I heard a creaking sound in the bedroom. Grabbing Jinx by the elbow, I led her in there. The creaking was coming from a window that was to one side of Terry's bed. He was up now, the shot having awakened him. His head was turned toward the window. There was a big blade stuck between the edge of the window and the shutter, and there was broken glass on the floor; the blade was prying the shutter, causing it to creak, and then crack. Skunk's stink was easing through that crack along with the blade.

Jinx lifted the pistol, holding it tight with both hands, and fired. It was such a big pistol, the shot made her take a step back. The shot hit the shutter and cracked it, went through, slammed into some glass, and broke it. The big blade was jerked away.

"You might have got him," I said.

"Yeah," Jinx said, "but I don't want to go open that shutter and look out and see."

"Me neither," I said.

"That means me, too," Mama said. She was standing behind us, holding the shotgun.

"I haven't any plans for an examination, either," Terry said, sitting up in bed, his good hand holding his arm above the amputation. I could feel Jinx shaking where her shoulder was pushed up to me, or maybe it was me shaking.

"We're safe enough in here," I said. "With all that rain, he can't burn us out. We're all right if we don't startle like quail. That's what he wants, for us to startle and make a break for it so he can pick us off. We just got to stay alert."

"If he's out there," Terry said, "and we're in here, he has the advantage. Not us. He can just wait us out. That bastard can live off the land. We can't even go out now to pick berries."

Me and Jinx pushed an old dresser with a tall, cracked mirror in front of the busted window to make it safer, and then we all sat up that night, listening. Now and again one of us would drift off, but there was always someone awake. Jinx stayed in the bedroom with Terry. Me and Mama sat in the big room. During the night, at least a couple times, I heard Skunk try the doorknob, rattling it so as to shatter our nerves.

Rattling the door, breaking the glass out of the windows, bits of it falling down between the window frames and shutters in little clinks, went on for most of the night; then a couple hours before dawn it quit.

When light come, I was scared and starving. It was still raining, though less savage than before. We dug the fish guts and that blackened head out of the fireplace and wiped it off, and the four of us had pieces of it. It wasn't much to eat and it tasted nasty. My stomach acted at first like it might not manage to wrap around it, but it did.

Mama found a tin with a little coffee in it, and she heated the water and made us some. It tasted like dirty water, but it was something to put in the belly to make you think you'd eaten.

About two hours after we was up, I ventured, against Mama and Jinx's will—Terry had fallen back into a wounded sleep— to open a shutter and look out. From that window I could see the woods. They was shadowy in the rising light. I checked as good as I could, but didn't see Skunk. I didn't see nothing but those dark trees and rain falling.

I locked up, went from shutter to shutter, checking to see if I could see anything. I opened one on the other side of the big room, and there was a face staring in at me, the nose poking through a broken pane of glass, the eyes dry and stiff. I jumped back and screamed. It was the old woman. She was still wrapped in the rug, but it had been peeled back so her face was free of it. Her white hair was wet as a fresh-born calf, and she was propped against the window by having her arms pulled up and bent at the elbow, pressed to the window frame. In her arms was the saw box. It was open, and everything that had been in it was gone except Terry's arm—the hand that went with the arm was gone, though. And the old woman's arms that held the box in front of her was stumps; her hands had been chopped off, too.

"He dug her up," I said.

"Hell," Jinx said, standing near me with the pistol. "We can see that."

"He's a monster," Mama said, easing over to take a look.

"You just now figuring that?" Jinx said.

"Jinx," Mama said, "you should be careful. I might knock the shit out of you."

Me and Jinx both looked at Mama.

"I've said it now," Mama said, "and though it makes me feel better, I prefer not to say it again, and would like to ask you to not remember I said it the first time."

The rain had started to slacken, and we could see the sun real good from that window, rising up in a thin gold line, dragging more blood-red light behind it. I closed the shutters and locked them.

I said, "There ain't no pattern to him. He's on deck all the time. Any other body would sleep sometime. But night or day, rain or dry, it don't affect him. How are we to deal with someone like that?"

I was starting to get a little crazy, and I had to make myself quit chattering like a squirrel.

Jinx went over and sat down cross-legged on the floor, laying the pistol across her lap. "There ain't but a couple ways for us to do, Sue Ellen," she said. "Someone has to go on into Gladewater and get help, or we all need to go. Or maybe there's a third idea, and that one is we split up and strike out in different directions, but that idea only works if Terry can go along, and he can't."

"So that brings us back to the first two," I said.

"It does," Jinx said.

"But if someone stays here with Terry," Mama said, "Skunk will eventually get in the house. One person can't watch both rooms and go without sleeping."

"Or the house will dry up and he'll set fire to it, burn it down," Jinx said.

"I believe I have a say in this," Terry called from the bedroom, throwing back the covers with his good hand. He was wearing only his shorts, trying to put his feet on the floor.

He started to walk toward us, but didn't get too far. He had to go back and sit on the bed. Jinx went in there and laid the pistol on the bed, helped him swing his feet back up, and covered him. We all went in there and sat on the bed by him.

"You couldn't whip a kitten if we tied one of its paws behind its back and put out one of its eyes," I said. "Lay down and rest some."

"All I do is rest," Terry said.

"All you're up for just right now," Jinx said.

I thought for a moment, said, "That log down there by the river. That could be a way."

"Log?" Mama said.

"It was there when we found the fish," I said. "We could use it to sail down the river. Me and Terry did a similar thing."

"I had two arms then," Terry said.

"That's true. But I think someone walking out—that's not so good, provided they're trying to get to Gladewater. I don't think it's real far by river, but on foot it might be a distance. All of you could stay here, and I could take the pistol and make a break for it, get to that log, push off and make it downriver to Gladewater, get some help. One person can make it easier than a bunch."

"That doesn't sound like that good a plan," Jinx said.

"I have to agree," Terry said.

"Me, too," Mama said.

"I'm a fast runner, and if I can get down to the river and push the log off, and if Skunk ain't right on top of me, and the water is running swift, I can get away."

"That's a lot of ifs," Mama said.

"If we stay here, we're all dead," I said. "I'll take the hatchet. I'm more likely to hit something with that, since I ain't a good shot. And the hatchet ain't so heavy."

I went over and grabbed up the hatchet by the fireplace. Mama said, "Now? You're going now?"

"Time ain't going to get no better," I said. "I figure Skunk ain't going to expect me running for the river when I got a perfectly good cabin to hole up in. That gives me an edge."

"That's not much of an edge," Terry said.

I hugged Mama and Jinx, and went into the bedroom and hugged Terry.

"You don't have to do this," Mama said as I came back into the main room.

"Yeah, I do," I said.

I went to the door and Jinx and Mama followed.

"Be alert," Terry called out from the bedroom.

I took a deep breath, told Jinx, "You open it, and I'm going to take off running."

She opened it, and I broke like a wild mustang, heading straight for the river, carrying that hatchet. It looked like good free running. I didn't see any sign of Skunk. All I saw was the slope of the hill that led down to the water. The grass was green and the wind was cool on account of last night's rain. I was almost enjoying myself. I was beginning to think things was going to be hunky-dory. That I was going to make that river and that log without so much as a grasshopper smacking into me, but right about then, coming out of the woods on my right, I seen him.

Now, it generally figures that things are scarier in the dark, which is how I had seen him before, at night, running along the bank, carrying a hatchet, same as I was now. But in the daylight, I got to tell you, he looked even scarier.

He was big and stout and was carrying the cane knife. He had on that derby and his hair was all coiled out from under it, twisted up and full of pine needles and leaves and dirt and such; that bird was there, too, dangling. There was a wink of light on his hat, which I seen now had a string fastened to it and was tied under his chin. That wink of light was Constable Sy's badge pinned to the front of the hat. He had a necklace made out of the hands he had recently chopped off, them that was Constable Sy's and Gene's, and the old woman's, and the blackened hand that had belonged to Terry; all of them had a strand of leather run through them, and they flapped against his chest as he run, like they was birds attacking him. He didn't have his pack on his back, having laid it aside somewhere, and there wasn't nothing to slow him down. His mouth was open and he had surprisingly good white teeth, and plenty of them. He was making a sound like someone trying to gargle with a turnip; that made the whole story about him having his tongue pulled out make sense. But that wasn't my concern then. My concern was the path in front of me and the river beyond that and that damn log. I could tell right away I wasn't going to make it.

I knew, too, if I turned around and tried to run back to the house I wouldn't make it there, either. He'd be on me with that cane knife.

I veered off toward the briar patch. It wasn't a good idea, but when I seen Skunk coming fast, I didn't have no more thought than that. I had to dive in or take that cane knife twixt the ears.

Just before I got to the briar patch, I looked back and seen Skunk with his cane knife raised, and glory hallelujah, he was right on me. And then there came a crack, and all of a sudden Skunk stiffened and then went down. I hesitated, looked toward where the sound had come from. I could see shutters thrown back on the house, Jinx's shiny black face at the window, that big revolver propped on the windowsill. That was a far and good and unlikely shot, considering she hadn't been able to hit him on the roof or at the window. It wasn't no more than blind luck, and it just as easily might have hit me.

Still, it wasn't a finisher. It was a flesh wound. Skunk got up and started after me again, walking like he had one foot hung up in a bucket of mud. I heard another shot crack, but this one didn't hit Skunk. It whined off toward the river.

I dove into them briars, swinging the ax, trying to chop a way through. All that was doing was slowing me down. I ducked and went through that shallow spot in the briars I had seen before, thinking that might get me away from him, but I could hear him coming, breathing heavy, making a sound that was godawful. I thought at first it was from pain, but it come to me that it was from anger. He was trying to yell at me with no tongue.

The briars and vines and bushes got thick, and I had to duck more than before to go through, and soon as I ducked, I heard a whistling sound pass over where my head had been. I knew by just sheer luck I had missed getting my head chopped off.

I hustled on through that low place on my hands and knees. Skunk grabbed one of my feet, tried to pull me to him. I kicked back, and my old shoe come loose of me, and I escaped.

The tunnel of briars was real narrow now, but that darn Skunk was getting through, coming close, smelling like an open grave. I kept scuttling, and finally the briars widened and there was room to move around, but I felt like one of those fish that had got in a trap and couldn't go back.

Getting to my feet, I tried to run, but there was just enough vines to tangle and trip me up. I almost dropped my hatchet cause the thorns had gotten into me, cutting me up something horrible. I saw right in front of me was the riverbank, and I wasn't no more than a step from it. It fell off there maybe twenty feet to a line of dirt running by the water. It was a good drop, but it seemed better than a cane knife in the head.

It didn't matter, though. I was wound up tight in those vines and thorns and couldn't pull free. I was like a fly in a spiderweb. I knew this was it. I was about to take the Big Siesta. I managed to get my feet under me, but those vines still had me. I leaped at them a few times, trying to break through, but they held me.

I glanced back. Skunk was hacking through the briar patch, getting closer. He had lost his bowler and the bird hanging from his hair had a lot of its feathers torn out. His face was as cut up as if he had been in a knife fight. He was grinning and right on top of me. He was so close I could see his skin was cracked up with wrinkles and scars; he looked ancient as Satan. He had the cane knife raised. I quit looking back and leaped at the briars again. I felt a terrible pain as the thorns ripped free and the vines broke, and I went tumbling over the riverbank.

I hit the bank hard on my stomach. The hatchet come loose of my hand and was lying nearby. I wanted to get to it, but couldn't make myself move cause I couldn't even breathe; the fall had knocked the breath from me.

I eventually got my knees under me, but all I could do was roll over on my back. Above me, Skunk was slashing his way through the briars at the edge of the bank, making a gurgling sound. He sprang off his toes to get a good jump, and down he come.

Well, almost. That big jump wasn't to his good. His leap carried him up into a tangle of briars that wound around a tree limb and dipped down; they caught up in his hair. One wrapped around his neck. His leap snapped some of the vines loose of his hair, letting him fall and ripping the bird free, but it wasn't a complete drop. The one around his neck was thick as a man's wrist. It caught and held him as surely as if he had his head in a noose. He kicked his legs, trying to twist loose. He dropped the cane knife. It fell right between my legs and stuck in the ground, weaving a little back and forth before it stopped shaking. He grabbed at his throat, trying to rip the thick vine off, but it was so tight around his throat he couldn't get his fingers under it.

I had my breath by then. I crawled toward the hatchet. I got hold of it, turned, and looked at Skunk. Due to all his kicking, he dropped some more—as far as the thick coil of vine around his neck let him. His eyes was bugged out and his mouth was open; the little nub of what was left of his tongue was thrashing around in there like a little man trying to climb out of a cave. His toes touched the ground, but not enough. He was hung good, and in a short time he quit gagging and moving.

With the hatchet cocked, I got closer to him, and all of a sudden, he shook a little. I damn near beaned him with that hatchet. But there wasn't no need. He was dead, and like a chicken with its head cut off, all that had moved him was his nerves and muscles coming unknotted. I could not only smell his awful stink, but the fresh stink of what he had let go in his pants.

When I realized he was done for, I fell over right there. It was like that time when I had sat down on the log and cried cause I was so overweighted with all manner of business. I started to cry this time, too.

26

When I was cried out, I walked along the bank, carrying my hatchet, kind of tiptoeing on my shoeless foot. I come to the spot where our boat had been, where the log I was going to ride was supposed to be. But the rain of the night before had lifted it up and washed it downriver. That gave me a bit of a chill, knowing if I had run down to the river slightly ahead of Skunk, I would have been trapped at its edge, and that even if I had jumped in, he could have swum after me and caught me good. Like it did for Brer Rabbit, that briar patch had saved my life.

When I got up over the rise and could see the house, I also saw Jinx, who was coming my way, toting the pistol.

I got closer to her, and then she started running, and so did I, at least a few steps, cause the foot that didn't have no shoe was full of stickers, and my legs gave out under me like they had on the riverbank. I just sat down and went to crying again. Jinx got to me and threw her arms around me and kissed me on the head, and I kissed her, and we both cried.

"You got him, didn't you?" she said. "I knew someone could get him, it would be you."

"He got his ownself," I said, and told her what happened.

"I started to come help, but then I was afraid if I got killed, wouldn't be no one to take care of your mama and Terry. Finally, I couldn't take it no more, and I was coming no matter what, then I seen you walking up."

"You did fine," I said. "It happened real quick. That shot in the leg slowed him down."

"Lucky shot."

"I figured as much."

"You stink."

"Skunk touched me."

"Ain't nothing soap and water won't take care of," she said, and helped me up. We walked back to the cabin, but I looked over my shoulder a few times as we went, just in case Skunk could come back from the dead. And I didn't let go of that hatchet, neither.

We had quite a reunion when I got to the cabin, though they was anxious for me to heat up some well water and bathe, and after a bit of airing, most of Skunk's smell went away.

We ended up staying at that house for a couple days. I found a pair of the old woman's shoes, which was pretty run-down but better than mine, and took to wearing them. We kept talking about how we was going to bury her again, but I'm ashamed to say we left her leaning up against the house. We just kept them shutters at that window pulled to so as to keep her odor out.

Me and Jinx caught fish for us to eat, and each time we was out, we went and looked at Skunk hanging where I had left him, just to make sure he was good and dead. And dead he was. Birds had been at him. His eyes was just holes. The flesh around the end of his nose, and his lips, had been pecked at, too. If I thought he stunk before, he stunk twice as much now.

When Terry had his strength up enough we thought he wouldn't be as much a burden to Mama, we laid in some squirrels we killed with the shotgun, knowing they wouldn't last more than a couple of days before they went rancid. But they was good enough eating for three days in a row. We gathered up some berries and some wild grapes. We left Mama with the shotgun. She was the best choice to take care of Terry, provided she remembered how to be a mother. As of late, she'd been right good at it.

Me and Jinx took a bit of the money from the can in case we needed it. I carried the hatchet, Jinx carried the pistol, and we went walking out. It was a long ways before we come to a road; about two days. We slept out in the open under some trees, and woke up full of red bugs that had crawled up and nested in spots I don't like to talk about. When we come to that road, we abandoned the pistol and the hatchet, as we felt these might not be the things to carry if we was going to try and bum a ride.

Well, that need not have been a problem, cause we walked all day and not one car came down that red clay road, least not until we was in sight of a town, and by then it was close enough to walk. The town was Gladewater.

"Here we be," Jinx said.

"It ain't much, is it?"

"No, it ain't."

But as we got closer we saw that it had some good streets and some buildings all along that street, and there were some dirt lanes that branched off of it, and we saw the bus station with a big bus parked out front.

We kept walking, and when we was in town good, the first thing we did was stop and talk to a man that had just finished parking his car in front of the general store. We asked him where the law was. He pointed out the police station, which was just a house with a battered black Ford in front of it.

There was a sign on the door that said COME INSIDE, and we did. There was a plump little man with a lot of black hair sitting behind a desk that was leveled out with some folded paper under the legs. He was holding a flyswatter and kind of batting it around at a fly, mostly out of entertainment, I figure.

There was a big white hat on his desk that looked like it would need a head about twice the size of his to fill it; maybe a pumpkin would have fit in that hat. There was a note tablet and a stubby pencil next to the hat. He had on regular work clothes, but there was a police badge pinned to his shirt, and he had a .45 in a holster on his hip. I saw it, because when we come in he stood up. He looked at us, said, "You girls need something?"

"You could say that," I said. "We got something we need to tell you."

He studied our faces, asked us to sit down. He adjusted his gun belt so his belly could live with it, sat back down, threw a boot heel with some straw-laced cow mess on the bottom of it over the corner of his desk, and leaned back in his chair. He cocked the flyswatter over one shoulder like it was a rifle. He told us his name was Captain Burke, which was an interesting title, cause it turned out he was all the policeman there was in Gladewater. I guess he was most likely the privates and the sergeants and all the in-betweens, too.

I started to point out the cow mess, but decided it wasn't worth it. I just watched the fly he had been chasing land on it.

"You look like you got wrapped up in some barbed wire," he said. "Or got laid into by a big cat."

"Thorns," I said, and then I started telling what we had come there for.

Without explaining how May Lynn died, or bringing her up at all, we gave him some background. What we told him was me and my mama had run away from home cause the husband and stepfather was mean, and that Jinx was traveling with us as a help. We told him about Terry, too. How he had run away from a mean stepfather and had his finger chopped off. How it got infected, and about the old woman that sawed it off. We didn't mention the money, and we held back the part about Skunk. We just said how Mama was waiting back in this cabin and an old woman had held us prisoner, and cut the arm off our friend, but that it needed doing. We stopped talking about there.

When we finished, Captain Burke almost jumped out of his chair, said, "Come here and look."

We followed him back to where there was a room that had been made into a jail, with bars on the door and at the window, and sitting in there on a cot was none other than Don Wilson, my stepdaddy. He turned and stared at us. He looked thin and pitiful and his face had sunk in at the cheeks and his Adam's apple poked out against his throat like a turkey wattle.

"Is this the fella you run off from?" Captain Burke asked.

Me and Jinx couldn't do no more than nod.

"Hello, Sue Ellen," Don said.

"Hello," I said.

"How's your mother?"

"Tolerable."

"Good," he said, then looked at the floor and didn't try to catch our eye again.

Captain Burke said to Don, "I'll get you supper soon, and you ought to eat it this time, not just play with it."

Don didn't say nothing, just kept staring at the floor.

"Come on back to the office," Captain Burke said.

We did, and we all got back in our same chairs, except Captain

Burke. He had an icebox in there, and he opened it up and got out three Co-Colas and used an opener from his desk drawer to pry the lids off. He set the Co-Colas in front of us, said, "There, now. Ain't nothing like a good Co-Cola to kick the thirst."

He sat down and we all sipped our drinks, as if on command. They were lukewarm, but right then I would have taken a big slug of spit if it had just a touch of sugar in it.

Captain Burke said, "That man back there, Don, he come into this town over a month ago. He come by and said he was look-ing for some kin, and had I seen them, or had any word. I told him no, and that I didn't have papers on anybody that was a run-away.

"Well, then, he didn't leave town. He just drove around in his truck, which had an old tarp over the bed. He'd sleep in the front seat of the truck, and now and again he'd go down to the river, where there's a place for boats to tie up, and look around, then come back and stay about. Flies was all over the back of that truck, so finally, I made him give me a look. Know what was back there?" Burke said, eyeballing me and Jinx like we might actually have some idea.

"No, sir," I said.

"It was the body of a man, and he was well rotted. He had a hole through his chest about big enough to drive a tractor through, even if it was dragging a pile of brush."

"That's a big hole," I said.

"Yep, it was a big hole," he said.

Captain Burke let that bloody, flyspecked picture he had painted settle on us, but there wasn't a thing we knew to do with it. Jinx, as if to feed the story, said, "Dead man, huh?"

"Yep. He had been dead some time and had heated up good un-der that tarp. So you know what I done?"

We shook our heads.

"I arrested this Don fella, your stepdaddy. I arrested him and I asked him who that was in the truck bed."

"That seems like a good way to go," Jinx said.

"I thought the same," Captain Burke said. "I said, 'Who in hell is that and how did he get dead?' He says to me, 'Why, that there is Cletus, and I shot a hole through him with a shotgun.'" He paused and looked at us. "How do you like the story so far?"

Neither Jinx nor I knew what to say, so we just waited, like birds on a limb.

"So I say, 'How come did you shoot him?' And he says it was cause Cletus had paid a crazy nigger named Skunk to hunt y'all down—that would be you—and that he didn't want none of you dead. He said there was some money involved."

"He didn't want us dead?" I said.

Captain Burke nodded. "What he said."

"There ain't no money," Jinx said. "That was all some kind of pipe dream of his."

"Say it was?" Burke asked.

"It was," Jinx said. "Cletus told him a pipe dream and for a while there I figure he thought it was real."

I wondered then if Jinx was being mighty clever, or just digging us a big hole to fall in.

"This Don Wilson says there was a girl got murdered, and that kind of set things off, though he didn't know exactly how it started the ball rolling, or anything else about it. Just that his stepdaughter—that would be you—and a boy, who ain't here, as I see it, and a little colored girl, which would be you, was all friends of hers. He said that girl drowned with a sewing machine fixed to her feet and that got things in motion."

"But he didn't know how it got things in motion?" I said.

"What he said," Captain Burke said. "Don said he figured it was Cletus what killed her. Said they wasn't a close family, and there was some kind of quarrel, maybe over some money, and Cletus killed her. Cletus claimed you had the money, and that brought this Skunk character into motion. I don't know I believe there's a Skunk character."

"There is," I said.

The Skunk part didn't excite him that much. "And you say there ain't no money?" He said that like he might like some of it.

"All we got is ten dollars between us," Jinx said, and dug the money we had brought from the can out of her pocket and slapped it on the desk. "That's it, and some pocket lint."

"Your stepdaddy said this fellow Cletus put this crazy killer on you named Skunk, the one you say is real, and he didn't want that. He tried to get Cletus to call it back. But that wasn't the way Cletus wanted it. So Wilson shot Cletus, said he went looking for this killer Cletus had hired, but didn't find him. He came here to see if you showed up to catch a bus or something. He was down at that bus depot, parked out front all day, until I noticed all them flies and had me a peek in the back of the pickup. I asked him why he didn't just toss the body. And you know what he said?"

We shook our heads.

"He said after he killed him and tossed him back there and covered him up, he just didn't think no more about him. Can you imagine that? That fella with a hole blowed through him, lying in the back of a truck smelling like an outhouse, flies all over the place, and he didn't think no more about him. There's a man with something on his mind, that's what I can tell you."

"There really was a hired killer," I said, thinking he hadn't paid attention the first time I mentioned it.

"This Skunk, you mean?" he said, and then it come to me that he might be circling around to see if we was going to change our story. I decided to add to it, and let the thing I added be the truth.

"Yes, sir. He killed two men that was working for Cletus, and caused another to get killed when a raft turned over on the river. The man on the raft was a preacher who tried to help us. His name was Reverend Jack Joy. He was an all-right fella."

"My wife ran off with a preacher," Captain Burke said. "So I don't know I feel the loss all that heavy of a preacher."

"We was running from Skunk. But he got his the other day. He's dead by the river, hanging."

"Hanging?" Captain Burke said.

I explained that part to him. When I finished up the story, I said, "What you going to do with my stepdaddy?"

"I don't know," Captain Burke said. "But your story and his kind of fit, except for the money."

He kept coming back to the money, and by then I had him figured. He had already taken that ten dollars Jinx had put on his desk, folded it up, and put it in his shirt pocket.

"Cletus just thought there was money, but there wasn't," I said. "His boy, who died not long back. He spent it up. Word was he stole it from a bank."

"Do say?"

"Yes, sir, that's the story," I said.

"So we can run all this by a judge if we like," Captain Burke said. "But Don tells me Cletus ain't got no next of kin to worry about things. Is that right?"

"Yes, sir," I said. "His whole family is deader than a doornail."

"Well, then. You said this fella that was after you . . . Skunk. You said he's dead and hanging?"

"Yes, sir," I said. "And Mama, and Terry, that boy with the one arm, they're still in the cabin."

I had told him this already, but he was a man that liked hearing a thing repeated, so I gave him his wish. I decided then to talk about how the old woman had died. I just mentioned before that she had cut Terry's arm off cause it was bad infected, and that she had held us captive, but I hadn't mentioned she had passed in her sleep. I told him now and told how Skunk had dug her up and we had left her leaning against the house.

When I finished, I wasn't sure he believed all or any of our story, but he nodded at things while I talked, the way you will to someone you think may not have all their marbles.

When I finished with it, Captain Burke ran his hand through his hair, said, "We got pretty much a mess here, don't we?"

Me and Jinx didn't argue with that.

"What we going to do about it?" he asked.

We didn't offer any words of wisdom.

"I guess I got to think on it before I decide," he said. "First, though, I reckon we need to go get your mama and this Terry fella, and I want to see this Skunk, and that old woman you say you left leaning up against the house."

I figured my criminal life was about to come to a bad end, but it didn't work out quite like that.

Here's what happened. Captain Burke hired a greasy trapper with three fingers missing (said a gator got them) and a motorboat; he motored us back up the river. Captain Burke looked silly sitting in the boat with his hat on, it being a ten-gallon. He had stuffed the inside of it with paper to make it fit, and it stood out from his noggin all the way around.

We stopped at where Skunk was hung up. They pulled the boat on shore enough so that it didn't float away, got out, and stood there and looked at Skunk, who was even worse for wear than before. His neck had grown thin, and it was starting to rot.

Captain Burke got him a stick and poked Skunk a few times, causing him to swing back and forth. He poked him another time and darn if his head didn't pop off, and let me tell you, that was a nasty sight.

"Who'd have thunk that there?" said the greasy trapper. "You'd think a head that big gonna have a neck that's not gonna wear so quick, wouldn't you?"

"He ain't got no better neck than nobody else," Captain Burke said.

"That there supposed to be that Skunk fella that comes to get folks and such?" the trapper asked, since Captain Burke—who, when it got right down to it, was kind of a blabbermouth—had told him the whole story.

"Yep," I said.

"Ah, he don't look like so much to me, he don't. No, sir. Not so much."

"Yeah, well," Jinx said. "He ain't alive. I don't reckon the dead look like much no matter who they was."

"Well, now," said the trapper, "that's a point you got there, it is. I'm just saying how he looks."

They left Skunk where he fell, and we motored on up the river some more to where we had stopped when we first come to the old woman's house. We went up the hill and to the house. I knocked on the door, and Mama answered it and let us in. Terry was able to get around better now, go to the outhouse proper, instead of going in a pan with the results thrown out one of the busted windows, as this was a thing he told us right away, right there in front of strangers. But I guess if I had had my arm cut off and had been having to do my business in a pan, I would have been pretty excited about the change as well. In the short time we had been gone, three days about, they had eaten up all the squirrels we had laid in, and the berries and grapes, too.

Captain Burke looked over Terry's amputated arm and nodded his head at the work. "You say that a woman lived here done that?"

"Yes," Terry said. "She's leaning up against the house, with what's left of my arm in a box."

Mama went over and opened up the shutters, and there she was, still in the same place, but shrunk some in the blanket, and good and ripe, with that saw box still cradled and open on her forearms, the remains of Terry's arm lying up in it.

"Uh-huh," said the trapper, looking out the window. "I knowed this old woman some, a time back. She was like an old poison snake, but without the sweetness. Nobody had anything to do with her come these last ten years. She'd done got so sour wasn't no one wanted anything to do with her. I thought she was done dead."

Well, we buried the old woman again, and the trapper said a few words over her. About how she was mean as hell, but still she was dead and we ought to be polite, or some such thing. While he was talking I sort of drifted away, watching a blue jay in a tree.

Finished, we walked down to where Skunk was. The trapper and Captain Burke buried Skunk and his head in the side of the riverbank, which seemed foolish to me, as it wouldn't be long before time washed him out of there. But to tell the truth, I didn't really care. I wasn't all that concerned about how Skunk had ended up, though there was moments when I'd consider how he had been treated when he was young; his tongue yanked out, hit over the head with a boat paddle, near drowned, and made to live in the woods. When I'd consider all that, I'd at least have a moment or two of some sad feelings for him. But they passed quicker than they came.

When they had Skunk buried, the trapper said to the bank where he had been tucked, "Good luck in hell," then we walked back to where the boat was. It turned out the boat wasn't big enough for all of us, which was a thing we had tried to tell Captain Burke from the start. But he had his mind set, so here we was. It was decided they'd take Mama and Terry to Gladewater, and it would be seen to that they got put up in a boardinghouse. Me and Jinx said we'd stay and wait our turn. When they was out of sight down the river, me and her went back up to the house and got the lard cans with the money and May Lynn's ashes. We dug a hole near the briar patch and buried them, and made some little markers with rocks.

I guess it was near dark when Captain Burke and the trapper showed up, and we got loaded and made our way to Gladewater. Mama and Terry was over at the boardinghouse. Captain Burke went and got Mama but left Terry there, cause he was still feeling weak from all that blood loss. The trapper went away, and me and Jinx just waited around in the street until we seen Captain Burke and Mama coming our way.

Mama had had time to clean up and wash her hair, and she had been given a dress by the landlady; she looked good and fresh, and Captain Burke, like most men, was smitten.

When we all got to the jail, Mama went in back and talked with Don. When she came out, she said, "I talked to him like you suggested, Captain."

"And?"

"He says he killed that man to keep him from having me and Sue Ellen killed. He said he doesn't like Terry and doesn't have any feelings for Jinx one way or the other."

"Figures," Jinx said.

Captain Burke looked at Mama. "Was he rough with you? Is that why you run off?"

Mama nodded. "Yes. Yes, he was, and that is why I ran off. But I think now he's done. He was just trying to protect us in the end. It might not make him a good person, but it doesn't make him evil. He was trying to do one thing right."

That was our complete story. Reverend Joy didn't come up again, and neither did Gene or Constable Sy. It didn't seem to bother Captain Burke at all. None of the story we told would have been worth a damn for any solid law enforcement, even if it was mostly true, but Captain Burke seemed satisfied with it. I reckon when it comes to police matters, law is pretty much where and how you find it. And how much work there is to it for them, and how much money there is or isn't in it.

In our case, there was too much work and no real money for Captain Burke, and at the bottom of it all, like lots of people in those kinds of positions, he didn't really give a damn.

"I'll cut him loose, then," he said in a big way, spreading his hands. "We'll call him killing that Cletus fella self-defense. Hell, we'll just call everything even and not hurt our heads too much over it."

"Sure," Mama said, like any of it made sense.

Captain Burke told Mama he wouldn't mind taking her to the café for dinner tomorrow if she was agreeable, and she said, "Maybe."

Don was let loose, given his truck keys, wallet, and his greasy cap.

"Your truck is behind here," Captain Burke said. "I think they buried that Cletus fella in the pauper's section of the graveyard, if you or anyone cares. I guess being the shooter, you might not want to give him any prayers."

Don looked in his wallet. It was empty. He said, "I had five dollars in there."

"No, you didn't," Captain Burke said.

Don decided it was best to take the loss. He went outside, carrying his cap. When we went out he was waiting on us.

"I appreciate the way you helped me out in there, Helen," he said to Mama. "I wouldn't mind if you came home now."

"You and I are divorced."

"We wasn't really never married by a preacher," he said.

"That's why we are divorced. Because I say so."

"You wasn't married?" I said.

"No," Mama said.

"We just sort of took up together," Don said.

"Mama," I said. "What else ain't you told me?"

But I didn't say it like I really wanted to hear any kind of answer.

Don tried to sweet-talk her some, but Mama told him it was done, and she better not see him no more, or she would press charges with Captain Burke.

Don grinned at her. "I got a bottle of cure-all in the glove box of my truck, if Captain Burke didn't drink it up. I know you must have been missing it. I'll buy you another case soon as we get home and the trader comes around."

"No more cure-all for me," she said. "That's what made me foolish. The river made me strong."

"The river?" he said.

"Yes, the river. And these kids. And another one that isn't here right now."

"I saved your life," he said. "I killed Cletus."

"Cletus couldn't find his elbow with a map," she said. "You didn't do anything to stop Skunk. Sue Ellen did that."

"That's right," I said. "And that Sight you're supposed to have hasn't helped you much, has it? I don't think you got any kind of future sight. I think you're just a big donkey's ass."

I had been wanting to say something like that for a long time, and now it felt good to have done it.

Don glared at me.

"So you go on, now," Mama said. "I won't cry for Cletus, but Don, I won't cry for you, neither. All I can say is I'm surprised you left the house and come this far. I'll give you that."

"I could take you home," he said, acting a little bit tough. "I could make you."

"I don't think you can," Helen said. "I'll yell out for Captain Burke."

"He ain't going to be around all the time," Don said.

"No, but he's nearby right now," she said. "And I am not afraid of you. You go get in your truck and you do what you want with your life, but I am done with you. I didn't protect Sue Ellen like I should have, up there in that bedroom in my stupor. I'm protecting her now. I'd die before I'd let you touch her."

"I didn't mean nothing by that," Don said. "I was just trying to compliment her."

"You meant everything by it, and I should have stopped you," Mama said. "If I see you around, I swear I'll tell Captain Burke and say how I protected you with some lies but have changed my mind, and that you were in with Cletus to kill us and get the money."

"Even though there ain't no money," I said.

"Yeah," Mama said, picking up on what I was doing. "Even though there isn't any money."

"Cletus made that up on account of Jinx hitting him upside his head with a stick," I said. "He wanted revenge." Damn if I wasn't getting to be a natural liar.

"And you did agree to have Sue Ellen hunted down and killed for seventy-five dollars," Mama said. "I heard you agree to it."

"I didn't mean nothing by that," he said. "Had I, I wouldn't have killed Cletus. That's just my way to talk like that. I wouldn't have let nobody hurt Sue Ellen."

"It's your way that annoys me, Don," Mama said. "You want me back so you can get me on the cure-all, keep me upstairs in that rotting house like a china-head doll. You won't change. Never. You'll hit me when you're mad, then you'll tell me how you didn't mean it and you'll change, but you won't change. For all I know, one day you'll do me like you did Cletus."

Don studied Mama carefully to see if he could spot any weakness in her position, but there wasn't any. He looked at me and Jinx. I stayed steadfast, and so did Jinx.

"You'll regret it," Don said. "You'll miss me."

"Haven't so far," Mama said. "I only helped you out here because you killed Cletus. That's a murder you're going to get away with. Now we're all even, you and me, and we're all done."

Don put his greasy cap on, turned around, and walked away.

"That's that," Mama said.

27

Actually, that was almost that. We did see Don around town a couple more times, driving by us when we was walking on the street, following us. Captain Burke got word of it, and the last time we seen Don he was driving by us on his way out of town, his face all puffed up and bruised. He didn't even turn and look our way.

Captain Burke set it so the town of Gladewater put us up for a few days at the boardinghouse and paid for our meals. It was a courtesy he gave to us because he said we had had such an ordeal, but the real reason was because he was interested in Mama. She even went to eat with him at the café several times, but one day, late morning, she come to us and said, "Sue Ellen, I want you to go with me. You two can come, too, if you want."

Mama had got up and gone out early that morning. When she found me, I was sitting with Jinx in Terry's room, which he had to himself. Me and Mama and Jinx had a room we shared. Missing an arm has its benefits, Terry said.

We all ended up going. It was the first time Terry had been out of the boardinghouse, having been up to that point ashamed of his missing arm. He didn't say he was, but it was a thing you could tell by the way he had quit looking us directly in the eye. But that day he seemed stronger. I think it was because the night before, Mama and Jinx and me and him had been talking about going to get the money and May Lynn, then buying some bus tickets and lighting out for California so he could spread her ashes, a mission of his I now better understood.

So we followed Mama out of the boardinghouse and walked with her toward the town square. When we got to the center of the square, she walked us to where there was a bench and a smattering of trees, one of them a big oak. The bench faced the courthouse. We all sat on the bench in the shade of the oak.

Mama said, "Now you just sit and watch the door to the court-house there."

We sat there not talking, because we could tell Mama didn't want that. There was a clock built into the top of the courthouse, and it showed us it was almost high noon. We sat there watching it click to twelve, and when it did the noon whistle was set off, and it blew loud enough I put my hands over my ears.

People started coming out of buildings along the square, including the courthouse. After a moment, Mama said, "See that man there?"

"The fat one?" I said.

"Yes," she said. "That's Brian. That's your daddy."

Now, I hadn't thought about the fact that he had gotten older, since Mama had aged so well. But there he was; a tall man with thinning hair and a big belly. As I looked at him I tried to see my face in him, but the truth was he was too far away for me to tell much of anything.

He stood outside the door of the courthouse and put one foot behind him, so that the sole of his shoe rested on the bricks.

"Have you spoken with him?" I said.

"No," she said. "He's not quite the Adonis I remember."

"It's still him, though," I said.

"Yes. Watch."

After a moment a nice-looking woman who was a little thick in the waist came down the walk with two girls trailing her. I figure they were a year apart, nine and ten was my guess, but I'm no good at guessing ages.

The woman smiled and my real daddy smiled. The woman touched his arm, and he let her slip it into the crook of his as he moved away from the wall. The little girls jumped up at him, so as to look him in the face, and I could hear him laugh even from where we sat. It was a happy laugh. The laugh of a man whose life had gone right and was good.

"He's going to the café with them," Mama said. "He was in there the first time I had lunch with Captain Burke. I didn't know it was him, but I remember looking at him and thinking he looked familiar, and the next time I was in there with Captain Burke, Brian came over and spoke to him, and Captain Burke introduced me as Helen Wilson. Then he introduced me to Brian. Course, I knew who he was by then, but he never figured out who I was. He didn't recognize me at all. I haven't aged that much, have I?"

"No, Mama," I said. "You look fine."

"I thought so . . . well, I think I look pretty good."

"You look real good," Jinx said. Terry nudged her with his shoulder, letting her know to butt out; this was just me and Mama talking.

"He didn't know me from nothing. I found out where he had his law office, in the courthouse there, and I knew he came to the café for lunch, so I came here to watch for him. And the first time I did his wife and daughters met him, right there. They hadn't gone to the café with him those other times, for whatever reason, but there they were, and that's where they went two days in a row."

"How do you know?" I said.

"I followed them. And when I did, it came to me that his life is made. It's all wrapped up neat in a bow, and I ought to leave it that way. I let him go back then, when I had a chance to keep him, and I have to let him go now, even if he would want something to do with me—and I doubt he would. Frankly, I wouldn't want him to. We're different now, and he's happy, and I'm going to leave him that way. But because I have to let him go, it doesn't mean you have to, Sue Ellen. He is your father."

I looked at Brian and his family walking toward the café.

I said, "Funny thing is, I don't feel nothing. Not a thing."

"I'm sort of disappointed," Mama said. "But I don't feel anything, either."

"Does this mean we're going to get the money and bus tickets and go away?" Jinx said.

Mama smiled at Jinx. "It does. And Sue Ellen, wherever we go, it might be nice if we got you some education."

We didn't actually leave right away. Me and Jinx walked out of town the next day, back down the road, and made our path across the stretch that led to the old woman's house. We knew our way now and made very quick time and didn't have to spend the night in the woods. We had some bread and cheese to eat, and a little water in a jar.

When we got to the old woman's house, it was mostly burned down. We walked around it and looked to see if there was anything to see, but there was just charred wood and the chimney standing up. There wasn't any way we could figure what happened for sure, but our guess was folks traveling down the river had used it to hole up in at night, and someone had been careless with the fireplace. If that was the case, they looked to have escaped. Wasn't any bodies in the burned wreck that we could see.

The shovel was still there where it had been under the house, though now the house had fell down on it and burned the handle off. We took the blade out of the ashes and went to where we had buried the cans and dug them up. They looked fine.

Walking down to the river, we carried the cans and eased along to where Skunk had been buried. We didn't discuss it, we just done it like it was in our heads all along, and it might well have been.

The side of the bank where Skunk had been buried was busted open, and there wasn't any sign of his body.

"Shit," Jinx said.

"I think he just got washed away," I said.

"Ain't been no serious rains since we left here," she said.

"That don't mean the body might not have fallen out, and there could have been enough water to carry it off."

"Can't be sure," she said. "And I don't see how there'd be any more water than there is now without there being any more rain."

"You're the one that don't believe in miracles," I said. "He didn't walk away. His head was torn off."

"I don't believe in miracles," she said, "but that damn Skunk might change my mind."

I supposed the body could actually have been dug out by someone who was curious, saw part of it poking out, though I couldn't figure the reason anyone would want him. Maybe wild animals dragged him off, or an alligator. That made some sense. But to tell you true, I don't know what really happened and never did figure it.

Bottom line to all this is, we walked out with the money and May Lynn, and back to Gladewater. We got there early night, and later that night in the boardinghouse, we counted out the money. There wasn't no way to divide it up right, cause there were a number of large bills. Mama wasn't in on the divide, but I promised her half of my third. Next day we took some of the money and bought bus tickets to ride out the next morning to California, with what Mama called some scenic stops along the way.

We talked about how we would take May Lynn's ashes and toss them at some famous Hollywood spot. We had talked about it many times, but for the first time, at least as far as I was concerned, it finally seemed real. While we talked, I peeked at Terry. He had tears in his eyes. I think maybe he had decided he wasn't a murderer, but that hadn't changed his feelings of responsibility. I decided then and there that I forgave him, and that he was going to punish himself plenty enough. I was also mad at May Lynn, even if she was dead; she shouldn't have treated him that way. But I forgave her, same as Terry.

Terry didn't tell Mama what he had done, and me and Jinx didn't want him to. We figured that at this point it was just best to let that dog lie.

Before bed that night, me and Mama had a private moment out on the porch of the boardinghouse. We was sitting in rocking chairs, taking in the breeze. After a while, I said, "Mama, you still dream about that black horse?"

"You know, after you killed Skunk, that dream mostly stopped, just now and again I'd have it. But when I told Don good-bye, next night I dreamed I caught that white winged horse and it took me away. What was odd, Sue Ellen, was that I was naked as the day I was born, riding on that horse up into a night sky, riding right up at the moon. I looked down, and behind me that black horse was coming, flying without wings, and then it come undone, like it was made of dry shadows, and those shadows were swallowed up by the night and were gone. Me and that white horse, we just kept on flying, flying fast to the moon. Next night, I didn't dream anything about it at all."

"I guess that's good," I said.

"Yes," Mama said. "It certainly is."

We slept with our tickets on an end table, the lard can with May Lynn's ashes holding them down, the bucket of money nearby.

During the night I woke up in my little bed thinking I was on the raft again, and that I was floating downriver. I looked around the room; it took me some time to realize that not only was I not on the raft, but that Skunk was no longer after us; wasn't nobody after us anymore. I got out of my bed and got dressed in my shirt, overalls, and shoes, and slipped outside.

I strolled down the street toward where the river was. It was a pretty good walk, but the night was nice and I enjoyed it. I could smell the river and hear it before I got to it. Where I ended up was the spot where Captain Burke had loaded me and Jinx in the motorboat and taken us back upriver.

I sat on a smooth part of the ground, in a spot where I could see the water. The river wasn't too far away from me. I could have spit from where I sat and hit the edge of that dark water without any trouble. It was not a bright night. All there was of the moon was a thin slice of silver, like a curved knife blade. Still, it was bright enough on the brown water I could see it good. The river flowed along like nothing had ever happened on it, to us or anyone else. It was just the river. I had the sudden idea it was like life, that river. You just flowed on it, and if there came a big rain, a flood or some such, and some of it was washed out, in time it would all wash back together. Oh, it might look some different, but it would be the same, really. It didn't change, but the people on that river did. I knew I had. And Mama had, and so had Terry, and maybe Jinx — but with her, it was hard to tell.

But that old brown snake of a river, it pretty much stayed the way it was, running from one end to the other, out to the great big sea.

I got up and brushed myself off and walked back to the boardinghouse. I went in the room and quietly lifted the lard bucket with May Lynn in it, held it for a moment, and silently thanked her, because in her own way, even if I was a little mad at her, she had put us all together, made a family of us, sent us downriver to find out who we was and where we was going.

I picked up my ticket and placed the bucket down tenderly. I sat by the window with the ticket in my hand, waiting for the first crack of light.

ABOUT THE AUTHOR

Joe R. Lansdale is the author of more than a dozen novels, including *Vanilla Ride, Leather Maiden, Sunset and Sawdust,* and *Lost Echoes.* He has received the Edgar Award, the American Mystery Award, the British Fantasy Award, the Grinzane Cavour Prize for Literature, and eight Bram Stoker Awards. His novella "Bubba Ho-Tep" was made into a film, starring Bruce Campbell and Ossie Davis and directed by Don Coscarelli. His short story "Incident On and Off a Mountain Road" was also adapted to film, starring Bree Turner and directed by Don Coscarelli, for Showtime. He lives with his family in Nacogdoches, Texas.

joerlansdale.com

Listen to the song "Edge of Dark Water," written and performed by singer-singwriter Kasey Lansdale at mulhollandbooks.com/edgeofdarkwater.

Reading Group Guide

EDGE OF
DARK
WATER

—⁓ɯ⁓—

A novel
by

Joe R. Lansdale

A CONVERSATION WITH
JOE R. LANSDALE

Edge of Dark Water *is set during the Depression era. How much did the time period affect the story? What do you enjoy most about writing about earlier times? What's most difficult about it for you?*

The Great Depression was the engine for the story. I didn't make a point of identifying the era, I just sort of let the story determine that gradually with clues the reader would pick up on. I think I originally wrote it with a year in mind, and slipped it in, but when I started rereading it, I took that out. I thought it stood on its own, and the time period would be evident, and that if it wasn't, it would stand on its own without it. But I think it's pretty clear. I grew up on stories about the Great Depression because my father and mother were born at the turn of the twentieth century, my father in 1909, my mother in 1914, I believe.

My dad was in his early forties when I was born and my mother in her late thirties, so they had reached their mature years during the Great Depression. My father had ridden the rails to go from town to town to compete in boxing and wrestling matches at fairs. It wasn't his primary way of making a living, but it was something he did because he needed the money, and he enjoyed it. For the record, those kinds of wrestling matches led to the invention of what is known as pro wrestling today. Only when my dad did it, the outcome was not ordained.

I remember hearing stories about people being poor and so

desperate. My mother said once they only had onions to eat, for a week or so. And my father told me about some relatives of theirs who were so hungry they ate clay, craving the minerals, I suspect. A lot of my relatives had gone through the Great Depression, and it impacted them. They saved everything, and were very careful with food, cautious about being wasteful. They saved string and stubs of pencils and rubber bands, you name it. Growing up when they did, and then me growing up with them, and knowing what they had been through, it had its impact.

People think times are hard now, and it certainly is for some, but on the whole, not like it was then. Those were tough times and our country was on the brink. It just barely survived. That said, I did enjoy writing about that era because I feel such a kinship to it, having grown up hearing about it all my life. I think it's more interesting to think about and write about than to live it, though it might be interesting to have lived through it.

Does the Sabine River, or East Texas in general, have special significance for you, and if so, how did that come into play in the writing of Edge of Dark Water?

I grew up in Gladewater, Texas, along the Sabine. It was a river I went down in boats, inner tubes, and a navy raft. I fished it and camped along its banks and hung out in the river bottoms with my friends. I was around it for much of my life. It was a river where bodies were found and people were drowned, and all manner of shenanigans occurred along its banks. So, yes, it's part of me, like an artery.

Many reviewers have remarked that one of the great pleasures of reading your work is your portrayal of the spirit of the American South. Is this something you've consciously worked at? Or has it come naturally from your upbringing and living in East Texas?

I started out trying to write stories that took place elsewhere. I was miserable at it. Ardath Mayhar wrote a story that I read, in an old Alfred Hitchcock anthology, titled *Crawfish*. It took place in East Texas and was written in an East Texas voice. It broke the ice for me. Later, my wife and I moved to Nacogdoches, Texas, and Ardath lived there and we met. I couldn't believe I was meeting the person who had written that story, as it had been so important to me as a writer. She was a great friend of mine for many years, until her death. But she taught me with *Crawfish* what it was to tell a story connected to my region and the people who lived there. When I started off in that direction it felt natural. Not all of my stories have taken place in East Texas, or the South, but most of them have. I feel comfortable writing about that era, and writing in the language and variations of that language that I've grown up with.

Did you choose Hollywood as the characters' destination for reasons other than May Lynn's ambitions for her life? What do you think a place like Hollywood represented to people in Depression-era, small East Texas towns like the one in which Edge of Dark Water *is set? Did you have something in mind for what Hollywood represented for May Lynn, specifically?*

Hollywood, especially then, the thirties, was one of those faraway places that seemed to offer something special. It was a place someone could go to and become something new and shiny and famous. Or at least that was the thought. It was like Oz. A magical place. It was a dream destination; it was very early on part of our American myth. I think for May Lynn it was that and more. It was a possible escape from poverty and the possibility of maybe working in a café and then becoming a wife and mother. Not bad ambitions, necessarily. But they weren't good ambitions for her; she felt she was something special, and that there was a magic cloak out there in Hollywood somewhere, waiting to be tossed over her shoulders.

Speaking of Hollywood, a few of your stories have been adapted for television and film, including the novella "Bubba Ho-Tep," which was adapted into the cult classic film of the same name, starring Bruce Campbell. Can you tell us a little about how it feels to see your writing transformed for the screen?

I much prefer prose, but I love film as well. I've grown up with it and loved it all my life. Along with comics and books and stories and music. It is cool to write something and then see an actor interpret it, in film or on the stage. I've had both of those pleasures. I also had a film made from a short story of mine titled "Incident On and Off a Mountain Road." It was made for Showtime, directed, as was *Bubba Ho-Tep,* by Don Coscarelli. Last summer, my son wrote a screenplay based on a story of mine, and it was made into an independent film titled *Christmas with the Dead,* and comes out soon. So that's a part of me as well—films.

As for "Bubba," I never thought it could be filmed. I was wrong. It was a pleasure to see what Don did with it. It's very faithful to the story, and most of the dialogue is from the story, and some of the dialogue is taken from the prose and turned into dialogue. Even where the film varies from the story, it is slight and right. Bruce Campbell and Ossie Davis were awesome in it.

Where did you come up with the idea of Skunk? Were you inspired by any particular characters from the canon? Do you have a favorite bounty-hunter character from other novels or films?

Skunk is that bad dream that is coming after you and will not stop; a juggernaut. He is mortality and death, a creeping doom that all of us suspect is waiting somewhere around the corner, or under the bed, in the night shadows. He is like an elemental, a nightmare that just might be there when you wake up. He is every dark thing I have ever imagined.

In addition to being a riveting story of adventure and suspense, Edge of Dark Water *can be classified as a coming-of-age novel. Was weaving together these two genres of storytelling difficult? Do you remember the writing of any scenes where the marriage of the two seemed especially natural or especially difficult?*

It is a coming-of-age story. I'm a great fan of young adult fiction and have read it all my life. Even wrote a couple of young adult novels, *The Boar* and *All the Earth, Thrown to the Sky*. I didn't find it difficult at all, because I've done that sort of thing before with adult novels. It seems to be in my DNA.

I think one thing that helps me write so many different kinds of fiction is I like so many different kinds, and have never seen one kind as better than another. It's not the type, it's the quality. So for me, it felt pretty natural.

Each of the young protagonists who set out on their journey to honor May Lynn is marked by difference—Sue Ellen by her tomboyish ways, Jinx by the color of her skin, and Terry by his reputation as a "sissy." Was this a conscious decision, or did it come about organically as you thought about the group's adventure?

I'm sure my writerly experience and subconscious came into play here. I wasn't aware of doing it, but when you've been selling writing for over forty years, you tend to develop certain instincts. You do things you're not aware of thinking about. I'm very much a writer who works out of the subconscious. I have a hard time sitting down to plot, so I don't. It happens each day as I write. I'm sure my subconscious is doing the planning. It just doesn't tell me what's going on until my fingers touch the keys.

The awards you've received over the course of your writing career are quite numerous—the Edgar Award for Best Novel, the British Fantasy Award, the American Mystery Award, the Grinzane Cavour Prize for Literature, and eight Bram Stoker Awards. Out of all those acclaimed works, do you have a favorite, or one whose creation you remember the most fondly?

I appreciate them all.

Can you tell us a little about your life outside of writing? I hear you're a member of the Martial Arts Hall of Fame, and music runs almost as strong in your family as storytelling.

I have been a martial artist for nearly fifty years. I still teach. I don't spend quite as much time as I once did at it, but I'm still active. I created a system called Shen Chuan, Martial Science, and another arm of that, which is a family system. I studied numerous martial arts in my lifetime, beginning with boxing and wrestling, which my dad taught me when I was eleven. I wasn't very good then, but I stayed with it and became very active by the time I was a teenager and on up until now. By the time I was in my late teens I was pretty dang good. I am a member of the International Martial Arts Hall of Fame and the United States Martial Arts Hall of Fame. I own a dojo and have top students who teach the regular classes for me. I mostly teach private lessons these days, and seminars, and now and again I go in and teach the weekly classes. It's a good life.

As for music, my mother loved it and sang around the house. She at one point wanted to be a singer, but the hard Depression life took over. My brother was involved in music early on. He's seventeen years older than me, and tried to make a go at Sun Records back when Elvis and Johnny Cash and Jerry Lee Lewis were starting out in the 1950s. My brother wasn't as successful, but he loved music. He worked in the field as a producer for a while, and these days is writing comics. My wife's grandmother was musical, and Karen was a clarinet player.

My daughter is a professional singer and songwriter. She is currently working on an album in Nashville, and she is extraordinarily talented. My son isn't involved in music. He's a journalist and writes screenplays and comics and runs his own online newspaper. As for me and music, I listen to it.

What writers, artists, or filmmakers inspire you? Did you have the work of any other writers or filmmakers in mind during the writing of Edge of Dark Water?

I have so many influences, but believe I am my own thing. I may be a blend of many things, but in the end, I'm me. I love a lot of the Southern writers. Harper Lee, Flannery O'Connor, Carson McCullers, some of Faulkner, Davis Grubb. I enjoy Ernest Hemingway's style over his content. Fitzgerald's *The Great Gatsby* and shorter works, especially "The Diamond as Big as the Ritz." I love Richard Matheson, Ray Bradbury, Charles Beaumont, Raymond Chandler, Dashiell Hammett and James Cain, Andrew Vachss, Neal Barrett Jr., Elmore Leonard. Writers like Mark Twain, of course, Jack London, Rudyard Kipling, and so on.

In films, I really love John Ford, Howard Hawks, John Huston, the Coen brothers, and Clint Eastwood, who I think is a great director. Comic books also have been a great pleasure and an influence. This list could become too heavy to lift, as I've only touched on the many writers and filmmakers who have given me so much pleasure and have been an influence, so I'll end it there. Oh, wait. I should say that as a kid the writer who inspired me the most and made me have to be a writer, not just want to be one, was Edgar Rice Burroughs. He's still my sentimental favorite.

QUESTIONS AND TOPICS
FOR DISCUSSION

1. Many reviewers have praised *Edge of Dark Water* by comparing it to classic works of American fiction. What is it about the book that draws these comparisons? Which novels did *Edge of Dark Water* remind you of?

2. What would you say are the larger themes of *Edge of Dark Water*? What does this ragtag group's attempts to preserve May Lynn's dream of Hollywood stardom suggest about America's ideals of success?

3. Who was your favorite character in *Edge of Dark Water* and why?

4. What did you think of the way Lansdale portrays East Texas during the Great Depression? Does his portrayal of the dangers of the road seem accurate to you? What about the state of race relations in the region? No year is ever mentioned outright in the novel—what do you make of Lansdale's decision not to pin down the story with a specific date?

5. What did you think of the author's use of oral storytelling in *Edge of Dark Water*?

6. Why do you think Lansdale chose the Sabine River for the group's journey? Would another means of transportation, such as a highway or trail, evoke a different mood or perspective?

7. What role does freedom play in *Edge of Dark Water,* especially in regard to Sue Ellen's coming-of-age adventure story? If you were Sue Ellen, do you think you would have set out on the same journey away from home, or wanted to?

8. Which villain in *Edge of Dark Water* did you find most frightening and why—Skunk, Constable Sy, or Uncle Gene?

9. What do you think *Edge of Dark Water* says about gender roles during the Depression?

10. What did you think of the role Terry played in May Lynn's death? Do you blame him for the crime or for withholding information from Sue Ellen, Jinx, and Sue Ellen's mother?